"I'm in the happiness business.

"That's what cookies are, you know. Bites of happiness. If I can make their day, they'll tell others or leave a good online review, and maybe more people will come in the door. It's all business."

Nick understood. "I ran a business. I sold it recently. Not sure if it made people happy, but what I did provided something they needed. So why did you tell them we're a couple? Would you like us to be?"

"It seemed easier. They're in love. Let them think the rest of the world is all rainbows and sunshine. No need to rain on people's parade. You said you're leaving soon, so until then, I don't care if people think we're together after one night. Even though it's none of their concern, the gossips in this town will make it so. So until you leave, let them think we're madly in love. No offense, but you're handsome. Let them be jealous. Men of your caliber are rare in this town."

Nick drew satisfaction from that and chuckled. "No offense taken. I'm happy to play along until I leave. You were kind to me long ago. I can spare some kindness your direction. And I find you quite attractive, too."

Dear Reader,

Charles Dickens wrote, "It was the best of times, it was the worst of times, it was the age of wisdom, it was the age of foolishness, it was the epoch of belief, it was the epoch of incredulity..." and while he wasn't talking about high school, the lines from *A Tale of Two Cities* totally fit. Zoe James Smith, former homecoming queen and new owner of Auntie Jayne's Cookies, worries she peaked in high school. She loves her family store and her young daughter, but she's struck out twice in the love department and no longer fits in the Beaumont social scene.

Nick Reilly hated high school. He grew up on the outside looking in. Now he's sold his tech company for billions and the geeky ugly duckling is a stylist-clad swan who makes women swoon. He remembers Zoe fondly for giving him free cookies. She remembers him not at all. But as the son of a single mom who struggled, Nick can't help but step in when parts of Zoe's life go haywire. Will Zoe, with roots so deep they can't be pulled, realize the third time's the charm? Or will she let Nick fly off into the sunset without her?

I hope you enjoy reading about Nick and Zoe. I wrote their story while serving on the committee to plan my high school reunion. And yes, you previously met Zoe's sister, Sierra, in *All's Fair in Love and Wine*. To sign up for my newsletter or find my other books, visit me at micheledunaway.com.

All the best,

Michele

Love's Secret Ingredient

MICHELE DUNAWAY

HARLEQUIN
SPECIAL
EDITION

HARLEQUIN®
SPECIAL
EDITION™

Recycling programs
for this product may
not exist in your area.

ISBN-13: 978-1-335-72469-4

Love's Secret Ingredient

Copyright © 2023 by Michele Dunaway

For questions and comments about the quality of this book,
please contact us at CustomerService@Harlequin.com.

Harlequin Enterprises ULC
22 Adelaide St. West, 41st Floor
Toronto, Ontario M5H 4E3, Canada
www.Harlequin.com

Printed in U.S.A.

In first grade, **Michele Dunaway** knew she wanted to be a teacher when she grew up. By second grade, she wanted to be an author. By third grade, she decided to be both. Born and raised in Missouri, Michele lives in her childhood hometown and travels frequently, with the places she visits inspiring her writing. A teacher by day and novelist by night, Michele describes herself as a woman who does too much but doesn't know how to stop, especially when it comes to baking brownies and chocolate chip cookies.

Books by Michele Dunaway

Harlequin Special Edition

Love in the Valley

What Happens in the Air
All's Fair in Love and Wine

Visit the Author Profile page
at Harlequin.com for more titles.

To Radio Madison, who plays the songs I love to hear on Alt Nation while I'm writing and who once tried to help me win a cruise, keep singing friend. You rock. And to Karen Pugh, Wendy Cederberg, Lark Brennan (roomies!), and to Jolene Navarro and Candace Havens—you all listened to me talk about this book at the West Texas Writers' Academy, and I am so grateful. And to Mika Lane and Maggie Cole, my beach buddies who are never far from my thoughts. All of you are the best. I couldn't ask for better friends.

Chocolate chip cookies are a tiny bite of heaven.
—*Auntie Jayne*

Prologue

Beaumont's historic Main Street wasn't the type of place for shopping, especially if you didn't have money. Looking at all the stores window displays turned on your *wanter*—that part of you that desired things you couldn't have.

Sixteen-year-old Nick Reilly wanted a lot. He wanted the heck out of Beaumont. He wanted his mom not to have to work so hard and maybe cook dinner once in a while. He wanted a really fast computer. He wanted… the list was endless.

He hurried along Main Street, on the centuries-old brick sidewalks running alongside the cobblestone-lined street dating back to Lewis and Clark's expedition. Nick wanted most to be a doer, a guy who got things done. Like those who'd built this town, put it on the map, and made something of themselves.

Nick ignored his reflection, one that showed clothes scrounged from bargain bins or resale shops. His mom hadn't resorted to taking charity—yet. In fact, she had a line on an opportunity that would get them out of this place. "California," she'd told him, as if the Golden State might be the promised land. For her sake and his, he hoped so.

Nick drew his jacket closer, one he'd paid for himself at a church rummage sale. About a month ago, he'd started washing dishes at Caldwell's, a bar on North Main, and he headed there now. Caldwell's didn't serve food as it was mainly a "drink booze and eat peanuts" type of a place. It was also filled with cigarette smoke. Nick had read some places around the country were smoke-free, but Caldwell's wasn't there yet. He'd decided money earned outweighed smelly clothes and a lack of free nights and weekends.

Too poor for a car, he had several more blocks to go, but with two dollar bills in his pocket, he could afford to stop today at his favorite place on Main, Auntie Jayne's Cookies.

After all, it would be a long time before he got home and ate something, and nothing, absolutely nothing, tasted as good as one of the shop's chocolate chip cookies. Nick's mouth watered at the thought of it.

He crossed the street, weaving between cars that were parallel parked, and climbed the steps. A jangling bell announced his arrival.

"Welcome to Auntie Jayne's," a light and cheery voice called, and Nick almost froze in his tracks. Zoe James was here today. But she wasn't looking at him because she was serving a woman buying three dozen cookies. For a moment he thought about leaving, but as the woman stepped aside and toward the door, Zoe caught his gaze and smiled expectantly.

Even though she saw him as nothing but another customer, there was nothing like a Zoe James smile. The clouds parted and heavens brightened. Nick felt the wattage down to his toes, which tingled in too-tight, worn tennis shoes. No wonder she'd been voted homecoming queen. Zoe was gorgeous, smart, and kind, and Nick had the biggest crush on her. Half the boys in the school did. She was the holy grail. The unobtainable. Perfection.

Even dressed in an unflattering Auntie Jayne's gingham dress and starched white apron, complete with the silly cap sitting atop brown hair that caught the light just so, no girl at Beaumont High compared. As a senior, Zoe ruled the roost. Unfortunately, Nick was so far down the pecking order he didn't even rate admission to the barn.

"What would you like today?" Her fingers caught an apron string as she waited, and Nick fought nerves. She was out of his league. Not only was he a grade behind her, but she was dating Ted Smith, homecoming king and varsity football quarterback. Nick was all angles and zits, lanky and geeky, the type of guy seniors picked on. Status quo meant the likes of Zoe James never went for guys with dirty blond hair worn far too long and tucked up under a ball cap. He found his voice, which had recently begun to deepen.

"Two chocolate chips cookies. One for now and one for later. Oh, and a third one. I should bring home one for my mom." He wouldn't have a lot of money in his pocket after he paid, but his mom deserved a cookie too. Especially after... Nick pushed aside the rage he felt at the marks her last ex had left on her face.

"That's nice of you." The bell jangled again as Zoe dropped three cookies into a small white bag and straightened. She greeted the new customers, and Nick worked to regain her attention.

"I wash dishes at Caldwell's so this is my snack." That sounded so lame and so he rushed out, "My real goal is to work with computers. I'm building one right now. Plan to major in computer science."

Zoe handed him the bag and moved to check him out. "Half the time I can't even figure out this new cash register."

He was actually talking to Zoe. "What are your plans?"

"To work here, of course. I'll own the shop. I'm going to River Bend for a double major in business and culinary arts. Then I'm going to take over from my mom, marry Ted and have a family. It's all mapped out."

"Well, I'm getting out of here," he declared.

"My sister, Sierra, is in the naval academy," she told him.

Nick took the crumpled bills out of his wallet and began to hand them to her. She waved them off.

"They're on the house. Least I can do to help you get out of here if that's what you want."

"Thanks." Not one to argue when it came to saving money, which was often in short supply, Nick shoved the bills back into his pocket. "You're pretty cool, Zoe."

He swore she blushed. Her cheeks flushed pink and her brown eyes darkened. But before he could add anything else, the door jangled and in walked Ted. Behind him trailed two more of his friends. Ted took one look at Nick and immediately went on the offense.

"This guy bothering you, Zoe?"

Nick heard the infinite patience and some strain in

Zoe's voice as the lady behind Nick edged away. "Stop scaring the customers, Ted. He's buying cookies for his mother. Leave him alone."

"You know I don't like you working the counter by yourself," Ted said.

Zoe was already handing Ted's two friends one chocolate chip cookie each. "My mom's in the back."

"What's going on here?"

Nick used the arrival of Auntie Jayne from the kitchen as an opportunity to escape. He darted out the door and speed walked to Caldwell's, clocking in five minutes late. His boss glared but said nothing. Few wanted the misery of this job and his boss knew it. As Nick ate both his cookies later, he tried to forget his earlier encounter with Zoe. Girls as pretty as she was dated guys like Ted. They certainly didn't date poorer-than-dirt nobodies who had nothing to offer. Nick's crush was as unrequited as it was stupid. Finished with the last morsel, Nick slid a load of tall beer glasses through the commercial dishwasher, the steam whooshing into his face and making him sweat as he pulled the green tray out when done. He hoped his mom got the job. If not, he'd simply have to work harder or guys like Ted would always be better than him, and frankly Nick's *wanter* wasn't going to be satisfied. He wanted a fine life and a woman like Zoe.

Yeah, come hell or high water, which was a distinct possibility if the Missouri River a block east got too much rain in the spring, Nick was getting out of this town.

Chapter One

Eleven Years Later

There were worst things than being alone. One was charred cookies, especially the kind with crisp edges, charred undersides, and underdone gooey centers that screwed with profits, and Zoe's margins were thin enough.

Zoe James Smith's disgusted exhale attempted to clear a nose filled with the acrid odor of burnt dough. One thing the famed Auntie Jayne, whose name graced the sign outside, had drilled into Zoe's head from birth was that the sombrero-shaped cookies must be perfect or they didn't go out onto the sales floor. Sometimes too much Missouri humidity could throw things off and ruin a batch, as could a finicky oven. Sometimes it was bad karma. Sometimes it was all three.

Sometimes it was something else entirely, some unknown variable, like a whisper in Zoe's ear that maybe, just maybe, she wasn't cut out for this job. That the starry-eyed childhood dream she'd achieved wasn't actually what she wanted.

Using far more thrust than necessary, Zoe slid the inedible treats off the baking tray, parchment paper crinkling its protest as she dumped the unusable batch into the trash. The inglorious heap mocked her—yet another testament to a string of disasters that kept finding her, no matter how hard she tried to hide.

Had she broken a mirror or done something she couldn't remember? If she was in for seven years of bad luck, she still had four or five trips around the sun left to go, depending on when she started counting. If she counted the demise of her marriage as the first disaster, that was better than having almost seven years left from when she'd ended her relationship six months ago with Jared Dempsey, the elementary school principal whom everyone thought her a fool let loose.

"Zoe, we need more chocolate chips." Jessica entered the kitchen carrying an empty display tray. She was one of the local college students Zoe had hired to staff the store's front counter.

"Coming right up." Failed cookies aside, Zoe had baked enough this morning to compensate for losing two dozen. Life had taught her to be proactive rather than reactive. What was that phrase? Shit happened. Or in this case, charred cookies. Always be prepared for something to go wrong. Murphy's Law was a *law* for a reason. *Stop quoting idioms, Zoe, and get to work.*

After all, this was her place now. In a fulfillment of a lifelong dream, she'd fully purchased the store from her mother. Jessica waited while Zoe retrieved the replacements from the temperature-controlled storage unit. "We've got a huge line. No clue where it came from. Tour bus? Anyway, we're going to need a lot."

Maybe Zoe wasn't as prepared as she thought. To keep their tall shape during baking in a 375-degree oven, their famous chocolate chip dough had to sit in the refrigerator for at least forty minutes. The batches currently chilling had been in for a mere twenty. She'd ruin another batch if she baked them early.

"We've been getting more and more of those buses lately," Jessica continued. "Beaumont's really getting noticed now that Clayton Holdings revitalized things."

Which was a good thing, Zoe reminded herself. More tourists meant more money. She swapped out the empty for an already prepped display tray and handed it to Jessica, who carried it to the sales floor. Given the current economy, Zoe had had to increase wages to keep her dedicated staff from going elsewhere. She didn't even want to get started thinking about the upkeep that came from owning a two-hundred-plus-year-old building. There was always something.

A timer dinged, and Zoe withdrew a batch of chocolate chip cookies from the commercial oven. To make up for today's mini-disaster, she'd come in early tomorrow morning. Her mom had done something similar when she'd owned the store, not that she'd ever messed up like Zoe. No, Jayne James had never really needed her daughters' assistance, but Zoe and Sierra had helped out anyway. Zoe's daughter, Megan, was a second grader, far too young to work.

Zoe tried to brush away the doldrums. She'd already ruined enough cookies for one day by letting her emotions run the gamut. She wiggled her fingers, in an attempt to relax them, before moving the cooled cookies—one, two, three, four, repeat—onto the specialty display trays. She stored them securely and exchanged her cooking apron for a white frilly one. All Auntie Jayne's employees wore aprons over either prairie-style gingham dresses or prairie-style tops and black pants, the latter of which Zoe wore today. She pushed through the swinging door out onto the sales floor.

A loose line of twenty people milled around, filling the tiny space. Jessica packaged the orders while Sarah, another college student, worked the register. One change Zoe had made to speed things along was that Auntie Jayne's was a credit-card-only business. Zoe began helping Jessica fill orders.

Some customers wanted two or three cookies. Some wanted six. Some bought the baker's dozen. Auntie Jayne's offered a variety of flavors beyond the famous chocolate chip, including double chocolate chip, snickerdoodles, M&M candy cookies, and sprinkles. Perennial flavor favorites also included peanut butter, white chocolate macadamia nut, and oatmeal raisin. Zoe had created a gluten-free chocolate chip and a gluten-free sugar version of the classics and added those to the menu, baking every cookie "with love," same as her mom had, using top-secret family recipes that had been created and passed down by Zoe's grandmother.

As Zoe packaged cookies, she smiled at customers ranging from young to old. Her brain registered each person only in passing. Even when she'd worked for her mom, Zoe had rarely recognized the regulars. While she didn't have face blindness, Zoe couldn't remember clients the way her mom had. Her mom had the memory of an elephant; unlike Zoe, she never forgot anyone, welcoming them to her store as if they were old friends. As Zoe took over the entire place, she prayed the fact she couldn't remember wouldn't matter.

By four thirty, Zoe relaxed as total receipts for a Friday moved into above-average territory. She could do this—run the place. When the incoming flow of customers slowed to a trickle in the half hour until closing time, Zoe told her employees, "I'm headed back to the kitchen to prep for tomorrow."

But an invisible thread tugged as the bells above the blue door chimed, and Zoe swiveled and her breath caught. Her feet rooted to the black-and-white square tiles as a handsome man stepped out of a Ralph Lauren ad campaign and into her store. He wore an olive-green bomber jacket over broad, husky shoulders. Dark denim jeans sculpted down long, muscular legs. His hoodie clung to a fit body that stood a few inches over six feet—she was five seven herself. Blondish hair, that appeared as if a sunset streaked through it, feathered over a perfect forehead whose tiny lines added character. Gently arched brows highlighted piercing light blue eyes with a dark outer gradient. The deep timber of his voice seemed to echo as he said, "Hey."

Butterflies flitted in her stomach. Tingles ran down her spine. She managed to close her mouth before gulping like a goldfish. She blinked to clear her view. He still stood there, larger than life and totally real. She gave him her best customer smile. "Hello. Welcome to Auntie Jayne's. May I help you?"

A clipped blond beard covered his pointed chin and climbed the hollows formed underneath high, chiseled cheekbones. A shadow of a mustache wrapped across a full upper lip that some lucky woman would nibble. He smiled one of those full white teeth, all-American grins, the kind that make women go weak at the knees. Sweet Lord. She'd buy whatever he was selling. "One chocolate chip, please."

His cookie order jolted her out of her silliness. Only the rare few walked into Auntie Jayne's and bought just one. Most customers might plan to eat only one, but they'd buy one or two "for later," or they'd buy another for "a friend." Ordering one cookie was awkward. Two said you belonged. Three said that you loved cookies and didn't want to choose your favorite. His order had been confident and clear, and she stared at him, this time for clarity rather than being overwhelmed by his beauty. Perhaps he didn't do carbs or sugar, so one cookie was a rare treat for someone that fit. "Just the one? We do have a special pumpkin spice cookie made special for Thanksgiving. Can I tempt you with that?"

A strange energy zinged between them and full lips that would make a woman crazy with envy formed a circle as the stranger began to speak. "Just the one. Want to see if they taste how I remember."

He'd been here before? When? He was like a jolt of bright sunshine, almost as if branding the space as his and washing away the remnants of how Jared had walked through that very door. Six months ago he'd upended her world with the announcement he'd been offered a job in Chicago, that he was taking it, and that he wanted her to go with him.

"It was long ago when I was here last."

Ah. He must be a tourist. Her fingers lost some of the tension. The store saw plenty of those. "Well, welcome back. My mom ran the store then. I fully acquired it this past summer."

"But you worked here on occasion before then, didn't you?"

"I did. Most of my life." So maybe not a tourist. A whiff of divine, panty-dampening cologne tickled her nose. He was sex-on-a-stick gorgeous. The type who could have a supermodel clinging to both arms. He could be a model himself. Whoever he was, he was way out of her league. She was home and hearth. She'd been with two men her entire life: Ted and Jared. Both were good-looking, but they couldn't hold a candle to this guy. Flustered, Zoe managed a polite, "Well, I hope this visit lives up to your expectations."

"It already has."

She hadn't even given him the cookie. Fingers trembling, Zoe reached inside the display case. She willed herself not to drop anything, to not embarrass herself. Using a wax paper square, she retrieved one cookie, gripping it with a practiced amount of dexterity to hold the treat securely yet without breaking it. She managed to place it successfully into a pastry sleeve. "Here you go. I baked this batch this morning. Should be extra fresh and delicious."

"I can't wait." His blue-eyed gaze held her brown one. A sizzling jolt traveled through her as his fingertips lightly skimmed over hers, the motion creating a giddy shiver and awakening dormant hormones.

Zoe wasn't like Sarah or Jessica, who had male customers their own age flirting with them nonstop. Zoe knew what she saw daily in the mirror. Her straight brown hair went up into a banana clip and her clothes remained worn jeans and comfy sweatshirts when not at Auntie Jayne's. Since she'd dated Ted since middle school, her male social circle consisted of her girlfriends' partners. Well, pre-divorce. Post-divorce, Zoe didn't fit in with the couples, and unlike her married siblings, for single women Zoe's age, Friday and Saturday night rom-coms were valid social plans.

Being with Jared had changed things for a short while. When that relationship ended, she'd endured all the speculative looks, which made her feel far worse than the sympathetic ones leveled her way. At least this man gave her neither.

Instead, he tilted his head and studied Zoe with an intense gaze that made her wonder if he was trying to read her soul. Never breaking their connection, he backhanded his credit card to Sarah as if paying was an afterthought. "You don't know who I am, do you?"

No way would she forget a man with movie star good looks and clothes to match, but she had. She fought for any memory, trying to place him. Born and raised in Beaumont, she'd gotten her business degree locally at River Bend College, the town's four-year university. Maybe she knew him from there, like maybe they'd been in the same class or something? The high school enrollment had been 1,850, and River Bend maybe a thousand more.

"I'm sorry, but I don't know you," she admitted. Was he someone famous? If so, why hadn't Sarah and Jessica said something, like they had when members of that boy band had come into the store. Both girls had turned into giggling, preening fans who'd wanted to give away half the product in exchange for free concert tickets. In the end, the band had provided endless selfies, awarded backstage passes and VIP seats, and paid for three-dozen cookies. Sarah and Jessica had told Zoe she'd missed a good time.

Zoe tried to soften her clear failure to recognize him. "We see hundreds of people every day."

"I figured as much." He sounded resigned rather than disappointed, which was odd. He didn't try to play off Zoe's answer by making some dramatic gesture, either, like pressing his hand over his heart and pretending to be wounded. He simply took the cookie from the bag and bit into the edge, wrapping his lips around the morsel before his tongue darted out to catch a stray crumb. Momentarily mute, Zoe couldn't bring herself to ask who he was and why he thought she might know him. All she could do was watch the most beautiful man alive eat the cookie she'd baked.

He held up the uneaten portion. "As delicious as I remember. See you around, Zoe."

He took another bite, turned heel, and strode out the door, the bell ringing in protest. The loss of his beauty left the space feeling oddly bereft, as if a light extinguished. When he'd said her name shivers had traveled along her spine—wait! How did he know her name? Who was he?

Shaken, Zoe faced her employees, finding them staring after him. Sarah spoke first. "Who was that? I'm not into older guys but wow. He was something."

"Older? He's around my age. And I thought you'd know." Zoe's voice sounded somewhat even and calm, a miracle. "Are you sure he's not some actor? Or in another band or something?"

Sarah shrugged. "I don't recognize him. Jessica?"

Jessica had no idea either.

"Check the receipt," Zoe instructed. "What's it say?"

Sarah punched in a code to open the day's charge card record. "Nick Reilly."

Nothing jolted. No instant name recognition. He was like John Doe. Then again, wait. Her forehead creased. Nick Reilly. Reilly, Nick. Had he gone to Beaumont High? Her brain worked frantically to place him, but she couldn't retrieve anything. "So none of us have a clue who Nick Reilly is?"

"You could see if he has a TikTok or an Insta," Sarah said. "I'd do it, but my phone is dead."

Zoe shook her head. The big hand on the large, Roman numeral clock inched toward the top as it marked the hour. "No, I'm good. It's about time to close."

Besides, being twenty-nine and having a seven-year-old meant Zoe had far bigger priorities than searching the internet for some gorgeous mystery man she'd never see again. She had a store to decorate tomorrow for the upcoming holidays, cookies to bake, parents to visit at some point soon, homework to check, bills to pay, hair to wash—her to-do list was never ending, and that was without things going wrong at the store, like the finicky oven timer that had failed to go off, causing her to burn the cookies. Or had she failed to set it?

Mattered not. Whoever the man was, the last thing she needed was a repeat of the way her insides turned into under-baked gooey cookie dough from his mere presence. In Zoe's life, Trouble was always spelled with a capital *T*, and fact remained that men like him did not go for women like her. She hadn't been able to keep her husband happy, and then Jared had put his career first, as had she. No sense in fantasizing over something with the probability of zero.

Zoe went over to the front door, locked it and turned the sign so it read "Closed". Then she headed into the kitchen, leaving the girls to the nightly cleaning. She had things to do besides worry about some man she'd never see again. Cookies didn't bake themselves, and the store didn't stay afloat without product. She'd sacrificed both of her relationships for this dream, even if it didn't keep her warm at night. Besides, Zoe reasoned, that was what fuzzy blankets were for.

After leaving Auntie Jayne's, Nick strolled down historic Main Street, taking a moment to drop the empty bag into one of the black metal trash cans present on each block. The cookie had been exactly as he'd hoped—delicious perfection. Perhaps he'd enjoyed it since he'd purchased the treat with an American Express Black card instead of the loose change he'd scrounged years ago.

Nick inhaled the crisp November air, which reminded him he wasn't in sunny Southern California anymore. His jacket kept him warm, unlike the castoffs from his past. How things had changed. These days, if he wanted, he had enough money to buy most of this block, should any of it be for sale. He chuckled, causing some passersby to double take. Nick sidestepped and kept moving, a satisfied smile on his face.

Truth be known, he could buy the entire town, at least the part Clayton Holdings hadn't purchased over the past several years. He appreciated the irony. It would serve some of the townsfolk right, too, seeing how the boy they never thought would amount to much owning it all. But Nick wasn't into buildings or streets or even local history. This side trip was to exorcise demons and create some revisionist history, to remind himself how far he'd come from the boy he'd once been.

It hadn't surprised him that Zoe hadn't recognized him. In high school, he'd been unworthy of notice and they hadn't ever hung out. Now he'd changed so much from that scrawny, geeky kid who kept to the shadows that there were times he almost didn't recognize himself.

No longer was he that sixteen-year-old charity case who'd washed dishes to help his mom make ends meet. Nor was he the guy who'd hacked into the school's computers to adjust his dismal grades so he could have a fresh start at his new school. While in the database, he'd also bumped Zoe's B+ in chemistry to an A-. Least he could do, especially since Mr. McWilliams was a jerk.

Nick told himself he should be glad Zoe didn't remember him. He'd been another zit-faced oddball far beneath the notice of the popular crowd. Minus a few scrapes, he'd kept his head down, skipping school picture day and becoming another faceless kid muddling through. No one had recognized his potential so he'd squelched it like a flower under a brick. He'd made himself invisible.

Yet, in a case of unknown paternal genetics blooming far too late for bullying classmates who judged books by their covers, and in one of those grand twists of cosmic irony, the flower bloomed anyway. The ugly duckling turned swan still hated photographs, preferring to have his former business partner, Kevin, serve as the face of their company.

As for Zoe, she was as beautiful as he remembered, with the same kind face that had once been a beacon in his dreams. His heart had raced when he'd stepped into the store. Then she'd smiled, and he'd once again been lost.

He credited today's fuzzy feelings to the nostalgia of seeing his first crush. Even though they'd never dated, kissed, much less talked, he'd placed her on a pedestal. He'd expected that, when he'd see her, he'd experience nothing. Instead, a rush of something indescribable had nearly knocked him off his feet.

Nick wandered into the bookstore, running his fingers along the stacks until finally purchasing a Daniel Silva thriller. He'd shopped the mile-long block most of the day, traversing one side and down the other, swiping his credit card if he found something interesting. He'd bought his mom some soaps in the store next door to the inn and shipped them to her in Malibu, in the beachfront condo he'd purchased for her.

She'd done her best given the circumstances, which included "not being good enough" for those whose traditional, two-parent households with plenty of disposable income. Beaumont families had seen themselves as charitable when they'd excluded Nick from party invites and other such things. Why put him in a situation where he couldn't afford to bring a birthday gift, setting him up to be embarrassed? Hadn't they realized that had been humiliating in itself?

Vowing to bring about change, he'd donated millions to groups that lifted people up, and still, if he checked his investments, his net worth would rank him as one of the top twenty richest entrepreneurs under forty. A week ago he'd been number thirteen. Or was it fourteen? Did it matter? He had more money than he'd ever dreamed.

He was also bored out of his mind. Financially, selling his tech company had made sense. He'd closed the billion-dollar deal a month ago. Not including residual stock options that would also pay him a passive income for years, he was grotesquely set for the rest of his life, even if he didn't work another day and bought sixteen mansions around the world.

But Bel Air mansions were so last week, so he'd sold his for an obscene eight-figure sum, climbed into his Cessna and started flying across the country. Beaumont hadn't been a destination on his nomadic itinerary, but then he'd found himself landing in Chesterfield to refuel, as if Fate herself had determined the flight plan. Since Beaumont wasn't that far away, what was an unscheduled side trip down memory lane when there was no agenda he had to follow?

He'd rented an Audi sedan and returned to the sleepy river town where he'd spent formative years best forgotten. Somehow his plan to stay a day had morphed into another, then another as he worked to exorcise childhood demons.

The gadget geek, they'd sneered at him in high school, along with other names. He hadn't been handsome or wealthy. Only Zoe had shown him kindness, and she hadn't even seen him unless he'd been buying cookies. Why should she have? She'd been a year ahead, dating Ted Smith. Smith was the type of popular kid who lorded his status, the kind that to this day grated on Nick's nerves. But it was simply a fact of life that homecoming queens dated homecoming kings. People settled into their social and economic classes, keeping those who didn't belong squarely outside. Hell, he'd been the dumb ass who'd fallen hard for Alexa Cimarron, dating the popular actress for two years before he'd caught wind of her cheating, gold-digging ways.

When confronted, she'd described her liaisons as nothing to worry about, saying "It happens in Hollywood. I'm building my career. You know sex is just sex. You're the one I love."

Turns out Nick discovered he had more Midwestern small town values than he'd realized. He wanted more. Someone to love him for him, not because he'd banked billions. He'd left a tearful Alexa behind and ignored her subsequent texts. He'd also done what most considered impossible—scrubbing the internet of all their images together. Amazing what a geeky kid with enough tech-savvy and hacking ability could do. He'd simply erased the proof of their relationship: image not found. Error 404.

The streetlights flickered to life and a black wrought-iron fence came into view, lining the postage-stamp front yard of the Blanchette Inn, the town's historic B&B located on South Main. Nick had planned on grabbing a hotel room at a place outside of town, but when he'd discovered the inn had a vacancy, he couldn't resist. He'd passed it too many times walking to work. Now he knew it was more comfortable than a five-star hotel.

Nick turned and opened the gate. The November days kept getting shorter, darker, and colder. He glanced at the marker paying homage to the early 1800s slaves who'd chiseled the stones forming the inn's exterior walls and fireplaces. His footsteps rattled the steps leading to the wide front porch. Large wreaths adorned double front doors made of polished wood. The wreaths contained a Thanksgiving cornucopia of yellow squashes, tiny orange pumpkins, and wooden turkey ornaments. Mrs. Bien had told him she made each month's wreaths herself. After pressing the code to unlock the front door, Nick made his way inside, finding the innkeeper straightening magazines in the parlor.

She gave him a welcoming smile. "Nick, how are you? Did you have a nice time shopping?"

"I did, thank you." He held up the bag with the book. Down the hall a clock chimed, indicating it was quarter after five.

"I put some hot apple cider and banana bread in the dining room if you're hungry for an afternoon snack."

"Thank you. I had a cookie at Auntie Jayne's."

"Those are delicious. I buy a dozen or two for the guests when I'm too busy to bake. That might be tomorrow. It's Christmas decorating day."

Nick frowned. While some of the big box stores had had Christmas decorations out since before Halloween, Main Street remained adorned in mostly fall colors with few hints of red and green. "I wondered why I didn't see any decorations."

"We make decorating Main Street a social event. Two Saturdays before Black Friday, well, in this case, tomorrow, all the shopkeepers decorate at the same time. On Sunday, it's fun to walk around and see the final results. Then, on Black Friday, all the shopkeepers start wearing historic costumes. We even have carolers performing. It's like the entire town transports back in time for a month. There's also a cookie bakeoff and a gingerbread contest the Saturday after Black Friday. It's a shame you'll miss it."

He'd told Mrs. Bien he'd lived here over a decade ago and was simply passing through. "Do you take guests over the holidays? Right now I have no Thanksgiving plans." Not even to see his mother as she'd be going somewhere with friends.

If Mrs. Bien was surprised by his admission about the holiday, she never showed it. "Your room is free so you can stay if you'd like. Until New Year's Eve, the holidays are a slow time. If you stay, you'll have the entire place to yourself on Thanksgiving unless we get a few more bookings. We're going to my daughter and her husband's or I'd feed you myself. If you want food, Miller's Grill does a carry-out meal until noon that day, so you could order one of those and pick it up."

Miller's Grill had the reputation of serving some of the best brisket in the state. All of Beaumont County's movers and shakers ate there, so Nick had tried the place for the first time yesterday. While he'd found the brisket and sides delicious, he'd decided that Beaumont was not exactly a hotbed of culinary innovation or presentation. One demon exorcised in deciding Miller's wasn't all the town thought it was. Not when compared to some of the Michelin star places he'd eaten.

The residual memory of Zoe's delicious cookie, though, remained fresh on his tongue. For a moment he wished he'd ordered one "for later." Maybe he should stay. Go see her again. Find out if his heart would race as it had earlier.

He sent Mrs. Bien a grateful smile. "I'm tempted. Is it alright if I tell you tomorrow morning? I might still leave like I'd planned."

"Of course."

Nick climbed the wide staircase. The second floor housed the guest rooms as the family quarters were on the third. He admitted his accommodations hit the right buttons. The masculine four-poster queen bed had a dark maroon comforter instead of the period replica pastel quilt and lace curtains he'd glimpsed in another guest room. The huge room contained a tall armoire and something Mrs. Bien called an escritoire. The ornate wooden piece of French furniture had a slanted top that when folded down formed a writing surface. A matching desk chair waited at the ready. Near the fireplace and its heavy wooden mantel, a large leather wingback invited sitting.

He kicked off his shoes, finding it interesting that this room held more charm than his former mansion. He'd certainly appreciated the good night's sleep. His childhood bedroom had been in a single wide whose walls would rattle in a heavy storm. His mansion had been cold and sterile. This room was just right. As for his childhood home, he'd discovered the trailer park was long gone, paved over and covered by high-end condos with excellent river views. It was as if the poor souls who'd once lived there had never existed.

He moved to the chair, not wanting to delve too deeply into why he kept extending his stay. Had Zoe even thought of him after he'd walked away? He'd seen the flicker of interest in her eyes. Then again, he knew he had that effect on women. Now anyway. And here in Beaumont, no one knew how much money he had. He'd give himself a week total, he decided, as he'd already been in town part of that. One week to bury Beaumont and cut its talons from his flesh. If worse came to worst and he couldn't figure out where to fly next, he'd winter the plane, buy an RV, and drive around the country. He'd head south, maybe down to Key West where it would be warm. Maybe he'd even get a dog for a traveling companion. He'd never had a pet. That was something new he could try.

Using the remote, he turned on the gas fireplace and

watched the flames flicker. Outside, night had fallen. He'd read for a bit, freshen up, and maybe try the wine bar he'd walked by earlier. That appeared more his pace than the bar scene on North Main, which would consist of college kids out for a fun Friday night. Caldwell's was no longer. It had become the Main Street Makerspace, which was owned by Mrs. Bien's son-in-law, Luke. Good riddance, Nick thought. Another demon vanquished. The bar had been a hellhole, and now it was a family-friendly venue where people could take classes and/or work on their arts and crafts. The place even had a darkroom and a 3D printer.

Yeah, a casual wine bar with food was more his style. Nick wasn't sure when he'd become an old man at twenty-eight, but perhaps that was from living in L.A.—like a vampire, the city sucked out the youth out of a person to keep itself young.

Nick shifted, the motion made his sleeve inch up along his forearm, revealing a white line that zigzagged across his inner wrist. He bent his fingers toward his wrist, watching as the line disappeared into the folds the movement created. He straightened his wrist and flipped to page one. No matter what he did while in Beaumont, it made no sense for him to dwell too much on the past. History could be a wound that never healed if one kept picking at the scab. He already had enough scars.

Chapter Two

Life certainly would be easier if it was a romantic comedy. As the TV show's credits scrolled, Zoe set aside the bag of popcorn, her fingers snagging the few pieces that had dared to fall on her oversized gray sweatshirt. She popped the kernels into her mouth—no sense wasting buttery popcorn, especially when it was the skinny kind.

Megan was at a sleepover at her friend Anna Thornburg's house, and it was oddly quiet without her. Zoe's life was go, go, go, so when the silence came, Zoe hated it. When she and Ted had first divorced, she and Megan had been a team. At first he'd made an effort to fly back to Beaumont twice a month, taking Megan with him to his parents' house. She'd filled the empty hours baking or visiting her parents. Now her parents had moved about fifty minutes away and Ted rarely came to Missouri, meaning Zoe kept Megan with her most of the time.

Zoe didn't mind. The less she had to deal with her ex, the better. Megan had everything she needed to be happy and well adjusted. Zoe was grateful Megan had a true best friend in Anna. Zoe wasn't even sure if she missed Lacey Dempsey, Jared's daughter. For a year Lacey had formed the third part of their Megan-Anna-Lacey trio, until Jared and Lacey had moved away. Zoe hadn't asked him to stay. How could she? His dream job was as important to him as hers.

The irony wasn't lost on Zoe that around this time last year she and Jared had agreed to date seriously, creating a world full of promise. She'd cooked many a meal, including Thanksgiving, in her house's tiny kitchen. She'd helped him make wine. She'd rediscovered what her body could do and how good sex could be with a tender and wonderful lover. She and Ted hadn't had much of a sex life even before Megan's birth, so being with Jared had been eye opening. Like fine wine, perhaps sex got better with age.

But when he'd asked her to move to Chicago with him, Zoe's feet had frozen like a pond in winter. She couldn't move to another part of Missouri, let alone another state. She couldn't leave Beaumont or the store. Ted had demanded she leave or else, so they'd divorced. Jared had asked, and she'd found herself unable to commit. She'd broken both of their hearts.

Something was wrong with her to have let him go, but she had.

Then she'd done what she'd always done: baked. After losing her big, beautiful two-story farmhouse to the divorce, she'd purchased a smaller, two-bedroom, century-plus house on Third Street. For the first time in her life, she became independent. She had a home loan she could mostly afford on her Auntie Jayne's salary. She had a small backyard with a carport off the alley. She had a living room and dining room that looked out onto an open front porch in a walkable neighborhood two blocks from Main Street and five minutes from the store. She'd painted the inside herself, including the ceilings.

She'd liked the house on sight. A decent and modern bathroom sat between two bedrooms. The updated kitchen was cramped but efficient. Zoe put the empty popcorn bag into the trashcan and rinsed her hands of the residual grease, using a faucet she'd swapped out herself. Living in town meant she could walk everywhere, like she had today. Anna's parents lived in a historic home on South Main, so Megan could walk over there and vice versa.

Beaumont was Zoe's hometown, which is why she'd stayed when others hadn't. Because of her dad's early-onset Alzheimer's, her parents had sold the family winery and homestead last summer to Clayton Holdings. Her dad now lived in a top-notch memory care unit in a suburb of St. Louis, and her mom lived with one of Zoe's brothers nearby. Even Zoe's sister, Sierra, and her husband, Jack, had moved into St. Louis County to be closer to Sierra's job. They'd married in the family vineyard—well, his family's now—in June. While Zoe had been initially skeptical of Jack's development of the area's wine country, she couldn't find many flaws in his plan. She'd also never seen her older sister so happy.

If Zoe was honest, she was a tad jealous. She'd been in love twice and neither had worked out. Now she paced her silent house, too restless to sleep and her head starting to throb with a massive headache.

She glanced at the microwave clock: 9:06. Good grief. In college and pre-Megan, she and Ted would be out partying at ten and staying out until dawn. Now she stood in her kitchen on a Friday night. Unless she watched another movie, played Spider Solitaire, completed a Sudoku, or cleaned the house yet again, she was twiddling her thumbs like some loser. She'd started to relearn German using a phone app, but she'd already done enough practice for the day. Heck, she was on a two-hundred-day streak. Clearly, she had too much time on her hands.

Usually she'd be putting Megan to bed by now, but Megan wasn't here. Megan was also growing up and becoming more independent. In a decade, she'd be a high school senior. It was only a decade ago that Zoe had been in college, and seven years ago that she'd been holding a baby in her arms. Time moved far too fast.

Idly, she wandered the small house, stopping to place a piece into the puzzle she and Megan had started on the dining room table. She reached for the romance novel she'd borrowed from the library, then set the hardcover down. She moved to the shelf and pulled down her senior yearbook, but no Nick Reilly existed at Beaumont High in the R section of the index. She yanked out two other yearbooks before giving up. Googling his name resulted in fifteen million, three hundred thousand results found in under a half second, and none were images of him. Finding him online would be a wild goose chase and an exercise in futility, especially for a man she didn't remember and most likely would never see again.

Frustrated, Zoe exhaled, sending a loose strand of

hair billowing. She rubbed her temples. If she didn't do something, she'd become that desperate loser many of those "mean girl" PTA gossips already called her. All those "poor Zoe" comments, usually followed by "What if she never finds anyone again? What if she's alone forever?"

Why couldn't they see her as a single mom running her own business with very little support? As a success? Burned cookies aside?

Zoe pushed aside the pang. No, the fact she was divorced somehow painted her as a failure as a woman and it irked her. Worse, divorced women didn't necessarily fit in anywhere. She wasn't single scoping out her first guy with the help of all her single friends. She wasn't part of a couple either. It was a limbo Jared had filled until she'd been unable to commit to moving with him. Had she made a mistake turning him down? There were days she doubted and second-guessed her decision, even though deep down she knew it was the right one.

The cuckoo clock she'd inherited from her grandmother chimed the quarter hour, and Zoe decided she couldn't take the oppressive silence anymore. There were worse things than being alone, and one thing was the nonstop processing going on inside her head, making it pound. Stomping her way into her bedroom, she thumbed through the hangers, moving them aside with rapid clicks. As proof she wasn't afraid to be alone, in the early days following her divorce, Zoe had forced herself to sit in one of the bars on North Main and watch a band. Tonight she'd do the same, but somewhere less meat market. She'd go to La Vita è Vino Dolce, a self-service wine bar a short distance from the store. She'd known the owner, Caleb Masters, ever since elementary school, not that they'd hung in the same circles. Zoe and Caleb had reconnected at one of the Main Street Merchants Association's monthly meetings, and he currently dated her cousin Andrea.

Zoe pulled her sweatshirt over her head and shimmied off her jeans. She pulled on a soft knee-length black sweater dress and zipped up her black dress boots that rarely got any use. She topped the outfit with a three-strand silver necklace. She swiped on some lip gloss, yanked her hair out of the clip. After giving it a fluff, she decided she'd made enough effort. If she lost momentum, she'd lose her nerve and not go. She took two acetaminophen. That should help with her head, as would going out. One glass of wine in an actual venue would prove she didn't need anyone to complete her but herself. She was a powerful woman. What could a man do for her that she couldn't do for herself? Well, besides *that*.

Zoe refused to settle. She wanted the fantasy. The perfect meet-cute. The attention of an attractive and interested man. She wouldn't find it tonight, and the realist in her doubted that, after Jared, she'd again find a high-quality man who loved her. But she'd at least get out of her house before the silence drove her crazy and her head exploded. She shoved her ID and credit card into the holder on the back of her iPhone, punched in the code to lock the front door, and stepped out into cool night air perfect for a short walk. Instantly, she felt better. The medicine must have kicked in.

Avoiding the empty tables, she found a seat at the end of a full-service bar. A quick glance showed her not much had changed. Caleb's place provided a welcome, after-hours niche safe for any size party. He'd created a low-key, comfortable place to drop in. With food limited to charcuterie boards and flatbreads, patrons felt no obligation to buy a bottle or eat an expensive meal. They could stop by for a break while shopping or frequent the place like they would a coffee shop, but with wine. Located in a historic store of some sort from centuries ago, the walls rose a story and a half and provided a feeling of space. Caleb had renovated and opened the flat rooftop last June, so in nice weather people could sit outside and watch boats traverse the Missouri River, which meandered by a block to the east.

Zoe passed over her credit card and the chip card embossed with the venue's name to a perky, college-aged bartender who greeted her with "I see you've been here before."

"I have. Please add fifteen dollars."

"Will do. You don't need me to explain how to use the thirty-two self-service wine taps, do you?"

"Nope, she's an expert," a familiar voice said.

"Caleb!" Zoe jumped out of her seat and gave him a big hug. "I didn't think you were in town because you and Andrea have been so busy opening all the other venues."

Caleb grinned. "It's been nonstop, but I wasn't leaving decorating to chance or to an unsupervised staff. Not after last year."

"Yeah, yours were pretty skimpy last year. The Merchants Association was aghast."

He grimaced. "That's putting it mildly. Mrs. Zappatta complained to my face and the rest did so behind my back."

Zoe winced. "Let me guess. One was Mirabelle Adams."

Mirabelle ran a boutique on Main Street containing high-end clothing most Beaumont residents couldn't afford and considered herself the official expert on all things a historic town needed. She and Zoe had butted heads several times at the Merchants Association over what Main Street needed versus what its merchants could afford, and Mirabelle had let Zoe know that dating the principal should be off-limits.

"She was one. Not that you heard it from me." Caleb reached for Zoe's credit card and handed it back to her. "Your drink's on the house. Add twenty."

The girl moved away to refill the card. "You didn't have to do that, but thank you. Is Andrea in town?"

"She'll arrive Sunday so she can inspect my handiwork. We might do some house hunting, but that's still up in the air. We have no idea where we want to settle. She can work from Beaumont and I can work from Portland. We're still debating."

"Whatever you do, don't let it break you up."

He winced. "Gosh, Zoe. I'm an insensitive clod. I'm still sorry about you and Jared."

Zoe gave a sad smile. "Me too. You and I can't seem to leave, can we?" Her offhand wave shooed away the thought. "Then again, why should we? Look at this place. This is your flagship. The store is mine. When we've got roots like this, it's hard to leave." She tried to lighten the moment. "Besides, who else will save me from sitting with Mrs. Zappatta at all the association meetings if you leave?" Mrs. Zappatta saw herself as the unofficial mayor of Main Street now that Zoe's mom had moved away. "You owe me."

A mock expression of horror etched Caleb's features. "The whole reason I've amped my decorating game.

And if I hear one more time about petunias and wooden planters, I'm going to drink all the wine in this place myself. How are things at the store?"

"Great." If she didn't count making the upcoming loan payment out of her savings. In a case of more bad karma, she'd not only had to replace three ovens last month but also pay for the needed extensive repair work on the old mortar between the bricks. It was, after all, a two-hundred-plus-year-old building. Still, the unexpected expenses had come at the worst time. But since this was her dream, she'd make it work. She would succeed. Already everyone thought something had to be wrong with her to have turned down a man of Jared's stature, believing she should have sold the store and gone with him. She couldn't let them be right.

Hopefully, the holidays would help pad the bottom line, especially if they were anything like today. While Auntie Jayne's Cookies made most of its yearly sales during the town's two festival weekends in September, and then again during the Halloween festival, the holiday "rush" period between mid-November and Christmas provided the boost that carried the store until April. Financially, if she could hang on until she provided cookies for the new Clayton Hotel and Conference Center, she might be okay.

Caleb glanced over her head. "Looks like I'm needed in the kitchen. Don't leave without saying goodbye."

"I won't," Zoe promised as the bartender returned Zoe's reloaded chip card.

Zoe moved to an area behind the main bar, where eight self-service wine cellars each contained four tapped bottles. Bar patrons could dispense a glass of this or that from one of the thirty-two vintages Caleb had available. If Zoe wanted, she could pour two vintages into one and create her own blend. Not that she'd suggest mixing a Boudreaux with a Moscato, but someone might want to try. She retrieved a clean wine glass from the shelf.

Moving to the red vintages, Zoe inserted the chip card into the payment slot. The wine taps dispensed in two-, four-, and six-ounce portions. As the amount of credit on her chip card displayed on the screen, so did the prices of each pour. She hovered her finger over a button for a four-ounce pour of old vine Zinfandel. Deciding to shake things up from what she normally drank, she moved her glass one bottle over and chose two ounces of a Malbec she'd not yet tasted. The red wine poured from its designated silver spigot and stopped once the portion dispensed.

Shivers on her arm indicated someone had moved beside her, and the deep and sexy voice she'd heard earlier asking for one cookie said, "That's a good choice. That vintage is one of my favorites from Washington State."

Startled, Zoe spun around. Wine sloshed in the glass but didn't spill over the rim as it would have done with a larger pour. She put the glass to her lips and took a sip to calm zinging nerves. No counter between her and Nick now. Instead, all six feet of him stood within reach of her forearm. If she pressed her hand forward, her fingers could touch that broad chest that was now covered by a Henley. Butterflies went crazy in her stomach, which had dropped to her toes.

Nick's piercing blue eyes held Zoe mesmerized. He'd pushed that sun-swept blond hair off his forehead. His right eyebrow lifted in amused query. "We both clearly had the same idea tonight." He put his glass under the spigot and dispensed the same vintage, opting for a similar two-ounce pour. "Both in the choice of the venue and the wine."

Goosebumps prickled and somehow her mouth formed words that came out more breathless than intended. "Hello, Nick."

He raised his glass in mock toast. "Ah, she remembers me."

Zoe shook her head. "Sorry, I won't lie and pretend I do. I read your name off the credit card receipt."

He gave a wry grin. "Ah, well, I'm flattered you tried. But no worries, I was a grade behind, and we didn't have classes together and it's statistically impossible for you to have met and remembered every person who was at Beaumont when you were there. Besides, I was not popular. We didn't run in the same circles. I stayed under the radar. Sat in the back of class. That kind of thing. And I've filled out since high school."

"That makes me feel a little better. I think. I still feel as if I should have known you."

A woman could drown in those blue eyes of his, especially the seductive twinkle, which could have been a trick of the light. Zoe hoped so, for she shouldn't be having this type of a physical reaction to a man, especially one she didn't really know. "I'm sorry I don't remember."

His deep husky laugh instead wrapped around her. "It's fine and my ego's not easily dented. Like I said, I've changed."

Whatever he'd looked like before didn't matter as Zoe's nerve endings fired rapidly. He was the type of good-looking man a woman fantasized about. But the fantasy never was as good as the reality. Before she did anything foolish like kiss him—his lips were that divine—she cut their reunion short.

"Well, it was good seeing you. I hope you have a good night." She returned to her seat, and found herself flustered when seconds later he slid onto the open stool next to her. Oddly flattered but somewhat wary, she shot him some side-eye. "I thought you were over there?"

"If you don't mind, I'd like to continue to reconnect." He produced that knee-weakening grin that created heat in places long dormant.

Did she want him to leave? Knowing Caleb would make sure she was safe, curiosity won. "Are you sure you want to tread down memory lane?"

"Why not? It's the town I really hated most. I couldn't wait to get out of here."

She wasn't sure what to think about that. "And I'm the one who gave up two relationships in order to stay. I can't imagine leaving. Despite some challenges, my life is here."

"And I wouldn't have had the life I lead now had I remained here. Interesting how things work out. And then here are we." As he sipped his wine, Zoe scraped her bottom lip with her teeth. Forget Trouble with a capital *T*. He was Danger with a capital *D*. Neurons sang. Butterflies flitted. All those romance clichés pounced. He was a heartbreaker, and she'd been there, done that. But she missed a man's attention, his scent, his lovemaking. She sipped half her wine and pointed the glass toward him. "I'm going to be honest. I'm not that interesting of a conversationalist. This is as exciting as my weekend gets. One glass of wine and I'm out. And you're right. This is a good wine."

"Glad you like it. And considering my night was

going to be reading a book in my room at the Blanchette Inn, talking with you is a huge improvement."

Her lips curled with dubious disbelief and she couldn't help but add the eye roll. She wouldn't delude herself by thinking that a man this handsome wanted her, but the fact he'd pursued her to sit at the bar did provide a thrill. She needed to keep it together. "If you say so."

His fingers twirled his wineglass, making light dance off the pour. "I do."

How had she missed him when she'd arrived? Then again she'd headed right for the bar as if she'd had tunnel vision. See no one. Get one glass and go home. All the proof she needed to convince herself she was not a loser. Now she couldn't have left if she tried. Long buried femininity demanded attention. What harm could there be in holding a simple conversation with a gorgeous man? "You live out of town now, I take it."

"California. Near San Francisco. I later moved to L.A."

"Ah."

She lifted her wine glass and sipped. Maybe she should have chosen a larger pour. She hadn't noticed that little dip in the center of his chin before, but with their knees almost touching, she noticed now.

As he sipped his Malbec, the perky bartender bounced—that was the only word for it, Zoe thought with mild annoyance, she literally bounced—over holding a small, round charcuterie board containing chocolate and nuts.

"Here you go," the bartender told Nick far too brightly as she set the wood platter down. "I take it you're sitting over here now."

"I am. Go ahead and send the other half of the order, thanks, along with another glass."

"Will do." The woman left with less enthusiasm as Nick had appeared not to notice her interest.

Nick shifted the board closer to Zoe, causing pleasant prickles. "Do you come here often?"

She thought back. "This is my second, no, third time. Last time I was upstairs on the roof with my family. The owner dates my cousin."

Their bartender returned, less perky this time, and opened a slim bottle of port on the wooden surface in front of Nick. He lifted the bottle and passed it to Zoe. "Your family owned a winery, right? What do you think of this vintage? I like port better than brandy as a nightcap, and tonight seemed to call for one."

"If Caleb's stocking it, I'm sure it's great. Andrea is a master sommelier." Zoe read the label. "Dried fig, toasted pecan and cocoa bean. And a hint of fruit preserves. Sounds delicious."

She passed the bottle back to him, and he poured two small glasses. He held one out. "Taste that and tell me what you think. You're the master."

"That's Andrea," she corrected automatically. "But my dad taught me some."

"Then share your opinion. I'm sure you know more than you think."

Perhaps about wine. She remained in the dark where he was concerned. They'd need far more than twenty questions for that. She pushed the dregs of the Malbec aside and held the port to the light. She swirled to assess the wine's color. She brought the glass to her nose and sniffed, inhaling a delightful, nutty bouquet. "If it tastes as good as it smells, it's going to be delicious."

"Try it and see."

She sipped, letting the sweet flavor flow over her

tongue. Her father always maintained that a good wine appealed to the entire palate, pleasuring each taste bud, whether those taste buds be the sweet ones in the front of the tongue, or the salty and the sour ones, or the bitter-tasting ones toward the back of the mouth. She closed her eyes, letting her senses of taste and smell take over. The wine was perfect. Sort of like the man sitting next to her.

She opened her eyes to find that Nick had moved the small wooden board directly in front of her. Instead of being covered with meats, cheeses, and nuts, this one held dark chocolate truffles, milk and dark chocolate candies, and chocolate-covered pretzels and peanuts. "Try one," Nick offered.

She chose a truffle decorated with a caramel swirl. As the bliss of dark chocolate landed on her tongue and mixed with wine residue, instinct made her close her eyes again. The candy softened in her mouth like a melt-away, coating her tongue with chocolatey goodness.

She blinked her eyes open, gave a tiny shake, and sighed.

That looked like a rather delicious and pleasurable piece of chocolate." "It was." Chocolate was often de-scribed as orgasmic, and she would not think of the orgasm that he might give her. Unused to flirting, she tried not to bask in his infectious and beautiful smile. Being here with him couldn't be real. He was too beau-tiful. Too gorgeous. She resisted pinching herself. This wasn't an alternative universe. She hadn't tumbled down a rabbit hole. "Try some," she urged. "You ordered it before you saw me so you must have wanted to plea-sure yourself."

He arched an eyebrow, and horrified, she slapped a hand over her mouth. "That came out wrong."

But he simply laughed, a deep rich sound she was quickly learning to like. "No worries. I can pleasure myself just fine. But it's better with two."

"I was talking candy." Zoe reddened more and reached for her port.

He brought his glass to hers with a little clink and then they both took a drink. "It's fine, Zoe. I'm teasing you. I'm sorry if I offended. Not my intention to make you uncomfortable. You used to give me extra cookies whenever I came in. Least I can do is share my chocolate with a beautiful woman, even if that's all the night is. I don't have any expectations or ulterior motives. We're simply two people sitting in a bar, sharing chocolate and killing time."

A memory danced on the edges but flitted away before Zoe could recall it. She gave free cookies to a lot of people, but somehow the fact she had given them to him seemed important. She also had a longing to do far more with him than kill time. Then again, maybe he meant exactly what he said. "I'm sorry. I have no idea if you're flirting, and I'm not sure you should be. I kept to my own crowd in high school, and we didn't put others first. In hindsight, my boyfriend was a jerk. I hope I didn't bully you. If I did, I'm sorry."

"You were always kind to me. I may have had a little crush." His thumb and forefinger formed a half-inch gap. "But you were dating Ted. And yes, he was a jerk."

"Still is at times." She took another sip and tried to place him. Still nothing. "I wish I'd known high school was going to be the most carefree time of my life. Maybe I wouldn't have rushed things."

He considered that seriously. "I couldn't wait to get out of Beaumont. I did all of my senior year and part of my junior year in California. But you had a good senior year, Ms. Homecoming Queen, and don't fault yourself for that."

The wine had loosened her tongue. "When I peaked, clearly."

"Of course not."

She patted the top of his hand. "You don't have to be kind or flatter me. It's been a long time. I'm not the person you think I was."

No. She was better. Nick flipped his palm, capturing Zoe's fingers and giving her hand a little squeeze. He hadn't believed his luck when she'd walked into the wine bar. She'd been like an angel crossing the threshold. He might not have seen her in years, but he was seeing her now. "It's not flattery. It's truth. You have nothing to worry about, Zoe. You're as beautiful now as you were then."

She was. The soft black sweater dress hugged and highlighted womanly curves he longed to touch but wouldn't because he prided himself on self-restraint.

Zoe might no longer be the fresh-faced, all-American girl she'd been, but she'd grown into her beauty. Her lips were as naturally lovely as ever, and when she'd bit into the chocolate, the movement had ignited his libido. He resisted the strongest urge to touch her shiny brown hair that shimmered and caught the light. The strands danced around her shoulders and he longed to push that one wayward piece behind her ear, where the hint of an earring sparkled in the lobe. The simple strand of silver that slid down the valley between her breasts

called to him more than the finest gems worn by some
of his failed dates. They'd been beautiful women, grac-
ing the covers of magazines. They hadn't attracted him
like Zoe did in this minute.

He'd noticed at the store she didn't wear a wedding
ring. He'd done an internet search and found her divorce. He felt bad for her, but then again, admittedly not
that bad. Ted had been a grade A asshole. Nick wanted
this second chance, especially as he was a man with
equal social standing. He didn't want her to see him as
he'd been in high school: poor and unpopular. A loser.
"Tell you what, let's skip the past stuff. How about we
focus on the moment as if we just met?"

"We can do that," she agreed, to his relief.

On firmer footing, Nick sipped some wine and followed it with a bite of solid dark chocolate. The flavor
exploded on his tongue. "You're right. Really good."

"Told you." As she relaxed, his tension dissipated.
Nick popped some cashews in his mouth. Around them,
a few people watching the two sixty-five-inch TVs
cheered as the home team scored a goal.

"Do you think the Blues have a chance?" he asked.

"Too early to tell but they have a good lineup," Zoe
said. "Are you in town for business?"

It was a fair question, and he had told her to focus
on the here and now. "I'm on an extended vacation of
sorts." Which was close enough to the truth. After being
burned by Alexa's gold digging, Nick kept his financial
status private. He didn't want people targeting him for
his bank balance. There were days he even wondered
if his mom would still be in his life had he not made a
large fortune.

Her eyebrow lifted. "You came to Beaumont for vacation?"

He shrugged. "Why not? Clayton Holdings is transforming the area and I wanted to see if anything was like what I remembered."

Zoe tipped her glass toward him. "But you didn't like it here."

"Exactly. But I'm liking it now." He shifted like a schoolboy with his first crush. Then again, she was his first crush, and he hoped she didn't figure out who he'd been. She'd see him differently. Maybe even pity him, and he couldn't abide that. Life in the background suited him fine. It was one reason he'd let Kevin be the face of the company. One reason he'd never told anyone about his impoverished past once he'd arrived at Stanford. "Tell me about yourself."

Her unvarnished fingers toyed with the port glass. Her rounded bottom wiggled in her chair and his libido sent blood pumping. "I should be asking that of you. You know far more about me than I do you."

"I'm honestly not that interesting and I hate talking about myself. Tell me about the cookie store. It's yours now, right?"

"Yes. I bought my mom's shop."

"You married Ted."

"I did. We're divorced and we have a daughter in second grade. If she wasn't at a sleepover, I'd be at home watching a movie or working on the puzzle we started. It's a bunch of kittens in a wicker basket. She picked it out."

He'd seen something similar today in the bookstore. Beaumont residents shopped close, mostly avoiding the superstores that dominated the landscape about a half-hour drive from town. "Once, when I was buying a cookie, you told me once you wanted to buy the shop. I'm glad you did. You were always so determined. I found that inspiring."

She sighed. "I wish I could remember but that's honestly one of my flaws. Even years later, my mom can remember everyone who walks in. I'm hating that something I did or said meant more to you than it did to me. It feels like I'm rude somehow. Already much of my life is a big blur. It's divided into pre-divorce and post." Zoe's fingers worked the beverage napkin, worrying it into a series of lumpy wrinkles. "Maybe all we do is go forward." Her short laugh revealed her nerves. "This wine is really loosening my tongue. I told you I'm not good date material. Not that this is a date."

Part of him wished it was. He liked getting to know the real her. "Maybe it helps to talk about these things to someone who's a semi-stranger. I'm in between careers, doing one of those philosophical tours of the country as I try to figure out what's next with my life. What if I've peaked before I'm thirty?"

"It could be worse. I'm twenty-nine. I peaked in high school."

He refilled their port glasses. "I totally disagree. There's no way you've peaked."

"Ted thought we did. He had his midlife crisis in his twenties rather than his forties or fifties. Declared Beaumont too small and suffocating. Didn't matter we had a house or a child. He found a job in Seattle. Said I must not love him enough if I wanted my shop or my career over his. He's already remarried. Seems happy. Never forgets Megan's birthday, at least."

Nick loosened the fingers that had tightened into a

fist he'd put through Ted's face should the guy walk in. "If I say he was always an ass, will that help?"

"We did already agree he was a jerk." Her hair formed a wave of grain as she shook her head. "I wish I'd realized earlier that Ted and I didn't have long-term compatibility. That sometimes the love you have for people you're with in high school doesn't necessarily translate into the kind of love that you want in your twenties and beyond. I had my whole future planned, you know? Now, I'm facing that thirty milestone in a few months and wondering what do I have to show for it?"

"A shop and a daughter. I'd say you're doing pretty good."

"Well, yes. Those. But is this all my life is? Is this my entire existence?" She swirled her wine. "Told you I'm in a funk."

"Then that's two of us so we're good company. My last girlfriend cheated on me. Said sex was a different concept from love. She begged me to stay and have an open relationship."

Zoe winced. "Ouch. That's wrong. I'm too old-fashioned for that."

"So am I. It's one reason I'm on this journey. I had to get away. I'm single and it felt time to make a change. Leave the past behind and move forward."

"Sort of like me tonight," Zoe admitted. She could understand. "I walked down here and told myself one glass. Now I've had way more than that." She lifted the port and studied the bottle. "This stuff is potent. It's like truth serum."

"Sometimes it helps to let loose. No worries about doing that around me. You're safe sitting here. I won't find fault." He waved over the bartender. "Margherita flatbread, please."

Surprised, Zoe grabbed her phone, slid the credit card out from the pocket on the back, and slid the plastic over. "You didn't have to do that. At least let me pay for half of it."

He placed his hand over hers and warmth fused his palm to the top of her hand. With the card flat beneath her fingers, he gently slid her hand and the card back into her space. He lifted his hand, the lack of heat immediately noticeable. "Let me treat. We can both use something besides chocolate and besides, I'm hungry."

An invisible wavelength crossed between them, and Zoe nodded. "Thank you. All I ate was some popcorn. Food sounds good." She gave him a shy, grateful smile. Then she shook a finger at him, her tone light and teasing with an underlying sincerity. "But I gotta warn you, don't think getting me tipsy and feeding me means you're getting in my pants."

He held up his hands like a Boy Scout and joined her in laughing. Then he sobered. "Let me make one thing clear. I have far too much respect for you than to want a simple roll in the hay. I don't want the night to end, but I'm not after the one-night stand either. You're worth way more than that."

"Oh." Surprise brought her perfect, kissable mouth so close. All he'd have to do is lean over. But he didn't. Zoe was a long-term type of woman and he didn't even know where he'd be in a week. "No worries, Zoe. While I might want to take you to bed and desire nothing more, for tonight you're safe. I wouldn't dare cross the line."

"No?"

"No. Even if I wanted to."

Chapter Three

As the night waned, Zoe couldn't remember the last time she'd had so much fun with someone she'd just met. She also reveled in the fact that an attractive and sexy man wanted to take her to bed. And the fact that, even though he wanted her, he respected her enough not to do more than flirt and occasionally touch her hand. He put zero sexual pressure on her while still making his desire known. She liked it.

Maybe she'd imbibed a smidge too much wine, but who cared? She felt young and carefree, sitting in a bar with a beautiful man who was an interesting conversationalist and had a great laugh. She could use a perfect night, and this fit the bill. Once the flatbread arrived, the tone of the evening shifted. They talked about all those things couples talked about on first dates: movies, books, favorite foods, and where they'd go if offered a chance for a dream vacation. They found themselves aligned on the merits of Lake of the Ozarks, deciding the fifty-four-thousand-acre lake to be a fun getaway if you were into boats, which neither of them was. He told her he had his pilot's license and talked about his travels, which included most of the United States.

She'd been as far as the Gulf of Mexico to see her sister at her naval base and to Chicago to see her brothers. He was a dog person; she liked cats. They both agreed the chemistry teacher, Mr. McWilliams, was a jerk. She knew the plan for her future: run a store and raise Megan. He'd admitted he had no idea what to do next, which was why he was crisscrossing the country taking remote jobs he could do via computer.

Even a man as good-looking as he had to have a flaw, so his lack of a plan for the future was, of course, a deal breaker. Sure, plans changed. But hers didn't. she knew what she wanted, but for some reason the men she met didn't. She'd been married to a man who'd had a midlife crisis and upended their future. She'd then dated a man who said he was settled in Beaumont, and then he changed his mind when something better came along. The last thing she needed was a man who had no clue about what he wanted to do next, who'd been honest that he wouldn't be in Beaumont past the weekend. Besides, since she didn't do flings, any relationship was dead on arrival. Because of this fact, she let go of her inhibitions and had fun. When she walked home—and she would do that soon—she'd have accomplished her goal in ways unimagined. Bonus, she'd attracted a beautiful man whose attention massaged and eased her bruised ego. Maybe she wasn't so over the hill as she'd thought. Amazing what having zero expectations had wrought.

"Zoe? Wow. It is you. I almost didn't recognize you! You're wearing makeup." At the female voice, Zoe stiffened. She sensed Nick's curiosity as a tall blonde approached. Elsa Toth was trailed by another woman, Mirabelle Adams. Great. The dynamic duo of destruction were beelining toward her.

Dread pitted in Zoe's stomach. Elsa, the leader of Megan's Brownie Girl Scout troop, was one of those super-skinny, stay-at-home moms who made anyone standing next to her look supersized, and Zoe was already extremely aware of the extra pounds she carried. "I never thought you went out," Elsa said. "It's so good to see you."

Was it really? Zoe accepted the awkward hug before Elsa stuck out her hand and introduced herself to Nick, adding, "Our daughters are friends."

Zoe's desire to avoid conflict defeated her denial. She wouldn't argue with Elsa, especially not here in a wine bar. Elsa ran both the PTA and Brownies, and no way would Zoe do anything that might damage Megan's social standing. Beaumont Elementary was too small for that, and Elsa had already done enough damage when Zoe and Jared had dated.

Nick accepted Elsa's limp hand. "Nice to meet you. I'm Nick Reilly. Zoe and I are old friends." While he kept his tone pleasant, Zoe heard the underlying message of "You've interrupted us and I'm simply being polite."

Either Elsa didn't catch his subtlety or she didn't care. Zoe figured it was the latter. "Really? Zoe never mentions having old friends."

Zoe winced. *Damn, Elsa. Look at you whipping out*

those claws right away. Maybe the wine had loosened Zoe's thoughts.

Nick's tone sharpened at the edges. "She grew up here so why wouldn't she? When I came back into town, she was the first one I wanted to see."

Zoe turned toward Nick to see if he was serious. But she didn't know him well enough to read his inscrutable, neutral expression. "Seriously?" Elsa asked, and Zoe held back a laugh at her dumbfounded expression when Nick parroted her "Seriously."

Zoe shrugged and smiled at Elsa.

"You are quite the example of still waters running deep, aren't you?" Mirabelle intruded on the conversation. Another East Coast transplant, Mirabelle held out her hand and introduced herself. "What do you do?"

"This and that," Nick evaded. He reached for his port and sipped in a way that said the interlude was over. He didn't ask them if they were having a girls' evening, or if they'd had a nice time tonight. He managed the situation so deftly, amazing Zoe by his complete lack of social pleasantry while still being genial. Zoe wished she could control a conversation as easily as he had. Within seconds, Elsa and Mirabelle told Nick they hoped to see him again and moved away.

"The current crop of mean girls, I see." Nick's gaze flickered back to Zoe.

"Since I was one in high school, I'll be nice and call them the country club set. They're newer transplants who warned me off dating Jared because he was the elementary school principal."

"Did it work?"

"No, but because they have money, they think they

should run everything. Mirabelle owns a shop and her husband is a CEO of some sort in St. Louis."

"Ah, new blood Beaumont finds the old guard bourgeois and useless."

"Something like that. I deal with Mirabelle on Main Street stuff. Elsa runs everything with the parent-teacher group. They think I'm a fool for not selling and moving with Jared to Chicago. First Ted, then Jared." She'd told Nick about Jared earlier.

"They still shouldn't be disrespectful people. It's not hard to be kind," Nick said.

"You'll get no argument from me there." Unlike Zoe's former classmates, whose prejudices Zoe knew inside and out, Mirabelle and Elsa's commentary had stung. Their actions toward her also declared that any high school heydays and power structures were long over. Being a couple with Jared had provided an anchor, a social safety net. The women's arrival tonight had again demonstrated Zoe's laurels were behind her. She wasn't part of the mom clique who loved to go out on the town and be seen. Even at the elementary school, the women worked to make her feel out of place, and she had to put up with them so as not to ruin her daughter's social standing.

Nick watched her with another unreadable expression, as if he could see far too much into her mind. "I should go," she told him. "I have cookies to bake early tomorrow morning."

"May I walk you home?"

She shook her head. "I'm good. Nothing happens in this town minus drunk college kids yanking the petunias out of the planters."

His hand moved to cover hers. Like when he'd refused her credit card, warmth flooded through her. A powerful zing traveled from head to toe. Sex with Ted had been teenage fumbling then perfunctory. Jared's lovemaking had been sweet and caring. Touching Nick even without being naked was like experiencing a blazing fire. She burned like never before, as if she were a phoenix ready to rise from the ashes. All parts of her body desired and wanted. If she turned her hand, she could put her palm to his and run her thumb against his skin. Despite longing to do that, she slipped her hand away to safety. Immediate coolness prickled, indicating what she'd lost.

"How about I walk you to the end of the block? I'm staying at the inn. It's nothing for me to walk back from whatever direction you need to go. I'm not going to pressure you, Zoe. But let them see us walk out together. Let you derive some satisfaction from allowing them to see you leave with me. It sounds vain, but people have told me I'm a catch."

She smiled and tilted her head in acknowledgment. "You are somewhat attractive."

He arched a brow. "Just somewhat?"

Zoe laughed. "Stop digging for compliments."

He laughed with her. "Who me?"

Their laughter slowly faded. "Thanks for retaining shreds of common sense. I don't want to give Elsa or Mirabelle any more ammunition."

"Then let's go." Nick settled the tab. His fingers grazing her back, he followed her as she led the way. Head high, she refused to turn to see if Elsa or Mirabelle watched them walk to the door.

She stepped out onto the brick sidewalk, Nick behind her. A thick mist haloed the antique-replica streetlamps, casting an eerie glow on the cobblestones. Zoe shivered as the damp fall chill seeped through her sweater dress. She should have worn a coat but hadn't thought it necessary.

As if reading her mind, Nick said, "Here. You'll want this." He draped his leather jacket over her shoulders, the woodsy scent of soft buttery leather a powerful aphrodisiac she had to resist. They walked side-by-side toward the cross street. Normally she'd walk the entire length of Main Street before cutting up to reach Third, but tonight she'd turn a street early.

"It's rather spooky out here," Nick observed. "I don't think I've ever seen it quite like this."

Zoe glanced around. "Me either. Keep your eyes peeled and maybe we'll see the Woman in White. This feels like her kind of night and this is her haunt."

"The town ghost? That's actually real?"

Zoe walked next to Nick. "Of course. We just finished a month of Halloween-themed ghost tours and people swear they saw her out searching for her lost love. She's trying to be reunited with him. It's sort of sad, actually."

Discussing the ghost gave Zoe something to talk about, which alleviated some of her worry. Part of her wanted to kiss Nick. Another part wanted to ask him to take her to the inn, to try her first one-night stand despite what he'd said earlier about not crossing a line. Another part feared doing either thing and wished she was already snuggled up alone under the covers.

"She's good for tourism then," Nick said.

"She is. Last month a ghost-hunting show filmed in town. I heard they got some readings. The town is starting to become a Halloween destination."

Shadows, created by the half-moon, danced along the bricks. Dead leaves rustled, tossed by a light wind. The inn's wrought-iron fence came into view directly ahead. "I'll walk you to the corner, if that's okay," Nick said.

Afraid to speak and break the magic, Zoe nodded. As they reached the cross street, Zoe felt the impending loss. Then the hair on the back of her neck stood up, and she glanced behind her. Unbelieving, she put her hand on Nick's arm, stopping him. "Stay still. Don't move," she whispered.

On the opposite side of the street, a woman approached them from behind. Dressed in period clothing, she glided past as a white apparition. Seconds later, she was gone, as if an illusion created by the mist or the fog rolling off the river. Zoe caught Nick's gaze. "Tell me you saw that. That it wasn't a trick of the light."

Nick's wide eyes blinked. "Uh huh. Maybe we manifested her. That was a tad creepy."

Between being this close to him and seeing the Woman in White, nervous energy gave Zoe a short fit of nervous giggles. She caught her breath. "Thanks for keeping me company. Had I seen that by myself, I'd be far more freaked out. And I am very freaked out. That's my first time ever seeing her."

"Mine too." Nick gave a huge exhale.

They approached the corner streetlight, and Zoe mentally planned what to say. She didn't want to walk away without some sort of goodbye, yet she wasn't going to take him home despite her earlier thoughts. She'd always been a "good girl." It was too late to turn bad. They reached the corner, and Zoe opened with a "Be sure to stop in for another cookie before you leave town."

Before he could answer, the harsh and blaring sound of sirens cut through the night as one of Beaumont's pumper trucks came roaring up the hill. The truck barreled over the cobblestones, coming from the fire station near the river, and lights flashed red and blue onto the brick storefronts as the ten-foot-high truck raced through the intersection. From their vantage point, they could see the truck go two more blocks before turning right onto Third Street, in the direction of her house.

"A ghost and a fire truck. Lots of adventure in this town."

Zoe didn't answer as she heard her cell phone ping. She pulled it out and saw she had a voice mail. No, there were more. She'd missed two calls from her alarm company. Fear clawed and she pressed the button on her phone for the second message that had arrived after a delay. "This is NC Security and we've dispatched—"

Zoe didn't wait to hear the rest. She began to run, the uneven nature of the brick sidewalks and the steep incline making her effort like running in molasses, especially considering the thick, high heels of her boots.

"What is it?" Nick easily kept pace.

"I don't know." Out of breath, she gasped the words, and reaching Third Street, she turned right and crossed the street. The sidewalk was flatter here, and farther ahead disco lights bounced off pavement and brick. Her phone shrilled and Zoe swiped. She tried to calm her erratic heartbeat and catch her breath as she answered the alarm dispatcher's questions rapid fire. "No, I'm not home. I'm almost there. I can see the fire truck."

Zoe ran faster, darting across another empty cross street and onto her block. Ahead, her neighbors gawked on the sidewalk, and they called her name as she reached them. She'd gone to school with Lieutenant Carl Cederberg, and he blocked her path to her front walkway. "Carl, why are you here? This is my house."

Carl was in rescue mode and didn't budge. "Is your daughter home?"

"No, she's at a sleepover."

Carl radioed his crew to let them know no one was inside the premises. The frenetic energy of the scene calmed. Firefighters wearing full turnout gear, including their masks, didn't enter or leave her house as urgently. Zoe craned her neck, trying to see the cause of the fire. She hadn't lit any candles. She hadn't left any appliances on. The wiring was old, but the house had been renovated twenty years ago. "Carl, what is going on?"

Carl saw Nick. "Good, you have someone to take care of you. Stay over here, Zoe."

Zoe bristled. "No one needs to take care of me, Carl. Tell me what's burning. What's happening to my house?"

Carl paid her no attention. Instead, he repeated, "Stay here, Zoe," and added, "I'll be back." He pulled on his mask and strode toward her house, the clomping of his boots causing the wooden front stairs to vibrate. He disappeared through a bright red door boasting a splintered frame and pry bar marks. Acid swirled in her stomach, joining the earlier, happier wine and chocolate. She felt sick, as if she could vomit.

"You okay?" Nick asked.

Biting back bile, Zoe swallowed. She'd keep it together even though she wanted to scream and rage at whatever god she'd pissed off. Her insurance deductible was two thousand dollars. Her reserves were already depleted. She shivered as reality climbed her back and sat on her shoulder like a bad omen. This claim would wipe out her savings. Zoe began to shake as the shock hit, that earlier fuzzy warmth of the wine bar fleeing. She was as sober as the day she was born and equally as irritated.

"Zoe, put my coat on."

She reached to her shoulder, finding the leather missing. She'd lost it sometime during the run home and was glad Nick had grabbed it. What a crappy way to end the evening. "I'm fine. I don't need anyone to take care of me."

His supportive demeanor never changed. "Of course you don't. But no point in getting sick."

True. She had a shop to run and a daughter to raise. She hadn't taken a sick day for herself in six years. Nick held out his coat and Zoe slid her arms through the sleeves. She snuggled into comforting, warm, soft leather that smelled like sage and musky male.

Her phone rang, and she answered the incoming call from her mother. The alarm company, unable to reach Zoe, had called Jayne James, the next contact on the list. "I'm fine, Mom. Megan's at Anna's. I don't know what's going on. I'm fine. You don't need to worry. I'll call you in the morning. Love you too."

"Zoe, here. Take this." One of her neighbors handed her a thermos containing hot lemon tea. Another brought her a fuzzy blanket, and Nick draped the purple-and-white striped throw around her shoulders and over his coat.

Zoe craned her neck before turning to Nick. "What's taking them so long? I don't see hoses. That's a good sign, right?"

"I believe so." He began to type something on his phone. At one point, when another neighbor brought Zoe some crackers, Nick moved a step away to make a call.

The wait was excruciating. Time slowed to a snail's pace. Firefighters entered and exited her home, their boots tracking soot from previous calls onto the front stairs and inside. She prayed they wouldn't damage the Oriental rug. She'd let Ted take most of the furniture, but this rug had been the one possession she wanted. She cared for nothing else.

After no flames appeared and the hour grew late, the onlookers faded away one by one as if they'd been ghosts themselves. Zoe slumped against her next door neighbor's fence, allowing the white wooden pickets to support her. Her feet ached from standing in heels. Nick took the empty thermos from her hand and passed it to someone.

"Why won't they tell me what's going on?"

"They will once they know," he reassured. He rubbed his hands together and blew on them.

Soon she and Nick were the only two left on the street besides the first responders. No wonder. It was freezing. Nick had to be cold. "Take your coat. I've got the blanket. You don't need to stay."

"I'm good."

"If you catch cold, I'll never forgive myself." She handed him the blanket and took off the leather. The chill hit her as she swapped the coat for the blanket. She wrapped herself tight. He slid his coat on and zipped it. "I can't believe you're still here. Thank you."

"What type of gentleman would I be if I didn't stay?

Shouldn't be long now. Appears like they're carrying in a fan."

"That can't be good." Zoe stomped her feet to get the circulation going. Her tall leather boots were not designed to be worn while standing outside in the elements nonstop.

"Let's wait and see what they say."

"Okay." Zoe hated to argue. She'd had enough of that in her marriage. But Nick proved to be the perfect companion. He didn't offer useless platitudes designed to make her feel better. He opted out of entertaining her in some misguided attempt to divert her attention. Instead, he stood by her side, a comforting presence she hadn't known she needed.

She watched Carl talk to a member of his team. She'd known him since middle school. Could tell the story about that time in sixth grade when Carl had gotten stuck after taking someone's dare to climb an oak tree. The ladder truck had raised the bucket to rescue him, sealing his fate. Now he was the highest-ranking officer when he was on shift. Zoe knew all these things about Carl, and about his marriage and kids, but she still knew little about the man next to her, who was again tapping and texting. Oddly, though, her gut said she could trust Nick completely. It was a strange, yet calm, feeling.

Carl approached, sans mask, and Zoe straightened. "What's going on? What burned?"

"Nothing burned, Zoe," Carl reassured. "We've been through the whole house with our thermal imaging cameras. You didn't have a fire."

"Thank goodness."

Relief was momentary. "Your alarm company alerted us to a carbon monoxide leak," Carl continued. "When we arrived, we found levels at four hundred ppm. Have you had any headaches or anything?"

Zoe placed her hand on her chest and swayed slightly. "Yes. Earlier. Right before I went out. I thought it was the stress of the day." Which was one reason she'd gone to the wine bar. "I'm feeling fine now." That was if she didn't count the strain of finding her house filled with invisible gas. She pointed at the ambulance that had arrived from another call. "I don't need to go to the hospital."

Carl peered at her and nodded. "Okay. Let's have them check you out, though. Maybe give you some oxygen."

"Can you tell us what happened?" Nick asked.

"I'm not an HVAC expert, but it appears that your furnace's heat exchanger overheated and cracked, sending carbon monoxide throughout your house. It probably happened tonight right before you left and built up while you were out. We've turned off your furnace and have started airing the house. While there was some smoke from the overheating, all you had was smoke. No flames. Once it cracked, the pressure was off. At eight hundred ppm, convulsions can set in within forty-five minutes. Higher levels can cause loss of consciousness and death. Someone upstairs was watching out for you. You're lucky you were gone for the night."

The cold had seeped into Zoe's bones long ago and Carl's words added even more chill. She shivered violently and her teeth started chattering. "When can I go back inside?"

"You can't." Carl said the words with absolute finality. "We'll leave when we get the house to an acceptable level, but then we're declaring your house off-limits until the system has been inspected and repaired and we test the air quality again. Until then, you need to stay somewhere else."

No. No. No. Panic bubbled. "Where am I supposed to go? My mom lives in Kirkwood. I have to bake tomorrow." She paused. She had no idea what time it was. "When you get the house aired out, it'll be fine for me to go back in."

Carl shook his head. "No, it won't. You have no heat, Zoe, and it's colder than normal tonight. We have your windows open. You can't go back inside until I check the air tomorrow, and you can't live in your house until an HVAC company services the heater. We need to make sure no carbon monoxide remains and that you don't have a natural gas leak. We've turned off the gas main. The system is not safe. And I really want the paramedics to check you out now that they're finally here from servicing a crash out on Winery Road."

"I hope everyone's okay. I'm okay." Her stubbornness took hold as uncertainty squeezed her chest. "Carl, the house is fine. I had the HVAC serviced in October. I have a service plan." One that came with a pricey monthly fee. "I'll be fine. I won't use the furnace. I have blankets."

Carl exhaled with the patience of a saint. "No, Zoe. It's not safe. And I'm not explaining to Megan what happened to her mom and why she's attending your funeral if you ignore my orders and go inside. Not to mention your mom would kill me, and I'm more afraid of her than you."

Despair took over. Zoe knew when she was beaten. She wanted to scream and wail, but Zoe did not cry— ever. Not when Ted had told her he was divorcing her, and not even when Jared had hugged her one last time before driving away. Ted thought it was proof of her being cold and bitter. "Carl, where am I supposed to go? My car keys are in the house."

"I can get them. You can drive to a hotel. The one out on Route Sixty-Six is pretty decent. If you're covered, your insurance will pay for a night's stay, maybe more."

Nick spoke then, his voice a beacon in the storm. "She can stay at the inn. Mrs. Bien has a room ready for her."

Carl nodded. "That's a perfect choice. I'll meet you there tomorrow morning and update you. If the levels are safe, I'll let you go inside for a few minutes and pack, so long as a member of my department is with you." With that, Carl strode off. Zoe watched as his men began hauling another large fan into her house. Her lips trembled, both with cold and futility. This could not be happening. But it was.

"Let's get you checked out," Nick said.

Zoe tilted her head. The world came back into focus. The flashing yet silent lights of the truck. The growly diesel engine. The damp mist settling deeper and making the cobblestones glisten. Nick staring at her, concern in those deep, beautiful blue eyes. She pressed her phone but it had died.

"It's late. It's around one-thirty in the morning." Nick led her over to the ambulance, and the paramedics checked Zoe out, gave her some oxygen and released her. As the ambulance readied to pull away, Zoe gazed around. Nick gently reached for her hand and laced his fingers through hers. "Come on. Walk with me. Mrs. Bien's waiting. I called her earlier. She's got some of

Shelby's clothes ready for you, said that you're about the same size."

"I have to be at the store at nine to bake."

He guided her down the street, the purple-and-white blanket billowing like a cape. "It's going to be okay, Zoe."

No, it wasn't, but she was too tired to argue. Her teeth chattered and her cold feet hurt from standing in boots this long. She wanted to close her eyes and wake up and have this nightmare be over.

Tomorrow—no today, she amended—was Saturday. She had to decorate the cookie store for Christmas or incur the wrath of the Merchants Association and picky Mrs. Zappatta and overbearing Mirabelle Adams. Zoe had to schedule the HVAC people for an emergency service call. She had baking to do, left over from the earlier disaster. She wanted to laugh hysterically but failed to summon even a whimper. She'd burned cookies and lost product. Her house hadn't burned, but somehow this disaster felt a million times worse even though she knew that was ridiculous. Her whole body shook. She stumbled slightly and Nick caught her. Even if she was the type to cry, she couldn't muster enough energy to create the tears that would mark her defeat. *Fork it, universe.* She surrendered. She'd been beaten down enough in the last few years to last a lifetime.

Nick draped his arm around her. She instinctively sank into him, his body a solid, reassuring mass as he guided her along the sidewalk toward Main Street. "Let's get you out of the cold."

They reached the inn, where Mrs. Bien immediately made a great fuss that Zoe was in no condition to resist. She soon had Zoe in a flannel nightgown and settled into the floral suite, which contained a lovely full-sized canopy bed. Zoe yanked the thick floral quilt to her chin and tried to stop her teeth from chattering. She'd brushed them with the toothbrush and paste Mrs. Bien provided.

"I'm sorry to be an inconvenience," Zoe said.

"It's nothing. Don't you worry. People check in at all hours. I'm used to it. Nick is here to see you. I'll see you both in the morning." Mrs. Bien headed to the third floor.

Nick came into the doorway, the hallway light silhouetting him in the frame. He held the door open, but Zoe didn't worry. Mrs. Bien liked Nick, and if she trusted him, he couldn't be half bad. Frankly, the way he'd been there tonight impressed Zoe to no end.

"I'm sorry this isn't the way you envisioned the night turning out," she said. She wished she could see his face but he remained in the shadows. "I was debating a good-night kiss when the firetruck went by."

"So was I. And no worries. We can talk in the morning. You need to get some rest rather than worry about wanting to kiss a guy like me."

Gone was the earlier flirtation. "I think I would have liked it. And you seem like a good guy to me. Not many would have stayed by my side tonight." Exhaustion won the war, banishing residual adrenaline. She fought to keep her eyes open. "Where did you come from anyway? How can I not remember you?"

"I wasn't worth seeing," he replied simply, pulling the door toward him. "Good night, Zoe."

She wanted to tell him that of course he was worthy, but he'd already shut the door.

Chapter Four

After fewer than four hours of sleep, Nick rose before dawn. Since daylight savings time had ended, he'd have almost an hour before the sun fully broke the horizon at six forty. The air was crisp against his high-tech running clothes made with recycled polyester fibers, as his feet pounded the hard-packed gravel surface of the Katy Trail. Created before he was born, the state had converted 240 miles of the former Missouri-Kansas-Texas railroad line into a walking and biking trail that crisscrossed most of the state. All the popular kids had taken their homecoming and prom pictures at the restored depot and the retired caboose located in the city's riverside park. He hadn't attended either dance, not even after he'd moved. Minus the occasional squirrel and a deer or two, Nick had the darkened trail to himself, the final streaks of a setting moon casting ambient light that reflected and guided his way.

Early morning was Nick's favorite time of day. When he'd been younger, those had been the few minutes when his mom hadn't been angry. Despite the harsh light streaming through grimy windows, the world had appeared bright and possible. By evening she'd been tired and beat, if she came home at all. Many times he'd scrounged for dinner.

In college, which he'd attended on need-based scholarships, he'd read Henry David Thoreau's *Walden*, and the work had changed his life. He'd hated high school English, finding the study of dead white men boring and irrelevant. Even though Thoreau fit firmly in that category and had many flaws when viewed from a twenty-first-century perspective, Thoreau's social experiment at Walden Pond formed the foundation for Nick's personal philosophy. The company he'd sold was proof he'd advanced confidently in the direction of his dreams, following Thoreau's line of "If a man does not keep pace with his companions, perhaps it is because he hears a different drummer. Let him step to the music which he hears, however measured or far away." When Nick had made his first million, he'd commissioned a plaque with those words. Now it was boxed away somewhere, collecting dust. Nick appreciated the irony.

He ran on, the runner's high allowing his mind to compute and process freely, becoming the physical epitome of Thoreau's "Morning is when I'm awake and there is dawn in me." Nick's best creativity came in the early morning. He refused to sleep through his life. He'd done enough of that in high school. He'd figured out that "to be awake is to be alive." Nick refused to let opportunities slip through his grasp again.

He lengthened his stride as he contemplated the previous night. When Zoe had entered the bar in that black dress, Fate had smacked him on the shoulder and whispered, "You're a fool if you walk away tonight."

Pitching to venture capitalists had been easier than approaching Zoe, but life was about risk. The result? A wonderful time. She was genuine. He liked her, no longer with a boy's crush, but with a man's serious and genuine interest. He'd wanted that kiss with as much fervor as when he'd wanted to escape Beaumont.

This, Nick decided, proved his relationship with Alexa had been a lie—one of his own creation. What the media and Hollywood sold viewers wasn't real, but Nick had wanted that life. Achieving the glamorous life had represented what he hadn't had in his childhood: money, power, and beautiful women. But all those had proved to be fake. Not his childhood though. All that had been real: the hatred. The bullying. The poverty. The hunger, both literal and figurative for both food and knowledge. He'd risen above until he wanted for nothing. Yet, instead of being satisfied, he felt empty.

With Zoe he'd felt seen. Her kind heart remained unscathed. If he'd needed proof of that fact, last night, before he'd shut the door, she'd apologized for the night not turning out the way he'd hoped. She'd also told him she'd been debating kissing him. That gave Nick's heart a little jolt.

He wanted to help her, but how? How to assist without offending her? Last night she'd wanted to kiss him. She'd leaned on him—Nick the man and not Nick the billionaire.

The whole night had been far beyond his expectations. During a delightful evening filled with margherita flatbread and port. She'd told him about her parents, how they'd helped her finance the shop, which also meant her mom micromanaged since it was owner-financing. "She may have moved to Kirkwood," Zoe had said, "but she's not lost touch with her network. You'd be amazed at how many people still report the comings and goings of Main Street back to my mom, including how the shop's doing. I want to be independent, you know? I'm not a plate that breaks."

He'd told her he understood, but he really didn't. From elementary school on, his mom had pretty much left him to fend for himself. His watch chimed, telling him he'd reached the halfway point. He reversed directions and headed back, his brain again filled with thoughts of how he'd almost kissed Zoe. He'd been ready to ask permission and place his lips on hers as the firetruck had raced by.

Nick ran faster, drawing the fresh morning air deep into his lungs. He'd started this cross-country journey to exorcise demons, not create new ones. Kissing Zoe would escalate things, change them. She saw him as a nice guy. He liked that. He didn't want her remembering he'd been that scrawny poor kid everyone laughed at. Didn't want her to feel sorry for him. He also didn't want her to know he was a billionaire. He wanted her to know the guy underneath, without the social and financial trappings coloring her vision. He reached town and jogged the hill from the river to Main Street. He stopped running at the corner, under that same lamppost that in the morning light appeared like all the others on the block.

Done running, he planted his hands on his hips, caught his breath, and began walking toward the inn. He found Mrs. Bien in the dining room, arranging the inn's continental breakfast. Her husband, John, sat at one end of the table, eating a plate of scrambled eggs and bacon and gave Nick a nod of acknowledgment.

"Good morning," Mrs. Bien greeted. "Good run?"

"It was." Nick went to the sideboard and poured coffee into a porcelain mug. "I know I said I was going to check out today, but I've decided to stay on. Is it possible to keep my room on a day-by-day basis?"

Mrs. Bien appeared pleased, smiling in a way Nick's mom never did. "Of course. I'm glad you'll get to see the Christmas decorations. They'll be up by the end of the day."

Nick didn't care about decorating, unless that meant Zoe had to decorate as well. He filed that fact away. "If her insurance won't pay, I'll cover the entire cost of Zoe's room. Say it's an anonymous donation or something if she protests."

He waited for her to question him, not about the money, for Mrs. Bien had seen his Black card, but about his motives. Life on the West Coast must have jaded him, for she surprised him by taking things at face value with a "That's very generous of you. We can do that," and nothing more.

"Thanks." Carrying his mug, Nick went upstairs to shower and change. When he returned to the dining room a half hour later, the older couple he'd met briefly yesterday sat on one side of the table. Honeymooners, he remembered. She rested her fingers lightly on his forearm. He had one hand on her thigh while his other hand fed her a strawberry. Both were in their mid-sixties. Wes and Kathleen had met in college, but not reconnected until a reunion about two years back, bonding over losing both of their spouses to cancer. They'd married a week ago.

Nick's mom hadn't ever married, but she had finally found someone worthy to keep her company. Nick had met the guy once and had found him a decent sort, thankfully not some gold digger after the investment stream of income Nick had established. He wanted his mom independent and financially secure while still protected. Even though she and Nick had never been super close, she was still his mom.

"Good morning," Nick greeted as he went to the sideboard and lifted a plate. "How are you today?"

"Great," Wes said. "This town's great. Everything we hoped it would be."

Nick's own trip had been surprisingly great so far, too. He served himself some scrambled eggs and bacon before moving to other choices. "How long are you in town for?"

"Just the one night. We're heading to Kimmswick next, and from there starting to make our way back home."

"We read about this place in Global Outdoors and added it to our list," Kathleen added. "We're touring Missouri's battle sites."

"And seeing its historic river towns," Wes threw out. He leaned over and kissed her cheek before glancing at Nick. "What about you? Where are you headed?"

Nick took a seat across the table from them. "I'm staying a few more days. I lived here until my junior year. Then my family moved to California. Oakland," he added, seeing their curiosity and trying to preempt any further deep dive into his past.

Wes reached for his coffee. "Never been there."

"Not as interesting as Beaumont." Nick forked some light and fluffy eggs into his mouth. "Did you have a chance to shop?"

"We did," Kathleen confirmed. "I bought everyone I know some of those cute little soaps next door and…"

Nick half-listened as she described the same stores he'd visited yesterday, her husband on occasion finding ways to insert himself into her travelogue. Nick had nearly finished his breakfast when Zoe entered. She'd put her hair into a ponytail and wore a large maroon River Bend College sweatshirt that swallowed her whole. Dark gray wooly socks contrasted with baggy light gray sweatpants. She was still beautiful no matter the ill-fitting outfit. Nick rose to his feet. "Hey. How are you feeling this morning?"

"Like I got hit by a truck." She thumbed the sweatshirt's hem. "Missing my clothes and my house. I look like a big red grape. But I guess it could be worse. I'll at least get to go home at some point and my stuff will be there. And not fried to a crisp."

He hated that she stressed over her possessions. He could buy her an entire wardrobe without scratching the tip of his wealth iceberg, not that she'd let him. Last night he'd had to convince her to let him pay and she'd made it clear to him how she hated relying on other's charity. He stood, introduced Wes and Kathleen. Nick pulled out the chair next to him. "Come eat something. Mrs. Bien made eggs, bacon, and pancakes."

"Is that a blueberry muffin?" She pointed to his plate and her tongue swiped across her top lip.

"It is and it's delicious. They're over here." To tamp down his desire for her, he retrieved a clean plate and handed it to her, taking care not to touch her. He topped off his coffee and watched as she began making her choices. He waited until she'd taken her seat before returning to his.

Zoe unrolled the silverware and put the linen napkin in her lap. "Did you at least sleep okay?" Nick asked.

"Please tell me I don't look like I tossed and turned all night." He shook his head quickly as her fingers tore a blueberry muffin into pieces. "I slept like a rock. I'm not hung over. But I am overwhelmed and it's not even eight. There's so much I have to do today." She put some of the muffin into her mouth. "Oh, this is good."

"I'm glad you like it." Mrs. Bien had returned to check on the breakfast buffet and her guests. "I'll send some muffins home with you."

"I don't get to go home." Zoe's lower lip quivered, and Nick gave her hand a sympathetic squeeze.

"How long have you two been together?" Wes said after Mrs. Bien went into the kitchen.

"Oh, we're not," Nick began.

"Since last night," Zoe interrupted, putting more muffin in her mouth.

Wes and his wife appeared confused. Nick couldn't tell if she was joking or serious. He studied her profile. Her head was down, and she focused on eating.

"Oh, so are you or aren't you a couple?" Kathleen appeared disappointed, and Nick figured that was the romantic in her.

"We went to high school together and ran into each other last night," Nick explained. "I'm leaving Monday for—" he paused. He had no specific agenda in mind and nothing appealed. He'd figure out where to go later.

"You're not leaving today?" Zoe stared at him.

He tried to appear nonchalant. "Figured I'd stay an extra few days. Thought you might have stuff to do at your house, and didn't you say you had to decorate the store? Thought you might like some help with that to try and take some of the load off. Unless I've overstepped." Worry had him rubbing his fingers together.

Zoe held his gaze before giving a shake of her head. "No, you're fine. Extra hands would be nice and would be appreciated. Thank you."

"What are you decorating?" Kathleen asked. "You have a store?"

As Zoe explained, Nick found himself grateful that her face grew more animated. Generosity had her telling Kathleen and Wes that they had to stop by for celebratory cookies as her wedding present for them. The couple hadn't visited the store on their previous shopping spree and promised to drop in before they left town.

"If you two are ever in Chattanooga, you'll have to look us up," Wes offered. "Young man, you take care of that girl."

"She can take care of herself. She's one of the most capable people I know."

"Most women are, son. You know exactly what I mean. You be good to her." With that Wes and Kathleen went upstairs and out of earshot.

Zoe arched a brow at him. She appeared surprised. "You really think I'm capable? Most people have their doubts."

Nick hated that she doubted herself. "Those people are fools. You've always impressed me. You're kind to do that for them."

"They seem like a lovely couple." Zoey rearranged the green grapes she put on her plate. "I'm in the happiness business. That's what cookies are, you know. Bites of happiness. If I can make their day, they'll tell others or leave a good online review, and maybe more people will come in the door. It's business."

"It might be business, but it's also more than that. I'm not sure if what I did made people happy, but I did provide something they needed. Why did you tell them we're a couple? Would you like us to be? I mean, I'm game to take you on a date."

Pink stained her cheeks. "I honestly don't know why I said that. It seemed easier. Did you see them? They're in love. They want the rest of the world to be as happy as they are. I refused to rain on their parade. You said you're leaving, and last night we pretended, so I followed through on an impulse, like we did last night."

"Why not? Let people think we're madly in love. I may sound vain, but I know I'm handsome."

"That's an understatement. You're gorgeous. Men of your caliber are rare. But sure, why not? Why not let them be jealous. Maybe for once all the people in this town will stop looking at me with pity in their eyes for a day or two. Do you know how much I hate that?"

"I believe I do, and I'm happy to play along until I leave. You were nice to me long ago. Call it a way to repay the favor. And for the record, I find you quite attractive too. I'm still thinking about our almost kiss."

Zoe's lips parted, but before she could respond, Mrs. Bien returned to the dining room with Carl in tow. "Look who I found at the door. Now you fill a plate and sit for a spell," she told Carl. "I'm also going to send you some food home for your wife and kids."

"Yes, ma'am," Carl agreed.

"See," Zoe whispered to Nick. "Easier sometimes to agree rather than argue. World's rough enough. I like to make things as smooth as possible."

"Then in that case, we're dating and in love." Besides, why not? Zoe intrigued him. And he had time to kill.

Zoe waited until Carl sat down with his filled plate. "You're going to tell me I can go home, right?"

Carl shook his head. "Not exactly. Not until we re-inspect and the HVAC is fixed. However, you can go inside and pack as long as someone in my department accompanies you. If you want, we can do it after break-fast. I told Wendy I was stopping by here to help you before I came home. I'm gonna have to text her that Mrs. Bien's sending food with me. She'll be thrilled. She hates to cook."

At that moment, Zoe's mom arrived. Nick recognized her. She hadn't changed much, minus now having a full head of gray hair. Older than her husband, Jayne James was in her sixties. She'd had her kids late, with Zoe the youngest. "Zoe!"

"Mom!" Zoe stood and accepted the hug her mother gave her.

"I'm so glad you're okay." As her mom stepped back, she gave Zoe a complete once-over. When her eyes lighted on Nick, they sharpened to a point as she tried to place him. Nick held Mrs. James's gaze until she turned her attention back to her daughter. "You had me so wor-ried. I almost drove out last night but knew you'd be fine if you were staying at the inn. I'm so glad Megan wasn't with you. What if either of you had inhaled the gas?"

"But we didn't. The paramedics said I was fine. I am fine. You didn't need to drive all the way out here to check on me."

Jayne wasn't persuaded. "Of course I did. You'll need help today with the store and decorating and such.

Who better to do it than me and your sister? Sierra will be along in a while."

Nick noticed the tension in the set of Zoe's shoulders. Based on what she'd told him, Zoe worried her mom would take over. "I have employees and the shop is fine. All I want is my stuff and Carl will help me. I can manage."

"Are you sure? I was always grateful to have extra hands. You know, they make light work and all that." Her mom's nose wrinkled as she took in Zoe's outfit. Nick's protective instinct immediately came to Zoe's defense and he rose to his feet. However, Mrs. Bien beat him to speaking.

"Those are my clothes," Mrs. Bien said in that easy, soothing tone that made her a master innkeeper. "I had some more stylish stuff of Shelby's in the closet, but realized it was all from high school. Shelby doesn't even fit in it anymore. I really should donate the items. I'll add it to the get-around-to-it list. Zoe simply needed something quickly until she could raid her closet."

Jayne's lips thinned but she remained silent, for even Nick knew one didn't criticize Mrs. Bien. As for Zoe, Nick had always thought the baby of the family got away with the most, but perhaps because she'd wanted to take over the store, Zoe had endured more scrutiny than normal. He wanted to offer his assistance, but held back, not wanting to insert himself without getting Zoe's approval first. Last thing he wanted was to make things worse.

"Besides not having my clothing, you can see I'm fine," Zoe said. A tiny, wrinkled *M* formed between her brows. "I have it under control."

That got a sharp response. "Just because you're

grown doesn't mean I don't worry about you and Megan. What kind of a mother would I be if I didn't? You're lucky you and Megan weren't home." Her eyes narrowed and swung to Nick again. "I heard you were with her."

Ah, the Beaumont grapevine. "I was. We were having a drink when we got the news. Surely that's acceptable." While he appreciated her mom's concern, Zoe was a grown woman. He understood Zoe's worry that her mom would again insert herself into managing the store. Her mom was clearly at loose ends from selling a business that consumed so much of her time. The days could feel long and empty, which was why he'd filled them by flying around the country. "I'm Nick Reilly."

Zoe's mom had a much firmer handshake than the mean girls from last night. "You appear familiar."

"I haven't lived here since I was a boy," Nick said. "Zoe and I go way back."

"I'm sorry I don't recognize you. I never forget a face."

"Mine's changed a lot. It's nice to meet you." Nick gathered he was dismissed when Jayne turned her attention back to Zoe. "I'll manage the store today while you sort things out. I told Nelson I'd bring you back to stay with us tonight. He's expecting us for dinner."

"Mom, no. I'm not going to Kirkwood tonight. The only other space is a Murphy bed in his office and I'd have to get up at three a.m. and then drive forty-five minutes out here. That's ridiculous. Megan has school this week. We'll rent something if needed."

"I can move a rollaway into your room for her if you want to continue to stay here. The room is yours as long as you like," Mrs. Bien said. "Actually, once Wes and Kathleen leave today, I'll move you into the suite. It has more space."

Thwarted, her mom gave a small huff. "Have you spoken to the insurance company? I figured you hadn't, so I called Hal and gave him a head's up. He's on his way over to talk to you."

Nick had no idea who Hal was but assumed he was the insurance agent when Zoe said, "I was going to call and see what insurance covered this morning. He didn't need to be roused out of bed."

"Oh, I'm sure Hal leapt at the chance to have one of my breakfasts," Mrs. Bien said, ever the peacekeeper. "There's always plenty of food, and you know his wife died last year. He probably jumped at the opportunity to get out of that house, and it's only a short walk."

"What house?" Nick asked.

Mrs. Bien gestured toward the front of the house. "He owns that three-story mansion down on South Main right next to Luke and Shelby. The historical landmark? Blue with the white trim?"

"Got it," Nick said. He'd walked by it many times.

"Hal's on his way and I called Larry and asked him to come over. That's where you have the HVAC plan, correct? With his company?" Jayne waited for her daughter's confirmation.

Mrs. Bien took the arrival of additional breakfast guests in stride. Zoe, however, appeared overwhelmed by the number of people coming to the inn. Nick gave her hand a squeeze, which she returned. "Mrs. James, how about you sit down and have something to eat? Zoe and I have some things to discuss. I'm sure her priority is seeing the damage to her house and packing her things, especially once Carl's finished."

Zoe shot him a grateful glance.

"I'm almost done," Carl said. Nick noted the fire-fighter still had most of the second helpings left on his plate. "We'll go in a few minutes. Unless you want to wait until after Hal gets here? I can have one of the other guys who are on shift take you and you can do it all in one swoop."

Zoe's mom shook her head. "Later won't work. You have to bake and the store opens in two hours. I'll head over and help you open. Do you have the decorating under control?"

Instead of answering, Zoe lifted her mostly eaten breakfast plate from the table and carried it to the service tray. Nick took that as his cue to do the same. Nick noted her fingers trembled as she ensured the tray jack remained steady. "You okay?" he whispered.

"Fine."

She was lying, betrayed by the twitch at the corner of her eye. She was nowhere close to being okay. Nick wouldn't be either if he were in her shoes. He'd once overloaded the circuits of a computer and watched it fry. Zoe's stress level appeared closer to a breakdown than being "fine." She'd had a huge shock last night. She needed time to recover. "I got your back if you need it. Use me as a buffer if you want."

"Really?" She turned and held his gaze. Her intensity threw him. She held herself tightly leashed, but he could see the fragility of her control starting to falter. The hints were in the rigidity of her posture and the lit-tle crease deepening across her forehead. "You'd do that for me? You don't even know me. I was joking earlier with Wes and Kathleen. Trying not to ruin their trip."

"I'd like to get to know you. You're safe with me

and so are your secrets. Tell me what you need. Let me help." He could afford whatever she required, be whomever she wanted. "Seriously. I can tell you want to be independent and you are. But sometimes even an island needs shoring up. Let me do something, especially if that helps you reach your goal. What was it you said? You wanted to be independent of your parents. Well, I'm not them, and everyone needs help sometimes, so give me something to do instead of having your mom do it. I've been where you are, Zoe, in one form or another. I know what it's like when things get overwhelming. But you won't break. Trust me, you got this."

"I want them off my back. I want them to leave me alone. I have enough to deal with without all the noise. I'm simply so tired all the time. When does it end? When is what I do enough?"

He could understand. He'd sold his company because it hadn't fulfilled his soul and instead had sucked it dry. "I don't know. Use me however you need."

She stared at him. "I still don't know why you're doing this, but thank you for helping me get some space."

He swiveled around with Zoe and they faced the crowd: Mrs. Bien, her mom, Carl, a man Nick assumed to be Hal and another who must be Larry the HVAC guy, both of whom had joined the fray the moment Nick and Zoe's backs had been turned. Wes and Kathleen, who'd decided they wanted more coffee before adventuring onward, were now in the dining room, along with Mr. Bien who'd wandered back in to see what all the commotion was about.

"Everyone, this is Nick. Well, some of you already met him."

Nick glanced at Zoe, sensing something had shifted.

He suspected Zoe had reached her tolerance limit, same as Nick's first computer. He raised his hand in a chest-height wave. "Hi."

"Zoe." Her mom's maternal tone said it all, He put his fingers lightly on her arm in support. Maybe that's what made her blurt out what came next, cutting off her mom before she got another word in edgewise.

"Mom. Enough. Nick and I are engaged. I know you want to run things, but we've got it from here, okay?"

Oh boy. When he'd made his offer of being anything she needed, he'd never expected this. But a lifetime of dealing with surprises meant Nick rolled with it. Nothing fazed him. If Zoe wanted them engaged, he'd play along. Surely, there'd be an exit plan.

"You're what?" Her mom's disbelieving expression was clear. "When were you even dating? How long have you known him?"

"I know it's a shock, but yes, we're engaged," Nick confirmed. *In for a penny...*

He dropped his arm over Zoe's shoulders and smiled at the group who stared at them with mouths open, except for Kathleen, who clapped her hands and squealed, "I could tell it was love at first sight."

In for a pound. He refused to leave Zoe stranded and he had been looking for his next challenge to alleviate boredom. Who knew it would be this? "Exactly. So, no worries. We appreciate all your help and we'll get to everyone in turn to work out the details. Zoe's strong and capable, and she's got it from here."

As Zoe observed all the surprised faces staring at her, she had no idea what had caused her to make such an outrageous declaration. No devil on her shoulder whispered in her ear. No internal monologue had preceded her blurting out the words. No one would believe her engaged after one night. This was no rom-com love at first sight. They probably thought her out of her mind.

But as Nick's arm settled comfortably over her shoulders, she went with the flash flood she'd created by parting the floodgates. She'd extract herself and mop up this mess of her own creation later. For now, she'd use anything to buy time and get the heck out from under her mom's overbearing scrutiny. Her mom was a fixer. If she knew Zoe was in financial straits, she'd swoop in like a guardian angel and take care of everything, exactly as she had been doing ever since Zoe had been little. Zoe knew it was high time to stand on her own two feet, even if it meant making a deal with the devil in tight jeans and a polo that sculpted every curve. Zoe shook off her indecision and began giving directions.

"Mrs. Bien, I'll take that suite if that's still okay. Carl, as soon as I talk to Hal, we'll go to the house. Hal, give me five minutes, and Carl, give me ten. That should be plenty of time for you to finish breakfast. Larry, if you want, you can come with me and Carl to the house. Mom, when you're done eating, if you want to go start the baking at the store, that would be great. I appreciate your offer to help. I prepped yesterday so things should be ready."

Since her mom clearly needed to do something, baking would give her a focal point and satisfy her need to help. Zoe knew her mom would also give her the third degree as soon as they were alone, but she'd cross that bridge later. With Nick acting as a buffer, maybe Zoe could put that conversation off as long as possible. Nick had told her he was leaving Monday. She'd make up something about his traveling for business and be able to get a few more weeks of peace out of their fake engagement. It was tough enough taking over the famed store and running it successfully without having her mom's added interference. While Zoe appreciated her mom's desire to keep helping, Zoe wanted to run the store her way, by herself, without her mom's beloved micromanaging. She was an adult. Time to stand on her own two feet, even if it took Nick's yanking her upward first.

"Well." Mrs. Bien broke the silence. "Of course, the suite is yours. Wouldn't you agree, everyone, that what Zoe said sounds like a good plan we should all follow?"

Like being in one of those dramatic plays where everyone freezes on stage and then suddenly begins moving again, conversation started to hum. Hal talked to her mom. Carl went back to eating. Mrs. Bien spoke to Wes and Kathleen about checkout.

Nick. She really needed to talk to Nick. Hopefully he would forgive her. He hadn't moved his arm and he had agreed. Hopefully that was a good sign. He was leaving. None of this would affect him long-term. As if reading her mind, his voice tickled her ear.

"Come with me." He led her from the dining room and to the second floor. He guided her into his room and shut the door behind him. "Sit."

Zoe sunk into the leather wingback. Nick perched across from her on the desk chair. "I'm sorry. I can go down there and explain everything," she said.

Nick shook his head, and a lock of that gorgeous sunset-colored hair swooped over his eye. He pushed it back. "Nah. Let it play out."

He appeared totally serious, which threw Zoe. She peered at him. "Okay. I mean, I hoped you'd say that.

Still, you're leaving so this isn't really your fight. You have an out."

A shoulder covered with a dark blue long-sleeved polo made a small shrug. "I'll be here as long as you need me. If not, it would ruin the optics and erase all the gains you made down there."

"What gains? I didn't do anything but lie to people. I'm known to be blunt, but I try not to lie. Well, maybe like with Wes and Kathleen. But not to my mother." Zoe experienced the full weight of guilt. She began to second-guess her impulsiveness. "Maybe that rom-com I watched last night invaded my subconscious and made me come up with this dumb idea."

"It's fine. I don't mind. There's nothing wrong with a few white lies along the way if it helps everyone in the long run."

Zoe scowled at him. "Even if we're stretching the truth, it feels unethical."

Nick gave her a killer smile and shrugged. "Perhaps. But it's not like you're telling me you love me and cheating on me. That's unethical. And some good already came out of it. Did you hear yourself down there? You told Mrs. Bien to prepare a room, Carl to eat, Hal to wait, Larry to have breakfast, and your mom to go bake. You took charge."

Zoe bristled. "I'm always in charge."

Nick arched an eyebrow and Zoe drummed her pointer and middle fingers against the leather armrest. He was right. Even in high school she'd let Ted lead. Then Jared. "I did, didn't I? I took charge." She reveled in the wonder of it. "Thanks for helping me do that."

"I didn't do anything. You did it all by yourself. One of the first things of being a boss is knowing how to take charge of a situation. You went about it in a rather unorthodox way, but you got there in the end and stuck the landing."

"My dad used to say that all the time. He was a Navy pilot."

That cute dip in his chin deepened as he nodded. "Well, it's true. People shouldn't doubt you. You know what you're doing."

"Are you sure about that? People say I should sell. Or I should have sold everything months ago and moved to Chicago with Jared. But I couldn't. This is my home. My dream."

"You don't owe anyone any explanations. You love your store and that's enough. There's nothing wrong with you, Zoe. It's them. Stop letting them in your head. Stop doubting yourself."

"You're the one in my head now," she admitted. "As long as we don't get serious. As long as this…" She gestured between them. "We can't let this get out of control. You're leaving and I have a daughter who can't have one more male figure in her life move away after she gets attached."

"That's more than fair. This plan can work."

"You have no secrets? Nothing you're keeping from me?"

"I'm not married, not dating anyone, and you'll always be perfectly safe with me. You're the boss, Zoe. You control how this goes."

Nick knew how to say all the right things, didn't he? She'd finally found a guy who seemed to understand her, they were fake engaged, and soon he was leaving. Story of her life: chaos and fate laughing. "You know, no simulation or class prepares you for what adulting is really like. You simply have to live it."

Nick grinned. "Exactly. 'Here is life, an experiment to a great extent untried by me; but it does not avail me that they have tried it.'" He caught her confusion. "Thoreau. *Walden*. Never mind. Basically he's saying that life is your greatest teacher, not other people or institutions. Thoreau thinks we live but a portion of our lives. Long ago, I decided I want to live all of it, you know? Good or bad."

"Mine's mostly bad and I don't have that luxury. Which is how I got us into this mess." Zoe nibbled her lower lip.

"I do. I'm considering this the start of a grand adventure. I've never been engaged. It'll be fun. Interesting. Novel."

"I hate lying to them." Really, that was the crux of the matter. It simply went against how she'd been raised.

"Then don't. Ask me to marry you."

The solution seemed so simple that Zoe stood and paced. "Are you serious?"

Nick rose and gave her a full shoulder shrug. "Why not? It'll be like Ryan Reynolds and Sandra Bullock in that movie. Ask me to marry you so you don't have to lie."

He meant *The Proposal*. "Do you want me on my knees?"

He frowned. "Of course not. That's silly. I'm not trying to humiliate you but help you. As a friend."

She could use one of those. "You do know they fell in love in the movie."

"That's Hollywood. I dated an actress. She was as fake as her performance."

Of course he had. But at this moment, he was what she needed. Zoe took a deep breath. "Nick Reilly, will you marry me?"

Nick came over and took her hand. Zoe felt the sizzle shoot straight through her as he gave their linked hands a little shake. "Yes, Zoe, I will marry you. Now that we've settled that, our engagement is not a lie. Let's go find Carl before he leaves and you have to deal with another firefighter."

Nick was so practical, which brought her down to earth from the surrealness of the moment. "Yeah, I don't want that."

"Exactly. Let's get your house straightened out. Remember, you're the boss."

"I'm the boss."

"You are. Now let's go face the horde. But one thing first."

Zoe blinked at the intensity she saw in his gorgeous blue eyes. "Yes?"

"We don't want you to be like a deer in the headlights when someone demands I kiss you. Which you know they will. So I'm going to kiss you, especially since we missed our chance last night. You ready for a practice run?"

Zoe's heart raced. Nick's words created the same rush as she'd felt on the Tornado water slide at Six Flags, her body plummeting at thirty-two feet a second as she swirled through the sixty-foot-wide, blue-and-yellow-checkered tunnel. The desire she was experiencing was scary and exciting at the same time, and he hadn't even brought his lips to hers.

"I guess." She tried to remain casual but adrenaline spiked. "Go ahead."

Nick palmed her cheek, his fingers feather light against her jawbone. He peered down at her, his mouth like an irresistible laser beam holding the promise of the world. Her breath caught as he angled his lips over hers.

Then flesh met flesh. Oh, softly at first, but Zoe experienced the immediate zing. Sensation traveled through her as if she'd been struck by lightning. As he nipped and pressed, desire swept like five-thousand gallons of rushing water carrying a raft along the rapids. She sighed with the thrill of it all, and when he probed gently into the small gap she'd just created, she captured the tip of his tongue and sucked him inside like a thirsty person finding potable water. Her hands threaded into his enticing, sexy hair—she found it extra silky and soft as it slipped through her fingers. Her body was on fire and she wanted more. Only Nick could quench this heat, this need. His hand slid to cup her hip, drawing her curves to him.

"Zoe?" A knock sounded on the door at the same time she registered her mom's voice. "Zoe? Are you in there?"

Zoe jumped out of Nick's arms as if spooked. She noted he appeared as dazed as she felt. "Coming." She made a poor attempt to brush wrinkles from the ugly sweatshirt and yanked on the doorknob to find her mom standing there, frowning.

Her mom smoothed out her expression. "Carl's done with breakfast and wants to know if you're ready."

"I'll be right down." Zoe closed the door to shut out her mom and leaned back against the wood.

Nick remained where he'd been when they'd kissed, his hair askew. He inclined his head. "Sounds like you're needed. Go get 'em, boss lady."

She fought the urge to press her fingers to her lips to see how swollen and puffy they were. "You're coming with me?"

To her relief, he nodded. "Of course. I said I'd help."

He'd already done far more. He'd given her a slate-wiping kiss. Who knows what would have happened had her mom not interrupted. Would Zoe have let him lift off her sweatshirt? Would she have removed his polo? Let him lie with her naked on that oh-so-close bed? That had been some kiss.

Recognizing she wanted all of those things made her give herself a hug, as if the action would ward off further disruption to her orderly, boring world. Nick ran his hands through his hair, which magically fell into place. She wished hers did that. Wished she had his calm and confidence. His sex appeal. His ability to be unaffected by knee-weakening kisses. He was so gorgeous, he could have his pick of all the single women out there. He'd dated an actress! Why had he agreed to this scheme? Why was she continuing it?

He studied her, his expression unreadable. As if sensing her hesitation, he gestured at the door. "I'll be right behind you. Ready?"

No, not necessarily. But she had no choice. It was called adulting.

"Good thing we got that kiss out of the way." Her quick laugh masqueraded as self-assurance even though she felt no such thing. That kiss had done things to her like no other. It was time to face the crowd downstairs, and to use a strength she hadn't known she possessed pre-Nick. She turned the door handle, ready to face the crowd downstairs. "Let's go."

Chapter Five

An hour later, the rapid-fire hits kept coming. Zoe tried to stay positive—she had her clothes, she had clothes for her daughter and she had a place to stay. What she didn't have was ten thousand dollars to replace the entire HVAC system. She blinked back the tears that threatened every time she thought of it. She did not cry.

Before her, sympathy etched the myriad lines crossing Larry's face. "You have a cast-iron furnace that's fifty years old," he told her in a firm tone that silenced all argument. "You have to replace the entire system, not just the heat exchanger. The system has to be brought up to code. It happens all the time in these old houses."

Of course it did. And of course, before she, Carl, and Larry had left the inn, Hal had told her that she didn't have systems breakdown coverage on her insurance policy, which might have paid for the repairs. She railed at her misfortune. She'd had a clean bill of health from the home inspector upon purchase. Somewhere she'd walked under a ladder, or broken a mirror, or crossed a black cat. Maybe she'd been born under an unlucky star or something.

"The town has a historic preservation fund. You can apply to it for help," Hal said before departing with a thousand dollar deposit charged to her emergency credit card. "Either way, I'll be here Monday to start. Moving you to the top of the list."

"Thanks." She dismissed applying for the fund, which was mainly used for buildings beyond repair. Maybe if it had been the store, but not for her house. Everyone would know her financial situation if she did, and she refused to allow that. If she wanted everyone's sympathy, she might as well make and publicize one of those online fundraisers, which in her mind was almost as embarrassing as standing on the street corner with a cup outstretched. Finances were to be kept private.

She'd handle this.

Because she had a maintenance plan with Larry's company, she could do a two-year, same-as-cash, no-interest payment plan. She'd be able to set that up with his office manager on Monday. She'd also built up five hundred dollars in credit from having the plan, so that would help, and once the work was complete, the gas company would give her a three hundred dollar rebate for becoming more energy efficient. Trying to stay positive with a "something was better than nothing" mentality, Zoe focused on the fact that, barring no more surprises, she'd be back home Wednesday afternoon.

One step at a time, Zoe reminded herself. Even if those steps seemed to be over canyons.

"How'd it go?" Nick asked as she brought her suitcase to the inn. He'd wanted to go with her but had respected her wishes of "I've got this."

She filled him in as they walked to Auntie Jayne's. "It's so rare I don't open," she told him. "I drop Megan at school and start baking."

As she opened the back door to the shop, fresh-baked aromas reached Zoe's nose. The angle allowed her to watch her mom. The famed Auntie Jayne was in her element. Mixers whirled. Her mom scooped rounds of dough onto brown parchment paper. Ovens chirped. Trays went in and came out with perfectly baked cookies. In what had been her element for decades, her mom dazzled. Always Zoe's inspiration, she'd built this store from a quaint little hobby into a Main Street institution. Was this what Megan might see if she stood in the doorway some day in the future and watched Zoe? Could Zoe maintain and grow the business? Or would her efforts lead to yet another failure?

Nick noted her hesitation. He whispered in her ear, his breath a soft tickle. "Hey. You got this."

Glad for his verbal fortification, she shook off her doubts. "You're right. Let's get decorating."

Zoe stepped fully inside the room. Her mom turned, scoop in hand. "How'd it go with Hal and Larry?"

"Fine." It wasn't a white lie, Zoe told herself. It had gone as fine as it could, which wasn't much but better than the worst. She could have lost her house. Nick placed a gentle hand on her waist. "I should be home Wednesday night."

"That's not too bad," her mom said.

"Zoe's got it all under control," Nick added.

She did, damn it. She'd beat this temporary set-back or go down swinging. "My stuff's at the inn, and Megan's going to spend the rest of the weekend with Anna."

"That'll give you some time together with Nick."

"Yeah." Zoe's adrenaline notched at the thought of another kiss. She gestured to the counter, which was lined with cookie sheets. "Are you good to continue to bake? If so, Nick and I will start decorating."

Her mom exchanged the scoop for a potholder and retrieved a baking sheet from the oven and set it on the cooling rack. "Yep. I've got this handled. Jessica is out front filling the orders and Sierra should be here soon. It'll be like old times. Now shoo."

With no time to tell Jessica that she and Nick had fallen "in love" in less than a day, Zoe led him to the basement storage area. When her mom had converted the upstairs to a commercial kitchen, she'd reinforced the stone foundation walls, turned the dirt floor into concrete, and added support joists to stabilize the main floor. With the lights on, the claustrophobic space didn't bother Zoe as much, but she hated it down here. The door had gotten stuck once when she'd been a kid and it had taken her five minutes of pure panic before she'd been able to escape. She pointed. "We need those plastic tubs."

"Gotcha." Making certain not to bump his head on the low beams, Nick made short work of moving everything. He had most of the decorating items on the small front lawn when Sierra drove into the back parking lot. As Nick carried the last tub and took it around the side of the building, Sierra walked toward Zoe.

"Well done," Sierra greeted. "So that's Mister Handsome. You know I want all the details."

Zoe pointed toward the kitchen before tugging her red cashmere cap further over her ears. The weather had turned far colder than earlier in the week. "You're helping on the sales floor."

"Not those details. He's something. I want all of the scoop. How you met, first kiss…"

Last night. This morning.

"No time. Check in with Mom. She's getting pretty comfortable in there. I'm going to have to remind her I'll want my pans back at some point."

"Yeah, I could tell when she called me that she needed to bake. She'd be out here more if she could, if it wasn't for Dad's memory care unit being in St. Louis. When you lose something you love, it sets you adrift. You remember how I was after the crash. Do you not want her out here?"

"Of course I do," Zoe said quickly. "She's better than me in the kitchen." Zoe paused and smiled wistfully. "I miss all the times we spent together. We did work together for several years so it's strange not having her. But I want to manage on my own. Every crisis it's like I'm still ten and needed stitches for my knee after crashing my bike."

"That's our family dynamic. Overbearing. You saw how she was when I first moved back from Pensacola. You just get it worse because you're the baby and we love you."

"Yeah, I know." Zoe knew how lucky she truly was to have such a great family. "I'm in a funk. You're all far from Beaumont and I hate it. Remember how I reacted when I heard Mom and Dad told us they were selling our home?" Following dinner, she'd stormed out of the house, Megan in tow.

"At least you didn't pour a bottle of wine on Jack's shoes at a party his parents were throwing."

"True, but I'd say that situation worked out. You've never been happier. And our home is still ours forever, even if it stays empty for a while." Jack had seen to her sister's happiness by making sure the family homestead remained in the James family when he'd purchased their winery. "But now that you're gone, I realize I didn't set boundaries. Not with Ted. Not with Jared. Not with Mom. But I'm torn. I get that people are only trying to help me. But part of it feels like I'm still being babied. It sounds crazy."

"It's not. But that's what families are for. If you need money for repairs…"

"No." Zoe was adamant. It was bad enough her parents would bail her out. She didn't need Sierra, who had a great job and a rich, real-estate developer husband, to start providing Zoe with handouts as well.

Nick rounded the side of the house. He slapped gloved hands together and blew on them. "Lights are up on the bushes. And hey, Sierra, I'm Nick."

Nick shook Sierra's hand and Zoe had to remember that the engagement was simply for show. "Zoe, I got a weather alert there might be flurries later. Nothing sticking but enough to make a mess of things. Give me another task."

Sierra took that as her cue. "I'm gonna say hi to Mom. And neither of you is off the hook for future inquisition. Remember, I want details." Sierra went inside and Nick swung his attention to Zoe.

"So that's the infamous Sierra Clayton. I read about the wine incident online."

"All true. But the way Jack tells the story, he'd never loved her more than he did at that moment. In fact, he quit his family company for a short while."

Nick followed Zoe around the building and to the front. "I'm glad it worked out."

"Me too. I'm happy for her. She didn't like him much in high school. Thought he'd made a bet about her, which is why he asked her to homecoming. That was what the money she gave him that night was about. Payment for a bet won." Zoe lifted the lid off a plastic storage tub. "I never realized what she went through, back then. I was in my own world."

"Some people love high school. Others can't wait to leave. I was the latter."

"And I was the former. If I'd known how hard adulting really was, I'd have figured out a way to stay forever." Zoe withdrew a cord reel wound with colorful Christmas lights. "If you look closely, you'll see the plastic hooks on the gutters. We run these across the front. The ladder is in that shed over there."

Because of the historic age of the shop building and the low slope of the roof, by the time Zoe had the display of singing Christmas carolers set up in its traditional spot at the front of the store, Nick had installed the lights. By 3:45, they'd finished the decorations. They'd worked around the steady stream of people entering and leaving, and they'd managed to smile and wave at Mirabelle Adams, who had the shop down the street. She'd walked by with a "Oh, Nick, you're still in town. And over here."

"Just helping my fiancée get her store ready."

"Really?" Mirabelle appeared stunned, and Zoe had to admit she liked seeing Mirabelle's shocked expression. However, after the woman had left, Zoe chided him, "Now it'll be all over town."

He grinned, not repentant in the slightest. "Isn't that what you wanted? For them to move on, to stop feeling sorry for you?"

"Yes." But already the ruse was growing bigger and bigger, and it hadn't even been a day. She might have asked him to marry her, but his saying yes hadn't made any of this real. Thankfully her daughter was still at her cousin's house and wouldn't hear any gossip. Zoe had time to figure out what to tell her.

"She's coming back," Nick said.

"Already?" Zoe asked. "What now?"

Mirabelle held a stack of flyers. "I forgot to bring these over earlier. Will you pass these out? We want a huge turnout for the gingerbread contest. It's held at the Main Street Makerspace the Saturday after Thanksgiving," she added the latter for Nick's benefit. "I'm assuming you'll be helping Zoe?" Then she focused on Zoe. "You are entering, aren't you, Zoe?"

Zoe hadn't planned on it and Mirabelle knew it. "I'll be working."

Mirabelle pressed harder. "Surely you can get someone to cover for you. You have to enter. You're a shoo-in for the cookie contest, and I'd assume with your skills you can build and decorate a gingerbread house. Probably better than most of us." She added a little laugh. "The association wants one hundred percent participation. It's for charity, after all. You don't want to be the only store without an entry, especially being a bakery and all."

"Fine. I'll be there."

As if frustrated by the entire conversation, Nick glanced at the sky. "Here comes the snow. We've got to go."

As the first flake fell, Mirabelle darted away. Nick steered Zoe behind the store, where Zoe found her voice. "When does it stop?"

Nick stopped. "What?"

"The pressure. I wasn't going to enter." For some reason she found herself close to tears, as if the waterworks decided to reassert themselves in an attempt to prove that Zoe James could break, that she could, in fact, cry.

"Then don't. You've got a good excuse with you heating system and such"

Zoe banged the flyers against her palm. "Did you hear her? One hundred percent participation." Zoe mimicked Mirabelle's voice. "I can't back out. The Merchants' Association would never let me live it down if I do. You should have heard them with Caleb over his paltry decorations. And it's a matter of principle, that if I enter, I have to win."

Nick's brow creased and he snagged the flyers and put them in a deep, front coat pocket. "Why do you have to win? These things are for fun."

Zoe rolled her eyes. "Please. Nothing's fun when it comes to Mirabelle. My mom never lost any baking competition. I'll never be able to show my face if I'm not good enough."

"Zoe." Nick placed gloved hands on her shoulders. "Zoe, you don't have to do anything you don't want to do. And you are good enough. You've always been good enough. You're being too hard on yourself."

Her lip quivered. "No, I'm not. Facts are facts. Just

because you don't like them doesn't mean they're not facts. There are days it feels that everyone in this town believes I'm a failure. I couldn't keep a husband. I rejected the elementary school principal, who was perfect by the way, except for the fact he's now in Chicago and I'm here. And the store? I'm maintaining the legacy, not building something new."

"There is nothing wrong with that."

She appreciated his attempt at a pep talk. "Deep down I know that, but it's like I'm under a black cloud that follows me around and turns me into an Eeyore. Why can't I be happy and bouncy, like Tigger?"

Nick drew her closer and leaned his forehead close to hers. "You are incredible. No one sees it themselves, but others do. I do. Tell you what. You use this time with me running interference to figure out what you want. Seriously. What does *Zoe* really want?"

"I don't know." The words broke forth before Zoe could stop them. "That's what bothers me most. I'm a mom. I want to make sure my daughter is safe and loved. But there has to be more than that, right? Or is that a lie all the romance movies I watch tell? Is this all my life is, raising a daughter? Running a store? What if there's nothing more than this?"

"I'm going to admit to being the last person who can answer those questions. I'm in town on my way to who knows where simply because I'm at loose ends myself. Maybe we can help each other figure it out?"

The snow began to lightly fall, dropping wet flakes on their hair and faces. "Come on." Nick grabbed one of Zoe's hands and guided her out into the open. "Look up."

Zoe tilted her head. Snowflakes dropped onto her

nose and her eyelashes. "I see nothing but gray skies and snow."

"Exactly." Nick stuck his tongue out. A flake landed and he sucked his tongue back inside. "Got one! You try."

"This is silly."

"Come on, Eeyore. Be a Tigger." Nick's tongue darted out for another. "Sometimes you gotta go with the moment." He raised his head, trying to catch more.

"Fine." Caught up in his childish excitement, Zoe stuck out her tongue. The lightest wetness dropped onto it and her tongue naturally recoiled so she could swallow. Then she tried again. And again.

By now, Nick was bobbing and weaving, his arms airplane stretched so he could catch more flakes. "I'm getting more than you," he called.

"I didn't know it was a competition," Zoe yelled as the heavens opened, sending more and more flakes falling toward the ground. She started racing around like a frog after flies. "I'm sure I've caught up by now."

"No way," Nick teased. "I've eaten more."

Zoe was beginning to get dizzy from her head being lifted and from running in circles. "You may have had a head start but I'm—Ooff."

As she accidentally smacked into him, he caught her in his arms. "Hey there."

"Hey." Her chest heaved from running, but she wasn't cold. Nick heated her in all the right places. Her face upturned, he captured her lips with his. He kissed her gently, and then his tongue slid inside her mouth, the heat of him mixing with the chill of the last snowflake she'd caught. He drew back, captured another snowflake and shared it with her in a sensation bordering on erotic. Zoe wrapped her arms around him and kissed him deeply until a deliberate cough had her stepping back, but not out of Nick's arms. Her mom and sister had joined them. Sierra grinned at Zoe. "Look at you two acting like crazy kids."

"We finished decorating and have everything put away," Zoe defended.

Sierra smirked. "You'll get no complaint from me. I kiss my husband every chance I get. Jessica left out the front, so we've got everything inside shut down and locked except for the back door. We'll let you do that and set the alarm."

"Thank you." Zoe glanced at the skies. The snow had already lightened. "Are the roads safe to drive?"

Sierra nodded. "I checked the highway department's app. Roads are fine. This is mostly flurries and the pavement is too warm for anything to stick. The streets won't even be slick. Mom and I will be fine driving home."

"You know she'll follow me anyway," Zoe's mom said. "I'll be back out tomorrow to help with the store. If you could get some chocolate chip dough prepped, that would help."

"Okay." Zoe didn't even protest. She'd seen little of her mom today and Zoe was down an employee owing to illness. "Thank you for everything today." She moved out of Nick's arms so she could hug her sister and mom goodbye. "Be safe and text me when you get home. Love you."

Nick followed Zoe into the quiet and sparkling clean kitchen. "Do you want a cookie?" she asked him. "Because I do."

She retrieved a double chocolate chunk from its air-tight container. "What kind do you want?"

"Whatever you got there looks pretty good."

"It's our chocolate chip recipe but with cocoa powder added. After all, there's no such thing as too much chocolate."

Nick took a bite and made an appreciative noise. "I'm partial to regular chocolate chip, but this is delicious."

Zoe nibbled. "It's my favorite. Thanks for your help today."

"You helped me too," he told her. "I ran around and acted like a kid. I can't tell you when that happened last."

She smiled. "That was fun. Crazy, but fun."

His chuckle was warm, rich and as delicious as the cookie. "Sometimes you simply need to channel fun in unexpected places. Tell the world to shove it and live in the moment. It never snowed in L.A. Maybe I'll rethink the fact I wanted to head south and be somewhere warm for the holidays. Maybe I need a white Christmas."

"I'm all for snow as long as it doesn't keep the shoppers away. Let it snow Christmas Eve. Until then, this is when I make most of my profit except for the two fall festivals."

Nick removed the flyers from his pocket, unrolled them, and flattened the thin stack against the steel prep table. "That cookie I just ate could win this baking contest."

Zoe pointed to the flyer. "It's a Christmas cookie contest. We change out the rainbow sprinkles for red and white ones on our sugar cookies, but that's about the extent of our holiday offerings. If I do this, I need something else."

One last bite and Nick's cookie was gone. "There's your answer. You should come up with an original Christmas cookie. A Zoe James Smith creation. A new addition to the shop that's all yours."

Zoe considered his idea. She'd never entered the contest, leaving that to her mom, and winning would allow her to make her mark. She'd have an original creation of her own for the store. A way to set herself apart from her mom. "You may be onto something."

"Think of the good publicity you'll get."

Zoe mulled over the idea. "I could use something that says this is my place now, beyond me baking the same old recipes. Maybe I could start there and then do a special cookie monthly."

"Now you're thinking," Nick said, and Zoe bloomed under his encouragement.

She pulled her phone from her pocket and performed a search. Then she held it out for Nick to see the picture. "I've always wanted to try Madeleines. They are cookies that are actually small, shell-shaped cakes. Even though they are baked in molds, the key is height and a light and fluffy texture. Our chocolate chip cookies are known for their height, so why not do something like these? We could dip the ends in chocolate and then decorate them. We could use food coloring and create cookies with two or more different colors. The ideas are endless."

Her mind raced, considering the possibilities. "Usually Madeleines are made with lemon, but there are tons of versions. Chocolate, coconut, and even rosemary. The molds are in the basement. I'm not sure why we have them as I can't remember my mom ever using them, but I saw them earlier today."

"It's fate." Nick's excitement was contagious. "Let's go get them."

He followed her to the basement, where Zoe found four madeleine pans in a clear plastic tub. The tub was on the top shelf, and she stood on tiptoe to grab the handle. Misjudging the distance, the tub slipped, and Nick caught it. He set it on a space where some of the Christmas decorations had been. He reached forward to where she massaged her hand and took it in his. "You okay?"

"Yeah. I think so. My fingers bent backward, that's all."

"Let me see." Starting with her forefinger, Nick rubbed his finger across the knuckle. He gently bent her finger at the knuckle joint and then, after straightening it, he massaged the skin down to the end of the nail. He repeated the process with each one of her fingers, ending with her thumb. "I don't see anything broken."

Zoe wouldn't have felt the pain anyway, she was so on fire from his touch. He hadn't done anything really, but the act was like that moment when Willoughby ascertained if Marianne's ankle was broken in the movie *Sense and Sensibility.* Nick's touch had all the hallmarks of innocence while at the same time creating unending stirrings of desire. Zoe needed to remember that Willoughby had broken Marianne's heart. She slowly disengaged her hand from his. "Thanks. I'm okay now."

"If you're sure. Glad I can help." The huskiness of Nick's tone let Zoe know she wasn't the only one affected by the sexual awareness electrons pinging between them.

She led the way back into the kitchen, where the bright lights and industrial steel counters gave her a welcome sense of reality.

"So Madeleines?"

"Yes. Maybe seeing the pans earlier put them in my head. They'll be different from what others will think of. They're French, and the first Europeans to settle in Beaumont were French. We might even be able to use some verjus in the cookies."

Verjus was a juice made from the immature grapes culled from the vines. Instead of tossing or letting them rot, vintners squeezed the unripe grapes into a liquid that could be used as a vinegar substitute or a non-alcoholic cocktail base. Traditional Madeleine recipes used lemon zest to provide tartness, as Madeleine cookies weren't overly sweet. Yes, Zoe thought, Jamestown's verjus might provide a unique fruity flavor. Her family really had perfected using verjus, something her brother-in-law Nick considered a growth area.

"You look like you've got an idea," Nick said. He touched her forehead with his pointer finger. "You get this little M right here."

"They're coming rapid fire, actually. I'll want to brown the butter and use it to grease the pans. My dad always charred the inside of some of our barrels to add a smoky flavor to the wine. We can do something similar with browned butter. It'll add more flavor. I'll need to shop for ingredients."

"Then let's go."

"Not tonight. The stores I need are closed until tomorrow." Her stomach growled. Lunch had been sandwiches from Vitale's Deli, hours ago.

"We need to get dinner," Nick said.

Zoe rubbed her hands on her jeans. "I'm not really dressed for going out."

"We can order takeout and eat at the dining room table back at the inn."

"You heard my mom. I need to mix some batter for tomorrow. It'll take about twenty minutes. I'd understand if you don't want to stay."

Nick remained rooted. "Tell me what I can do to help."

"Start by getting some butter from that refrigerator." Within a few minutes, she had two stand mixers beating the butter into a creamy submission. Into the whipped butter went light brown sugar, followed by a smaller quantity of white granulated sugar. The sugar and butter batter spun until light and fluffy. She showed Nick how to scrape down the paddle and add vanilla and eggs. Then came the flour, baking soda and salt. While many recipes called for two and a quarter cups of flour, Auntie Jayne's recipe called for three and a quarter. The extra cup of flour allowed for a thicker cookie, and for the scooped dough to hold its shape when baking. Finally came the chocolate chips. Auntie Jayne's recipe used three cups per batch.

Nick poured the chips into the bowl. He set the mixer speed to four and the paddle went round and round as it blended chocolate chips into the dough. During his pour, a few chips had missed the bowl. They rested instead on the stainless steel countertop. Nick popped one into his mouth. He then held out two more and brought them to Zoe's lips. She accepted the offering. The chocolate dissolved on her tongue while her gaze held his. He lifted another semi-sweet chocolate chip and fed it to her as well.

"Nick." She breathed his name softly, and with that his lips found hers. He tasted of chocolate and heaven.

His kiss landed somewhere between soft and sensual and plundering and passionate. It was simply perfect, and Zoe lost herself in the just-right moment until a buzzing and thunking of the paddle against the dough made her pull back. "I can't ruin the cookies. That would be bad."

"It would." He stepped away, allowing her space. She removed the bowl from the mixer and transferred the contents into an airtight container she stored in the refrigerator, where her mom would grab it tomorrow. Her mom had perfected the art of using chilled dough.

Zoe waved away Nick's offer to help clean, so he tapped on his phone while Zoe washed up.

"I ordered two filet mignon specials from the Beaumont Bistro. The food should be ready in five minutes." Then he groaned.

Zoe looked at him in confusion. "What?"

"I'm sorry. I acted without thinking. I should have asked what you wanted. I got them medium temperature. Will that work? If not, I can call back and order something else."

"I'm not picky," Zoe told him, pleased by his thoughtfulness. The Beaumont Bistro was even higher-end dining than Miller's Grill. Zoe had eaten there once with Ted and the food had been delicious. She hadn't been back since. "I'm surprised they had time to do a carry-out order given that it's Saturday night."

"Well, they did, and before you offer to pay your share, I picked our dinner so I get to pay. Got it?"

For once Zoe didn't argue. Her mouth watered too much instead at the thought of the delicious food. "My budget and I thank you. Ready?"

Nick assisted Zoe into her coat, his fingers light on

her shoulders. After locking the back door and setting the alarm, they went the opposite direction of the inn on clear sidewalks, the snow having stopped and melted, as she'd known it would. They walked by a darkened building several doors north of the cookie store. On the inside of a paper-covered front window, someone had tacked a For Sale sign. The place, unlike the rest of the block, wasn't decorated and stood out like a sore thumb.

"What was this place?" Nick asked.

"A chocolate shop. Remember those chocolates we had at Caleb's? While they weren't from here, he used to buy them here. Now he has another source. One day the owner decided he didn't want to be in business anymore, so he picked up and moved to Florida. What would it be like to have so much money, you can just vacate something? Anyway, I wish you could have tried some. This place made authentic French chocolate in small batches. So good. It's sad when Main Street stores close. Makes all the rest of us worry that it might domino. We're stronger together."

"Seems a shame he didn't sell first so the shop could keep going." Nick and Zoe reached the bistro, and the hostess handed them their order. Nick carried both bags by the handles, and despite the outdoor chilly temperature, the food remained warm when they began setting the carry-out containers on the dining room table.

Mrs. Bien came into the room as they'd finished removing the last container, and overriding their objections, she lit some candles and lowered the lights. Instead of using plasticware, she'd also brought them real china and flatware, and a bottle of wine and glasses. She studied the table, and satisfied, left them with a cheery, "Enjoy your date."

"It's not a…" Zoe started to say, but she stopped as Nick caught her hand and brought her fingers to his lips. She and Nick were engaged, so instead she told Mrs. Bien "Thank you." When Mrs. Bien left the dining room, Zoe immediately missed the warmth of Nick's fingers. Nick sat to her left, and as he served the food, she poured the wine.

"Thank you for this," Zoe said as they began to eat. Nick sat to her left. "If I forget to tell you later, I really appreciate you. Thank you for doing this."

Nick paused from cutting his steak. "You're welcome. I enjoyed being with you today."

She'd lifted her fork and paused pre-bite. He appeared serious and her heart missed a beat. "I'm not sure who else would have helped a stranger out as you did."

"Plenty of people, surely. But you forget, you're not really a stranger. I'd like us to be friends, Zoe. I was thinking I might stick around for a bit longer, maybe through the holidays. I didn't have a good childhood here. I'd like to make some better memories. None of my plans were firm. Would that be okay with you? Would it be ok if I stayed longer? I know you said yes to our engagement because I'm leaving. But I like you, Zoe. I'd like to get to know you more."

Her heart gave another thrilled leap, only to have her practical brain smack it down. "It's been twenty-four hours. And I'm a mess. My life is one disaster after another right now."

"Then we'd be quite the pair, wouldn't we?"

"I'll think about it." She could commit to that. Forking a morsel of delicious steak into her mouth, she lost herself in gastric appreciation as the spiced filet hit her tongue. When she opened her eyes, she found Nick watching her. "It's that good," she told him. A tingle of awareness shot through her, caused by his heated gaze. "Ordering from the bistro was a good idea."

"I'm an idea man." Nick cut another portion of steak. "Have you ever thought of expanding?"

Zoe shook her head and reached for her wine. Mrs. Bien had brought out a Jamestown Norton, one bottled about three years prior. This vintage had been one of the last years her father had been able to be hands-on in all parts of creating his award-winning wine at his vineyard. Now, he often didn't recognize Zoe, and she'd stopped bringing Megan to the memory care unit as he never recognized his granddaughter. For Zoe, the last few years had been one of constant heartbreak and heartache. Nick had blown in like a breath of beautiful, fresh spring air. He thought of things, like their need to eat, providing a meal when she would have been fine with a peanut butter and strawberry jelly sandwich.

"Perhaps you should look to diversify," Nick said. "You told me you'll be providing cookies to the Clayton Hotel. What if you bought the chocolate shop?"

"I don't know anything about chocolate. Even if I did, I'm already meeting myself coming and going running the store. Add to it the disaster in my house and not enough cash to fix my heater, I can hardly get back up from being knocked around, much less buy another business. Businesses involve product, employees, and all sorts of other nightmares, and I have enough of those with running Auntie Jayne's. But it's a nice thought. Having an empire."

Nick didn't seem too perturbed by her rejection. "Just something that jumped into my mind. You don't get anywhere without brainstorming. Some ideas have merit. Others are simply thrown out there to be discarded. No harm. No foul."

She was glad he understood. "Exactly."

They turned their attention to other topics, enjoying light conversation as they continued to eat the delicious food. Nick told her about learning to fly, something he'd started doing about four years ago. "I gave myself a lesson for my twenty-third birthday and got hooked."

Not for the first time, Zoe wondered exactly what Nick did for a living. Last night at the wine bar, he'd indicated his job had something to do with computers. Clearly he made good money, given that he'd paid the wine bar bill and for dinner tonight. Flying lessons also didn't come cheap.

"My sister, Sierra, was a Navy flight instructor. She followed in my dad's footsteps. Now she works for Boeing doing something for a military contract she can't talk about."

"That's cool. My company did some contract work for one of Boeing's competitors. Involved a lot of top-secret tech."

"Do you work remotely then? Is that what allows you to travel? You go to the jobsite?" He'd never told her exactly what he did, minus that he was traveling on a wherever the whim took him schedule.

Nick toyed with the stem of the wineglass. "I'm on sort of a sabbatical. But that's a good way to describe it. All I need is my computer and I can go anywhere."

Zoe wished she could go places. She sighed, the wine mellowing her and bringing nostalgia and its partner, melancholy. "I can't remember the last time I took a real vacation. My honeymoon maybe. I do take days off here and there but I don't go anywhere."

"Tell you what, pick a day and let me plan something."

Zoe was touched. She sipped some wine, tasting the hints of spice and oak that were her dad's trademark. "I'll think about it," she said, caving. What would it be like to go on a real date? With Nick? "Okay. Let's do it. Why not?"

"Great." They'd finished eating, and Zoe leaned back in her chair. Her stomach felt satiated and full. "What's on tomorrow's agenda?"

Tomorrow was Sunday. "Same thing as today," Zoe said. "Baking and selling. It's my life. At some point, Shelby and Luke will bring Megan here."

"Could I meet her? Take you all out to dinner?"

"Nick, you've done so much already."

She began to clear the plates to the side tray where they'd set the breakfast dishes. "If we do this…" she paused. Found the words. "You're a very tempting man, Nick. Even if you stay for a month, even if you find me tempting as well, my priority is always going to be my daughter and the store. I don't have a good track record with men. I can't let whatever this is between us take on a life of its own."

"I understand," Nick said, and Zoe got the impression he did. "Doesn't mean I still don't want to kiss you all over."

Oh Lordy, she wanted that too. And tonight she had no plans, no obligations and half a bottle of wine left. She could give herself a palate cleanser, a break from her past and a segue to her present. If she kissed Nick and let things go naturally…it was only one night. Megan would be with her from here forward. *Do it,* something inside her whispered. *Grab the adventure for once.*

Zoe held out her hand and Nick grasped it firmly, as if determined not to let her go. As Nick's blue eyes darkened, she spoke and sealed her fate before she completely lost her nerve. "Follow me upstairs."

Chapter Six

In those Saturday night romance movies Zoe loved, especially the ones geared for "family," any lovemaking existed off stage. The couple appeared in the kitchen the next morning, coffee cups in hand. On other networks, sex was graphic and intense. Someone got pushed against a door, clothing flew, and hands went everywhere.

In proof that life wasn't a TV show. Zoe's current reality was much more basic and fraught by nerves. Her first time with Ted had been a consummation of unbridled teenage lust, hormones, and adrenaline. Jared had taken her away for the weekend to a B&B in Hermann, and they'd shared a bed with no expectations. Once the lights had gone out, they'd started kissing and what ensued had been tender and natural.

With Nick, Zoe stood in her beautifully appointed

suite, the gas fireplace flickering for ambiance. She almost wished that Nick had whirled her around and pressed her against the door. That would have been easier than taking that first step. With Ted and Jared, she thought she had a future and sex was a natural step. Whatever she felt for Nick, aside from his kisses making her go weak at the knees, wasn't love. She'd be giving in to her urges with essentially a semi-stranger, someone she desired in a fundamental way: passion and lust. She was confident sex with Nick would be mind-blowing. But then again, what if it wasn't? What if it would be one more miscalculation in the life of Zoe James? She wasn't like Nick, leaping Thoreau-style into new adventures. She was rooted. Grounded. Liked her well-worn path. But in the end, life was too short not to eat the cookie, and Nick was a delicious man waiting to be sampled. What would it hurt? She'd regret it either way—so why not regret it for having enjoyed herself?

She'd gripped the bottle of wine by its neck and loosened her fingers. Nerves made her want to tip the bottle and drink from it directly. Instead, she placed her empty wine glass and the bottle on the side table next to the small loveseat. Nick stood with his hands tucked into the front pocket of his jeans. He hadn't even carried his glass upstairs. "You okay, Zoe?"

Was she? Besides the orange glow of the fireplace, a bedside lamp provided the only other light. A huge, Victorian canopied bed dominated the room, the comforter turned down and a mint placed on both pillows. She sank into the loveseat and gazed at the orange and red flames. "I'm nervous," she confessed.

"We don't have to do anything you don't want to do." He dropped into the arm chair to the left of the loveseat.

Zoe wasn't certain if the warmth on her face came from the heat of the fire or the inferno burning inside her.

"But I want to do things," she admitted, her voice notched above a whisper. She couldn't look at him when she said the words, but she meant them. Why hadn't he pressured her by sitting next to her? Because he was perfect, that was why. This was her decision, and Nick was giving her the space to make it. "I'm not very good at situations like this. I mean the awkward moment stuff, like this conversation. Not the sex." She flushed all over. "I'd like to think I'm good at that."

"I have no doubt." Did she imagine it, or had his voice dropped an octave? "Zoe, there's no rush."

But there was. He would leave, and then where would she be? She'd once walked by a toy store's front window display and seen a one-of-a-kind doll, one of those porcelain ones with beautiful blond hair. She'd begged her mom to buy it—it really wasn't that much—but her mom had said no and wouldn't let Zoe spend her own money. Every day for a month, Zoe had walked by that window to see if the doll was still there. One day it wasn't and she'd never seen it again, until post-divorce on an episode of *Antique Roadshow*, where the appraiser said it was worth a small fortune. Zoe had almost cried.

This oddly felt like that, as if she'd be passing on something important if she didn't take advantage while she had the chance. As long as she was realistic and didn't try to make this relationship into anything deeper feeling-wise, no one would get hurt. She patted the brocade fabric of the empty loveseat space next to her. "Join me. Please."

Nick obliged. The moment he squeezed in beside her, some nerves calmed while others flew into frenzy.

She reached for his hand, the weight providing comfort. "Why don't you lead," Nick suggested.

It was a novel concept. Even in high school she'd been a follower, with Ted dominating the social scene. Her popularity had been attached to his. Her store's popularity was attached to her mother's. "Take advantage of me as little or as much as you want. You tell me what to do," Nick continued. "Just know that I want all of you. There's nothing you can do or say that will make me like you any less."

His words created a balm for a weary soul while at the same time stoking a fire Zoe hadn't known existed inside her. She lifted her hand to his cheek and he leaned in, the prickliness of his beard caressing the inside of her palm. She swiped a thumb over his mouth, testing the soft and smooth texture. His lips parted and he sucked her thumb lightly inside, his tongue wetting her fingertip before she moved to explore other places. She slid her hand along his jawline. She traced his eyebrows, watching how his eyelids lowered to cover the deep blue gaze locked on hers. Zoe inched toward him, and instinctively he met her halfway as her lips found his.

Like with every kiss they'd shared, desire overpowered each sense. She curbed her passion, though, holding back by breaking away so she could instead plant a series of kisses along his jaw and over his face. She tasted his brow, kissed each eyelid, and nipped the tip of his nose. Finally she returned to his lips, which parted for her probing tongue. He tasted of heaven and sunshine and all good things. She reveled in how it mattered little that they'd created no promises. There were no declarations of undying love, which didn't exist if Zoe's history was anything to go by.

Tonight was about fulfilling her body's needs and the simmering sensualness kissing Nick aroused. She shifted, straddling his legs so she faced him. Her mouth returned to his neck and a small moan slipped past his lips. Encouraged, she ran her hands under his shirt, her palms flat against a chest sculpted by the gods. A thrill ricocheted as she unlocked pure, feminine power. Nick held himself tightly leashed, letting her set the pace. Nothing had turned her on more.

She tugged on the hem, and reading her intentions, Nick shifted, his biceps flexing as he stripped his top half naked, sending his shirt to the floor. Zoe marveled at his beauty. She planted her palms, his rock solid pectorals sending her neurons into overdrive. She was wet, her breasts were heavy, and her body burned hotter than the gas flames behind her. She lowered her lips and kissed her way across his chest, moving her body lower as she did. Nick tenderly threaded his fingers into her hair, gently massaging her scalp as she trailed kisses down to his belly button, before following the trail lower. He spread his legs and Zoe moved between them, her fingers on the fastener of his jeans.

"Zoe." Nick groaned her name. "You don't have to."

"But I want to," she told him. Her bold libido was a welcome shock to her system. She meant every word. She knew that with Nick she wasn't obligated, so what she wanted to do was a gift, both to him and to herself. He lifted and kicked away the last of his clothes, minus his athletic socks. Zoe had never seen anything sexier. She held him in hand, reveling that this masculine part of Nick was as gorgeous as the rest of him. He was absolutely perfect. Divine.

"Zoe." Nick let loose a low moan of pleasure.

She lifted her mouth and caught his gaze, her hand continuing to stroke. "Yes, Nick?" she asked, her voice wicked.

He shook his head, whatever he'd wanted to say unable to slip past his lips as she worked her magic. By the time she took him to the moon and beyond, she was heated and ready. Her inhibitions had fled, replaced by a confident sexual being that had been waiting years to debut.

"What does Zoe want?" Nick asked.

"Everything." Still fully clothed, she stood and poured herself a glass of wine. She took a drink and passed him the glass. Nick sipped and set the glass aside.

She stretched out her arm, and taking her hand in his, Nick planted his feet on the floor. "You're a little too overdressed for everything."

She arched an eyebrow. "Perhaps you should do something about that."

He wrapped her in his arms, his mouth on her skin. "Are you giving me the lead?"

"For now. Undress me. Do your best."

His grin was as wicked as the desire coursing through her. "I'll do more than that."

"Good. Sounds perfect."

In an instant, Nick's lips were on hers. He kissed her gently at first, and then with more passion as something new built inside Zoe. Who knew earlobes could be so erogenous? He dominated her mouth, trailed kisses to the hollow of her throat, and then planted kisses along her stomach as he removed her clothing. He dropped to his knees and brought his mouth to her core until Zoe's legs quaked and she could no longer stand. He guided her to the bed, where he unwrapped the mint and placed it on his tongue before bringing his mouth to hers and sharing the wealth. Passion cascaded over her in waves, and by the time Zoe surfaced for air, her chest heaved.

She lay on her side watching as he shucked the socks. He slid in beside her and faced her, his legs intertwining with hers. His hand snaked out and pushed her hair behind her ear, His breath tickling her ear. "You are incredible."

He was good for her ego, Zoe realized. Her hand pressed against his cheek. "You're not so bad yourself."

He chuckled. "Good to know I wasn't a disappointment."

"Far from it." His hand slid to her arm, then found her breast. His thumb and forefinger began to work magic on her nipple. "May I?"

She could only nod. His mouth replaced his fingers. He shifted his hand lower, working to lessen the urgent tingling between her legs by creating another, scintillating pressure. "Tell me what you want, Zoe. Tonight's about you."

"You," she gasped. "All of you."

He left the bed, retrieving a condom from the wallet he took out of the back pocket of his jeans. He returned to capture her mouth with his, and Zoe lay back as he moved over her. Then they were joined, and her body trembled from the fullness of him. "Tell me how you like it," he told her. "Faster. Slower. Harder."

Zoe didn't care. She was already there. He filled her completely and all she could do was thank the stars she'd walked into the wine bar. As if sensing he knew the pleasure he gave her, Nick grinned and kissed her deeply. He drove her up and over and into the place where oblivion is a delicious delicacy the rare few get to sample. Nick not only wiped the slate clean of her past lovers, but he set new standards Zoe couldn't imagine achieving again.

That was until he made love to her later that night, once both of them had rested, easily proving that the first time had not been some fluke. And then yet again before the light of day. She discovered herself in his lovemaking. Felt powerful and feminine. Desired for herself. He wrapped himself around her, cuddling as the bedside clock flickered to six a.m. "Get some sleep," he said softly, and with her eyes heavy and her body satisfied, Zoe caved and began to drift off.

"Don't leave me," she whispered, the subconscious thought finding vocalizations on the last vestiges of the night as she succumbed to sleep.

"I'll be here as long as you need me," Nick said. "As long as you want."

Nick had never been one who needed tons of sleep. His early life in Beaumont had been one of survival, so he'd learned to sleep in short bursts rather than finding eight hours straight. California had been slightly better. By the time he'd moved into the dorm at Stanford with bedding sourced at a charity shop, old sleeping habits were hard to break. Besides, Nick's brain never turned off. It ran constantly—solving problems, developing code, and executing plans.

Never in a million years would he have thought his returning to Beaumont would have resulted in making love to Zoe James. But here she was, naked and sleeping in his arms.

As he marveled at that, Nick had no clue what to do

next. What did you do when you achieved the impossible? When the fantasy became the reality? Wasn't he in this town in the first place because, once he'd achieved everything, it had all seemed hollow and empty? Alexa was a gold digger. His former company didn't need him, and he hadn't liked building it anyway. He had more money than he knew what to do with. He was at loose ends.

Tonight he held his holy grail in his arms, and it was everything he'd ever hoped it would be. He'd made love to Zoe, and he'd never had such a sexual experience, one where the entire event catapulted him to the stratosphere. He hadn't simply "gotten off" or orgasmed. It had been far more than some physical pleasure or a necessary release. He'd transcended to a higher plane. For a time, his head had quieted. He'd felt both on top of the world and at peace, finally finding the Zen that had always eluded him. He'd chased that feeling his whole life, only to find nirvana in Zoe's arms. He watched her breathe, her chest rising and falling in a soft rhythm. He moved a stray strand of hair off her face, and the small movement sent heat to his groin. He wanted her again. His desire hadn't abated. But the sun crept around the curtains. It was after seven. She'd need to shower, eat, and head into the store. Later tonight Megan would arrive.

This had most likely been their one and only night.

It hadn't been enough time. With that revelation, Nick knew that he was in far too deep. He stroked her cheek and Zoe's eyes fluttered open. "Hey there. It's after seven."

She shot straight up, a panicked expression covering her face. "I'll be late. My mom's coming. I can't be late."

He ignored how delicious her breasts looked and how he wished they could be tardy so he could take time to feast on them. "How about you do whatever you need to do and I'll bring up a breakfast tray?"

She nodded. "That sounds like a good plan."

He put a thumb to her lips. "It's all fine, Zoe. No awkwardness from me, got it?"

Relief crossed her features and her shoulders loosened. "Thank you."

He gave her a quick kiss. "You're welcome. I'll be back."

He pulled on his jeans, zipping but leaving the top button undone as he gathered his clothing. "I'm going to shower and I'll bring us some breakfast. Say twenty minutes?"

By the time he returned, Zoe wore a fresh pair of black slacks and her Auntie Jayne's uniform top. Her long hair was damp and straight. He carried in a full tray covered with two of everything: plates of food, glasses of orange juice, and linen-wrapped flatware. Nick had turned the gas fireplace off in the middle of the night, and they sat at the suite's small two-top table to enjoy Mrs. Bien's cooking.

"I enjoyed last night very much," Nick said.

Zoe turned pink. "Me too."

Nick knew he'd have to treat Zoe as if she was fragile, for in a sense she was. "I'd still like to take you and Megan out to dinner. Your mom, too, if you'd like. You all have to eat."

"Let me ask her when I see her."

With that, they ate mostly in silence, each to their own thoughts. Nick gave Zoe the space she needed, which as it happened, was space he needed as well.

Despite their having made love, he didn't want to rush her or pressure her into anything. His plan was to leave eventually, right? Right? He was still leaving, yes?

For the first time, he entertained the idea that he didn't have to leave if he didn't want to. He could stay. Maybe he and Zoe would fall in love. His brain raced as it contemplated various outcomes, performing a process that Nick had once described to a professor as visualizing which way dominoes would fall so that they could be engineered to fall that way once stacked to do so. But with Zoe, Nick had no idea how to order his life to keep her in it. He wasn't good with love. In hindsight, he hadn't even loved Alexa. Dating her had been about pride and feeling successful. As for Zoe, each time he ran a scenario through his brain, the results came back, "can't compute." Too many variables existed, and Nick hated variables.

One thing was obvious: at some point he would have to come clean with Zoe about who he was. Maybe he didn't need to reveal his pathetic past life in Beaumont—something he worked to exorcise daily—but he should clear up any misconceptions that he was some remote-working drifter, a guy who didn't know what he wanted to do next. He had to tell her the truth, about who he was and his finances, even if she didn't take it as well as he hoped.

But he didn't think the walk to the store was the best time. Or when Zoe showed him how to use the point-of-sale credit card system—a program for small businesses he'd had a hand in refining and updating. He wanted the moment to be right. Checking out customers after Jessica boxed their cookies, while Zoe and her mother baked in the kitchen, was not the right time either. Neither was the half-hour lunch break he used buying sandwiches from Vitale's Deli, feeding everyone the same as he had the day before.

Record crowds had turned out to see a fully decorated Main Street, meaning the store was nonstop busy. Somehow, Zoe had found time to leave for about twenty minutes to purchase all the ingredients she needed to make Madeleines. She was back before members of the Main Street Merchants Association had come to inspect the store's decorations.

Nick had met the famous Mrs. Zappatta, and he'd caught the visible tension between the older woman and Zoe's mom. "Mrs. Zappatta thinks she runs things now that Mom's gone," Zoe had whispered. To everyone's relief, the committee had given their approval and beat a fast trail elsewhere. The store closed at four on Sundays, and fifteen minutes later, Nick and Zoe were alone in the kitchen.

"How'd it go today?" Nick asked.

"Fantastic. We had excellent receipts. I also had some time to bake. Try this." She held out a shell-shaped cookie with alternating green-and-red-striped dough. One end, besides being dipped in chocolate, was covered with festive green, red and white sprinkles. "I swapped out the lemon for Jamestown's verjus and adjusted the sugars. Tell me what you think."

Nick bit into the fluffy cake. The cookie's tart yet buttery flavor contrasted with the chocolate the same way drinking the port had been accentuated by eating the candies. "This is really good. Incredible." He ate the last of the cookie. "Did you do the browned butter?"

"I did." She put one of the cookies in her mouth and chewed thoughtfully. "It's good. But is it enough to win? Something about the texture is off. I'll try tweaking it this week."

"I'm happy to keep taste testing." He'd missed his morning run since he'd been cradling Zoe in his arms, but that didn't mean he couldn't eat another cookie. While he tried another—frankly, he couldn't find anything wrong with it—Zoe placed the final three cookies in one of the store's signature boxes. "I sent the rest with my mom," Zoe said. "She'll take them home to my brother. Nelson and his kids will eat anything sweet. Drives my sister-in-law up the wall."

"It tasted fantastic," Nick said.

"But will the flavor work with milk? Santa's cookies aren't complete without being dunked in milk. I don't think it's there yet. I'll figure it out."

"Of course you will. Come here." It had been a long time since the morning, and he drew her close. He wrapped her in his arms and planted a kiss on her forehead. "If there's anything I know about you, it's that you are one of the brightest and most capable people I know."

"I appreciate your confidence." Zoe tipped her face, and he found her lips.

"You're a boss. Never doubt it," Nick said between kisses and darts of his tongue. "I'd back you against that counter and prove it, but I don't even want to think about how we'd have to sanitize things afterward."

Zoe laughed. "You really know how to talk dirty to a girl."

"Come on." Nick gave her one last kiss and then helped her into her coat. "It's time to go meet your daughter."

The moment Megan walked through the front door of the inn, Nick, of course, won her over in an instant.

Just where and when had he gotten that stuffed rabbit anyway? Probably when he'd been out for lunch. Zoe watched Megan clutch the toy before saying thank you. She then showed the bunny to her friend Anna. His thoughtfulness endeared him even more to Zoe.

Nick had also impressed Shelby and Luke Thornburg who, along with their daughter, would eat dinner at the inn. After giving Megan a hug goodbye, Anna had run into the arms of her grandmother, Mrs. Bien, and Zoe had taken Megan upstairs. "This is my bed? I like it." Megan bounced onto the single rollaway that was now in the upstairs suite. She set the rabbit on the pillow. "When will we go home?"

"Soon," Zoe reassured. "Until then, it'll be like we're on a vacation."

"Okay." Megan didn't appear fazed, for which Zoe was grateful, especially as they really hadn't gone on a vacation in years. "Nick's nice," Megan said. "Is he your boyfriend?"

"Nick and I are just friends." There was no evidence to the contrary. Even before housekeeping had come into the room to straighten, Zoe had cleaned, ensuring her suite didn't blatantly advertise the previous evening's activities. "And yes, Nick is very nice."

Anyone who realized that Zoe hadn't had time to grab any of Megan's stuffed animals was a superhero in her book. "He's going to take us to dinner at Miller's."

Megan grew excited. "I like Miller's. They have good chicken tenders."

It was a rare treat when Zoe and Megan ate out. "Mrs. Bien has some chapter books in the parlor downstairs. How about we bring one just in case? That way, if you finish coloring, you won't get bored when the grownups talk."

"Okay." Megan loved to read.

"Go wash up and then we'll get a book." Zoe pointed to the bathroom and Megan padded her way inside. They met Nick downstairs and walked to Miller's. The Sunday night crowd was always casual, and Zoe had changed into a soft knit sweater and her favorite jeans.

They were seated immediately. The waitress brought a kid's menu designed for coloring and four crayons. Megan got to work coloring a Thanksgiving scene with a cornucopia and a turkey. Zoe ordered a pulled pork special, which came with two sides. Nick opted for brisket. Megan chose the children's chicken tenders and mac and cheese. The food arrived quickly, and Zoe listened as Nick drew her daughter into conversation. He made a genuine effort, talking to Megan about flying, books, dogs, her favorite subject and all sorts of other things.

"My business partner has kids," Nick told Zoe when he saw the speculative lift of her eyebrow. "I spent a lot of time with them."

Zoe wanted to ask more, but Megan chattered on, monopolizing Nick's attention. With good company and good food, Zoe relaxed. She didn't even protest when he took the bill and paid the total plus tip, knowing he'd reject her effort. When they stopped by the restroom on the way out, Megan told her mom "I can do it by myself" so Zoe stood outside the entrance to the hallway with Nick.

"How am I doing?" he asked.

"You've completely charmed her. Where in the world did you find time to get that rabbit?"

Nick gave her a mischievous grin. "I have my ways. And are my charms working on you?"

"Maybe a little," Zoe admitted softly. "You're pretty hard to resist."

"It's an art," Nick teased.

He leaned closer, but before he could drop a kiss on her lips, someone called his name. "Nick? Nick Reilly?"

Both he and Zoe turned to see a beautiful blonde standing there. She peered at Nick as if he were a mirage she wasn't sure would disappear. Zoe worked to place the woman. She seemed oddly familiar. "Oh my goodness, it is you."

And with that, as Zoe's heart dropped to her feet, the interloper tossed her arms around Nick.

Nick had survived almost a week without being recognized. But time had run out. From the shock on Zoe's face, he needed to damage control, stat. "Zoe, this is Ashley. Ashley Rill. She was in most of my classes junior year."

"Actually, it's Buffa now," Ashley corrected with a huge smile, and Nick had never felt so much relief when he saw the flash of a diamond on her left hand. "You don't remember me, do you?" She stuck her hand out and Zoe shook it like an afterthought. "But you're Zoe James. You had the best homecoming queen dress ever. I was on court the next year, but I didn't win."

"We must not have run in the same circles."

"Oh, we didn't. I did cheer rather than dance like you did." Ashley focused her attention on Nick. "How are you? You look fantastic. I couldn't believe it a few minutes ago when you walked by my table. I thought I was seeing things, but no. You went away junior year and none of us saw you again. You're not on any social media either. Dan and I looked."

God forbid, Nick thought. Those algorithms and the data those companies collected... Nick shook his head. "Nope. Sorry. But it is me."

"It's kismet!" Ashley didn't lose enthusiasm. Her husband approached and Nick recognized him as another of his classmates. "You remember Dan."

Nick didn't really, minus that the guy had taken every science class. Had Dan dated Ashley in high school? "Good seeing you again. How are you?" Nick politely shook Dan's hand.

"Dan's a doctor," Ashley boasted proudly. "And I teach first grade in St. Louis County." She named the school, but Nick had no idea where it was. One thing hadn't changed about Ashley—she'd always had an upbeat, sunny disposition. "Oh, and Claire Cross is a loan manager. Married. Three kids. You'd know these things if you'd show up at a reunion now and then."

Another thing Nick purposefully avoided. Claire hadn't given him the time of day except when she couldn't do the work. Ashley had at least acted like his friend, although he'd never seen her in the hallway or anywhere else when outside of the classroom. Still, it was funny how a decade made some of those bad memories fade while others remained as strong as ever. But before he could get a word in edgewise, Ashley kept going, same as she had in high school.

"You should come next weekend," Ashley invited. "We're all getting together at Jamestown. Zoe, you should come too. Drag him, would you? I want to know what he's been up to. Nick, you got me through so many math classes! I owe you! Please do say yes!"

Megan came out of the restroom then, giving Nick the perfect opportunity to extricate himself from the situation, especially as Ashley and Dan had gotten up in the middle of their dinner to intercept Nick before he left the restaurant. "Seriously," Ashley directed this at Zoe. "Please get him to attend." Then to Nick, "We've all changed so much. We'd love to see you."

Using Zoe's go-to line, Nick said, "I'll think about it."

With that, he, Zoe, and Megan left the restaurant and walked home. The night held a chill but no Woman in White glided by under the streetlights. Megan skipped her way toward the inn, safely about twelve feet in front of them. "So you and Ashley?"

"Never," Nick said sharply. "Not my type. And she wouldn't have given me the time of day outside of class anyway. Same for Claire."

"Same for me," Zoe said. "I didn't see you. I didn't see anyone but those in my own circle."

Nick reached for her hand, enjoying how her fingers laced with his. "Nor did I expect you to do differently. As for them, they were people I knew. They needed math help. I wanted to fit in and didn't. I had something they wanted. Smarts."

"In hindsight, popularity can be its own trap."

"I learned that far later." He'd been a kid in the candy store when women had finally started noticing him because his looks had evolved into something considered sexy. Then later, he'd let Kevin do all the face time with investors because Kevin enjoyed the schmoozing that Nick hated.

Zoe turned his hand so the lines on his wrist showed. "You never told me how you got this scar."

"Put my hand through a pane of glass." He didn't add it was to unlock the door so he could protect his mom from an ardent ex-turned-stalker. That was a memory he'd rather forget and one reason his mom had finally moved them far from Beaumont.

They'd reached the inn, and Megan was waiting on the porch by the front doors. Nick punched in the code and she ran all the way to the second floor. He shut the front door behind him before too much cold seeped into the foyer. Zoe unwound her scarf. "She's usually out like a light. I could come to your room."

He wanted nothing more. "What if she wakes?"

"I wonder if Mrs. Bien has a baby monitor."

And before he could think to stop her, Zoe asked Mrs. Bien for just that, making Nick realize how much Zoe had already changed since they'd reconnected. He also experienced a strong emotional attachment when Megan initiated a goodnight hug. Would this be what it would feel like to be a father? He distracted himself by reading his book until, about an hour later, he heard a tap on his door and Zoe slipped through. "Hey," she said.

Even in sweats, she was a sight to behold. She set the monitor down and he drew her into his arms, inhaling and imprinting her floral scent. She had no hesitations now, not like the first time, and Nick made love to her with an urgency he hadn't felt previously. She was growing on him, becoming an important part of his life. Being with her as close as two people could be was like coming home to a place he'd always dreamed about but never had. Now that he had experienced the sensation, the truth of the matter was he didn't want to let her go. He was becoming attached. Before she'd been a crush. An unobtainable dream.

The reality was far better than Nick could have ever imagined. How could he leave? How could he let her go? But he did, as she slipped from his room to go back to hers so she could be there if her daughter woke up. He hated how empty and big his queen-sized bed felt.

Unlike her weekend schedule, Zoe had told him she went to the store after she took Megan to school. The store opened daily at eleven, so she baked all morning. Because of that, by Tuesday, she and Nick had developed a routine. He tagged along for the baking time and then made himself scarce during the latter half of the day. Kevin had reached out, and Nick was doing some remote work for his former partner. Nick liked the challenge the work presented, and the money wasn't bad either, not that he needed it.

He, Zoe, and Megan ate dinner together—usually something carried out and eaten in the inn's dining room. Then Megan went to bed and Zoe would slip into his room. Her HVAC repair was delayed and going to be more costly because of a part issue—Larry expected to be finished Friday afternoon. Nick knew she was disappointed the repair had taken extra and increased in cost, but he enjoyed having the extra time with her.

The week flew by. Friday also marked the last day of school for Megan—Beaumont Elementary gave students the entire week of Thanksgiving off as a holiday break. Once Zoe moved back into her house, it would change everything. She wouldn't be across the hall, able to slip into his room for lovemaking. He felt the loss every night when she left. It would be miserable without her there at all once she moved home.

But he'd make the best of it, as he always did. Keeping this in mind, he walked into the store at closing time Friday evening to find Zoe slamming baking trays around, clearly upset. He rushed over to her. "Hey, what's wrong? Is your house not ready?"

"That's not it." Zoe shoved the clean trays into their rack with more force than necessary. Everything was put away for the day and she was finishing up with cleaning the kitchen.

"Is it the Madeleines?" She'd been working to perfect the recipe all week. Nick couldn't have imagined how she was going to improve on her first batch, but she had. The following weekend she'd enter the competition and Nick felt in his bones she'd rock the judges' world with her entry. He'd tasted the update versions and they were delicious.

"The cookies are fine. Ted is coming to town Tuesday. He wants Megan."

Nick's forehead creased. "But it's the holiday."

She glared at him. "Exactly. But the judge gave him Thanksgiving and me Christmas. Except for since I had her double last year, he's saying I have to let her go and that next year we'll go back to switching. The nerve of the man. He never comes to town, but suddenly his whole family is celebrating the Thanksgiving holiday together, so he's bringing the new wife and baby and..." Zoe threw her hands in the air, frustration clear. "He told me he'll get a lawyer if I don't agree."

Nick had been a latchkey child, but since he had no idea who his father was, he'd never been transferred from one parent to the other. "Megan's resilient."

"It's not her I'm worried about."

"Ah." Nick gathered her in his arms. "You thought you wouldn't be alone."

She trembled. "I had fun things planned."

He assumed she meant Thanksgiving at her brother's house and then being with her daughter at the gingerbread contest on Saturday. He could go with her to both but hesitated. Once Zoe moved home tonight, his part in this engagement charade might be over. They hadn't talked about it, and he had no idea if she wanted him to remain in her life beyond his original purpose. What would it be like to be with her without the subterfuge? To make things real? To share all his secrets and have her love him fully as the man he'd become, and the one he'd been? "You'll have her for this weekend and Monday. I know that's not what you wanted."

"I'm used to him not showing up. Now he suddenly decides to be present and use the time the court gave him?"

Nick got it. The nerve of the man to decide to inconvenience her at the last minute and threaten to involve a lawyer, especially given Zoe's finances. "I'm sorry. How can I help? Do you need me to stay?" She'd never answered that question after telling him she'd thing about it, and he hadn't wanted to press.

"Don't you have plans?"

"None necessarily to speak of." Kevin had invited him to spend the holiday with his family as always, but Nick had said no. "I can stay as long as you need me." However long that would be, he had no clue, and he feared to ask. With Zoe, he'd take things one day at a time.

"I called my mom. Megan was excited about seeing

her cousins in Kirkwood, so I'm going to take her there this weekend. She'll stay overnight."

Nick tried to make light of a serious situation. He wanted Zoe to laugh. To not be weighted down. He developed an exaggerated playful accent. "Miss Zoe, are you asking me to go home with you and keep you warm?"

As he'd hoped, Zoe burst out laughing. "I sound so pathetic. But yes. Yes, Nick Reilly, I want you to come and shack up with me in my love den. As long as we attend your reunion."

"Oh no." Nick shook his head, his hair flopping into his face. "I can think of much more pleasurable things to do than go to a reunion." Besides, he didn't want the exposure.

Zoe waved a wooden spoon at him before setting it in a drawer. She had the kitchen sparkling clean. "You said you were exorcising demons. You spend the weekend with me helping me exorcise mine and I'll go with you and help you banish yours. That's fair."

"I'm not sure how so," Nick protested. "I don't even like these people."

"But they seem to like you. And honestly, what do you have to hide?"

Tons, Nick thought. About how he'd been that kid. The scarred one whose past traumas still taunted him. That, no matter how much he'd changed, no matter how much money he had, he'd never fit in. He'd never be good enough or worthy. He'd never belong socially or emotionally to a crowd or to a person. Heck, his looks and dollars hadn't kept Alexa from straying. In the end, what if what was on his inside was rotten from years of neglect? Like he couldn't repair it? Just cover it up with fancy clothes and things?

Zoe puckered her lips and blew him a kiss that went straight to his groin. "It'll be fine. Besides think of the rewards."

Those teasing words did it. He grabbed her and kissed her until they were both breathless. She was wearing her Auntie Jayne's gingham dress and an apron today, and Nick scrunched her skirt and with a fast movement had her panties at her knees. Zoe's eyes had gone wide, but she was an eager participant as her hands were yanking down his zipper. He backed her against the countertop, donned protection, and entered her wet and ready heat in one slick stroke.

She splayed out before him, her uniform askew. He leaned in to kiss her and drove them straight to heaven. Afterward, she lifted onto her elbows, her eyes glassy from the explosive orgasm. "Those kind of rewards?" Nick asked.

"Yeah, those." Zoe breathed heavily and Nick helped steady her as she found her footing. "So we're going, right?"

Nick caved. He was putty where Zoe was concerned. He'd give her the world if she'd let him, no matter the cost. He gave her another long kiss before they started sanitizing the kitchen. "Yes. We're attending a reunion."

Chapter Seven

Zoe couldn't believe she'd had sex on the countertop of Auntie Jayne's. As Nick disposed of the condom and the rest of the trash in the dumpster behind the store, Zoe used disinfecting wipes to sanitize the stainless steel surface. When had she turned into this desirous woman? One smoldering glance and she wanted Nick with the heat of a thousand suns.

She'd certainly never considered having experimental sex with Jared. He wasn't the type to have had anything but conventional sex in a bed, with the door firmly shut. Nick brought out a wild side she hadn't realized she had. She liked it. She liked who she was when she was with him, too.

He returned to the kitchen and gave her a grin. "You ready?"

"Down, boy," she teased. "I'm ready to walk to my house and meet Larry."

That easy smile she was so fond of widened. "That's what I meant. Look at you misreading everything."

She swatted him gently on his arm. He responded by giving her a huge kiss. When they broke apart, she locked the store and set the alarm.

They found Larry standing on the sidewalk outside her house, his company truck on the street. He gave both a big handshake. "Welcome home, Zoe! You have heat and the city building inspector has signed off. You can move back in. Let me show you your new system."

Zoe and Nick followed Larry inside. The first thing he did was show her how to work the new digital thermostat and waited patiently while she downloaded and installed the app. "You can set times and temperatures. It'll save you money to program things."

She felt like a participant on one of those home improvement reality TV shows, except hers was simply an HVAC upgrade. Downstairs, the old cast-iron furnace had been removed, replaced by a slick modern one that occupied half the space. "You have a high-efficiency heating and air-conditioning system that, depending on the temperature you set, works automatically. We upgraded everything, including installing new ductwork. You also have a humidifier for the winter and an automatic dehumidifier for the summer."

He gave a short laugh. "You'll need it. I know you didn't want the upgrade, but this is Missouri, after all. You'll also notice a difference in air quality with the filter unit we put in."

Zoe was overwhelmed but grateful. She hated the price tag, which had increased greatly, to the point that monthly payments would be painful. However, she appreciated how worry-free she'd be now.

They returned to her kitchen. "Just have some paperwork for you to sign and I'll be on my way. We've already filed the gas company rebate for you. You'll get that gift card in a few weeks."

"Thanks so much for working me in. I appreciate everything you've done for me," Zoe said as Larry handed her a packet containing the owner's manual, warranty and other papers.

Larry opened an iPad and brought up an invoice. He pointed to a line. "Sign here."

Using her finger, Zoe signed her name. Larry pressed here and there on the iPad. "I've emailed you the receipt."

"Do you know when I'll get the first bill? Next month?"

Larry closed the iPad cover and peered at her strangely. "Zoe, you're getting your deposit back. It should show up in a week."

That made no sense. Nor did Larry when he continued. "You don't owe me anything, Zoe. Your bill is paid in full. An anonymous donor."

If Nick hadn't been supporting her, Zoe would have landed on the floor, her shock was so great. "What? Who?"

Larry gave a small shrug. "I don't know. Someone called the office and paid your bill and swore us to secrecy. Sorry, Zoe, but I can't tell you."

"I don't want charity. If it's my parents, you send it back and put it on my credit card."

Larry looked her straight in the eye. "I swear on my wife's life that it wasn't your parents, Zoe. Take the gift. Sometimes there are angels out there and you simply have to roll with it. Someone was paying it forward.

Eventually, you do the same when you can. I'm leaving now. Promised the wife I'd take her to a movie." Larry glanced over her head and nodded at Nick. "Both of you take care."

"Thanks," Nick said, a word Zoe echoed when she closed the front door behind Larry. She wandered around her house. Minus a thin layer of dust, everything else remained exactly as she'd left it when she'd walked out with Carl.

"You okay?" Nick asked. "That was a shock. A good one, though."

Zoe removed the clip holding her hair and shook her head so the strands fell on her shoulders. "It's overwhelming. Who would do such a thing? Did you see the invoice? It's over fifteen thousand dollars."

Nick shrugged. "Someone paying it forward, like he said."

Zoe ran her fingers through her hair, her nerves getting the best of her. "This isn't like buying someone's drive-thru order or donating to clear student lunch accounts."

The front door opened, and a voice called, "Yoo hoo, we're here!"

"Mom!" Megan shouted as she raced inside.

"Thanks for getting her from the Brownie meeting," Zoe told Shelby.

Shelby wheeled in a suitcase. "It's no problem. And since Luke's with me, we brought your luggage. We figured since you'd already packed and left it with Mom that we'd bring it along and save you the trouble of going back."

"That's so kind." It would save her a trip, which was especially welcome as she still had to wash everything and pack Megan's suitcase for an overnight in Kirkwood. Her Friday night would consist of the domestic bliss of chores and more chores. This weekend, besides being the one before Thanksgiving, promised to be mild weather-wise. At least she and Nick had gotten some of her outdoor Christmas decorations done while waiting for the inside repairs. Already, many of her neighbors had their holiday lights running, and Zoe's house had been a forlorn dark spot. But no more.

Nick glanced at his watch. "I'm going to pick up dinner."

"Are we having Miller's again?" Megan asked hopefully.

"Of course, because you said it's your favorite," Nick said with a grin that melted Zoe's heart.

"Yay!" Carrying her bunny, Megan lifted her tiny suitcase and took it to her bedroom.

Shelby and Luke took their leave, and Nick turned to Zoe. "You good? Do you need anything while I'm out?"

"Sanity?" Zoe asked. "I'm in shock. More so than when it happened." She took a deep breath. "It's a huge weight off my shoulders to be back home. And to have that bill paid. I'm still pinching myself."

"You've got a huge weekend ahead of you because I'm holding you to that date tomorrow. That's the price for my attendance at the reunion."

Zoe held her right hand out in protest. "I'd like you to know I took off work. Something I almost never do. I made enough product so Jessica and Sarah can easily cover for me."

"Perfect." When Nick grabbed his coat and set off for Miller's, Zoe began to clean. She and Nick and Megan would have a good dinner and watch a movie, and then he'd leave for the inn. Tomorrow morning she'd drop Megan off at Nelson's in Kirkwood. She and Nick would then embark on whatever he'd planned for them. She wanted to attend the reunion, hoping it would give her some clues to his past. His classmates clearly recognized him. Since he never wanted to talk about his past, she hoped someone could fill in the gaps.

As for her taking a rare day off, even she should let go once in a while. The store would be fine. She'd be back on Sunday morning, bright and early. If her house could survive the last week, the store could survive one day.

"You still haven't told me where we're going," Zoe protested.

After waving off an invitation to lunch at her brother's because they'd been running late, Nick drove his sedan west with Zoe riding shotgun While he drove in the general direction of Beaumont, they were not on the most direct highway route because they weren't going to Beaumont.

"I told you it's a surprise." Nick shot her a grin, returning his attention quickly to the road. He liked that she remained in the dark. "You'll have to be patient. The mystery is half the fun."

She gestured with her phone. "We've only got six hours before the reunion starts. You're not trying to get out of it, are you?"

He wished. But a promise was a promise. "We'll have plenty of time to get back and get ready." He'd arranged everything to ensure that. He exited onto the ramp for Spirit of St. Louis Boulevard, and stayed straight when they reached the cross-street light at Chesterfield Airport Road. He saw her turn her head in confusion. "No, we're not going to the outlet mall. That's not my idea of fun. I hate clothes shopping. Especially on a day as nice as this one."

One good thing about L.A., plenty of stylists who could shop for him. A short distance later, the road made a T, and he turned right and then left into a parking lot. Zoe, who'd been texting something, craned her neck as he opened her passenger door. She stepped out onto the blacktop and read the sign for a private aviation company. "Why are we here?"

"We need a plane to get where we're going. And before you start worrying, you're dressed fine."

They were both in jeans. She'd topped hers with a red sweater set and he wore a dark blue long-sleeve Henley over a white t-shirt. He led her into the building and retrieved a duffel from a woman at a counter. Taking Zoe's hand, he led her through a door and outside. The day was sunny and in the low sixties, which was about average for St. Louis this time of year. They didn't have far to walk. Nick pointed to a plane with a blue stripe. "There's our ride. She's a Cessna Skylane. Seats four. I didn't need anything bigger but I'm certified for larger aircraft."

They walked around the propeller. He opened the passenger door and pointed to the beige leather seat. "Climb in. It'll be a comfortable ride once we get going. I've got some work to do before we can get out of here."

He ducked under the wing and went to his side. Opening the left-side door, he set the duffel on his seat and removed two sets of headphones, various charts, and spiral-bound books. He passed over a set of the headphones to Zoe. "Even though lots of things are digital these days, I also like having hard copy. I'm going to perform all the pre-flight checks and then we'll take off."

He went through the entire exterior routine before returning to her door. "While this is one of the safest aircrafts out there, we do have to go through the safety protocol." He showed her how to operate her door. "If something happens, which it won't, we meet by the tail. He leaned over to give her a quick kiss. "Don't worry. I won't let anything happen to you."

Returning to his side, he made short work of stowing the duffel bag and her purse. He'd had the plane fueled, and he made short work of his final preflight. The cockpit screens flared to life. "Put your headphones on." He put his over his ears, the silence immediate. "Can you hear me?"

Her voice floated into his ear. "Yes. Loud and clear."

He reached over and gave her hand a quick squeeze. "Good. We can talk the entire way. But first, I gotta get us out of here so we can get there." The engine started smoothly and the prop whirled. He radioed the tower, and following the air traffic controller's directions, he taxied out onto the runway. "Unlike a jumbo jet, we won't need much to get off the ground," he told Zoe. "She'll pop right up. You're going to get a great view of St. Louis."

Permission to take off came from the tower, and Nick increased the speed and pulled back on the yoke. It was a beautiful day with practically no wind. They'd have smooth skies. A little bump and the plane began to lift. "We're off the ground," he told her.

"Wow." He heard Zoe's breathlessness as the plane

began to climb. "I've been in the 737s, but flying in those is nothing like this."

Nick made a few adjustments. "You mean flying with over a hundred people you don't know? This is far better. Intimate. You'll have a great view from the eleven thousand feet we'll be flying at. If you look over to your left, you'll see some planes getting ready to land at Lambert Field."

Lambert was St. Louis's international airport. Zoe leaned slightly so she could see. Then she peered down at the world. "We're almost over Creve Coeur. Give it a few minutes and you'll see the Arch off to your right."

"Are you finally going to tell me where we're going?" Zoe asked after they crossed the Mississippi River into Illinois.

"Springfield. We've got a reservation for a tour of Abraham Lincoln's house."

"You were listening at dinner the other night," she marveled. Megan had been learning about the sixteenth president in her class and she'd told them all about it.

"I always listen," Nick confirmed. "Neither of us had been there, and I figured why not? You could preview it. Take Megan later. It's a quick flight, especially since we're at about two hundred miles per hour. We're going to have fun. I've got the entire day planned."

Almost as soon as they'd taken off, to Zoe it felt as if no time had passed before they were landing. She'd enjoyed the flight. The ride had been smooth, the seat extremely comfortable, and she and Nick had talked about anything and everything. He'd explained the various screens in front of him. One showed the horizon and how the plane was in level flight. The other screen displayed the terrain, weather and other aircraft around them.

She'd never liked flying, but her sister had loved it, and now Zoe had a better understanding of why. What would have been a two-hour drive had taken a fraction of that. She couldn't hear Nick when he spoke to the tower, but soon the screens showed him banking and straightening, and dropping altitude as, out in front of them, a runway came into view on the ground below.

Nick landed and taxied away from the main terminal and instead to a private aviation hangar. Soon they were on their way, parking the courtesy car in the lot for the Lincoln Home National Historic Site visitor center. "What's that?" Zoe asked as Nick pulled from his jacket a small, blue, spiral book with gold lettering.

"It's a National Park Passport booklet. When you visit a national park or historic site, you stamp the page." Once inside, he showed her how to find the date stamps the site provided. After stamping his, he insisted on buying her a book of her own. "I find it addicting. There are a few historic sites in St. Louis. One's the Ulysses S. Grant house. We'll need to go so we can get the stamp."

Pretending he wasn't leaving eventually, Zoe agreed.

Their adventure started with a movie. Then the National Park Service guide directed them outside, where they joined a queue of twelve other people. A short walk later and they climbed the front stairs to enter the yellow house with green shutters where the sixteenth president of the United States had lived for seventeen years with his wife, up until they'd left for the White House. The forty-five-minute tour took guests throughout the house, showing them the formal parlor, sitting and dining rooms, Lincoln's bedroom, Mary's bedroom, and then the boys' room. After passing the hired help's room, they went down the narrow back stairs to the kitchen, where the guide showed them Mary's black, cast-iron cook stove, purchased in 1860. The stove had an oven, apron front, and four cook holes. When they moved to Washington, D.C., Abe had convinced her the stove needed to stay with the house when Mary wanted to take it with them.

Zoe gave a shudder. "I can't imagine cooking on that," she told Nick.

He laughed. "It was the top of the line then. Did you see those clusters of oak leaves on the doors? Fancy."

"Um, no thank you to any time period before mine. I'd be the first one to have died on the Oregon Trail. Do you remember that game?"

"But of course," Nick said. "It was pretty basic."

The tour ended in the backyard, with the guide telling them about what items archeologists had found buried there. Once it was over, she and Nick took self-tours of two other homes. Then they walked to the end of the block and ate at the Springfield Carriage Company, which was a family-owned restaurant located in an old house. Nick and Zoe chose a spot on the front porch, and each enjoyed a "horseshoe," which was the name of the local sandwich. Both ordered an Italian beef pony shoe, which was beef topped with french fries and covered with homemade cheese sauce and pepperoncini. The stack was served open-faced on bread, and it was delicious. Full, they walked back to the parking lot and drove the short distance to the Abraham Lincoln Presidential Library and Museum.

Zoe found the tour enlightening, with its replica of Lincoln's childhood cabin to the ability of participants to follow the fate of several Civil War soldiers. Zoe clutched Nick's hand as they entered the sobering replica of Lincoln's coffin lying in state. Then they went out into the waning sunlight to drive to one more stop, Lincoln's tomb. They walked through the tunnel to the crypt, and then once they exited, they stopped at the bronze statue of Lincoln's head and rubbed Lincoln's nose for good luck, like many who'd come before them.

At the airport, Zoe watched Nick perform his preflight, and soon they were in the air, chasing a setting sun. Below them, the terrain had changed from green fields to black nothingness that was occasionally broken by flickering lights. Besides seeing the river on the GPS, she could also tell when they crossed over the Mississippi for it appeared like a dark snake weaving its way south to where it would dump into the Gulf of Mexico. Far off St. Louis was an illuminated strip on the horizon. Shortly after they crossed over the Missouri, the plane touched down. Zoe gazed around as Nick taxied the plane. She saw a few hangars and a small building, but this was not the same place they'd flown from. "Where are we?"

"Beaumont. The airstrip Clayton Holdings built. It's towerless."

"But the car's in Chesterfield."

"I had it delivered. It should be over there. Come on. You don't want to be late, do you?"

Zoe absorbed the implications. "No, I don't want to be late. But Nick, moving cars costs a lot of money."

Overhead light filled the cockpit once Nick parked. He killed the engine and removed his headphones. She did the same. "It's nothing, Zoe. Let's get going."

He came to her side of the plane and opened her door.

He put his hand on hers and helped her out, making sure she didn't bump her head on the wing overhead. He carried her purse and his bag to the small building and pressed in the code that unlocked the door.

"I'll be right back. Still have to secure the plane." Setting his bag on a table, he closed the door and left her in the plush lounge. The space also held a kitchenette with microwave, sink and refrigerator stocked with water, and Zoe discovered the ladies' room also contained changing facilities and showers. Her sister's influence, no doubt, Zoe thought.

She settled onto one of the couches until Nick returned. A short drive later, he walked her to her front door. "I'll be back in an hour." He dropped a light kiss on her lips.

"I'll be ready." Zoe closed the door behind him and leaned against the wood for a moment. It had been the best day. They'd had fun. She'd felt close to him.

But the trip had proven how much she still didn't know about him. He owned a plane. She had no idea how much that cost, but it was certainly beyond her budget. He'd had his rental car moved. He'd paid for everything with a Black card. American Express didn't hand those out to everyone.

Nick was a mystery. Hopefully she'd figure out some of his secrets tonight. If not, she'd ask. She'd pry. They were sleeping with each other. Even if her discovery didn't lead to anywhere good, and even if her gut said it was fine to trust him, the doubts in her head clamored louder and louder, demanding attention. Finished with her shower and blowing out her hair until it was straight and fell around her shoulders, Zoe located and donned the dress she'd long ago shoved into the back of her closet.

Perhaps she had a demon of her own to exorcise by wearing it. The designer, long-sleeve silk *V*-neck fell to her knees. The purchase had been a rare splurge made when she'd been married to Ted. She'd tried it on and fallen in love with the gold, maroon, sea foam green, and tan floral pattern. One-inch ruffles lined the deep-*V* neckline, and the skirt had three tiers, each with the same ruffle going around. Subtle ruffles capped the sleeves, accenting her wrists. The dress wrapped and tied with a belt. She'd have to go braless and tape herself into the bodice, but Zoe didn't mind.

She looked hot. Classy yet sexy. She zipped the tall boots she'd worn to the wine bar. She added a thin gold chain that held a tiny heart-shaped locket with the letter *Z* etched on the outside. The locket landed directly above the valley of her breasts. She dug out her makeup and worked to put on a face that was understated beauty. She knew she'd succeeded when she opened the door and Nick gave a low whistle. "You look fabulous."

His compliment reached her soul and she tried not to preen as she let him in. "Thank you."

"That dress." He leaned over and gave her a kiss on the cheek. "You are beautiful, Zoe. I'm going to be the luckiest guy at this thing."

"Flatterer," she said, deflecting and trying to make light of his obvious attention and her desire for it "You don't look so shabby yourself."

If anything, he was more bad boy dangerous. He'd worn a double-breasted wool and cotton structured jacket with ribbed cuffs and hem. The deep navy blue jacket, worn open, topped a tight crew neck t-shirt in the same shade except for some sort of embroidered logo on the chest. He'd tucked the shirt into deep navy blue trousers that had a flat front, elasticized drawstring waist. He shoved his hand in one of the two side pockets. The bottom of the pants had small zippers at the ankle. He wore no socks, but had put his feet into blue lace-up tennis shoes, complete with a white bottom.

Like the first day when he'd stepped into her shop, he looked like he walked off the catwalk and into her living room. "Wow," she said. It took guts to wear that type of outfit in Beaumont where most of the men would be in khaki pants and oxford button downs.

He appeared slightly nervous. "You don't think this is too much?"

"No. You'll knock them dead. You look like you could be at a movie premiere." She would've stripped him naked if they had time and if she didn't want him to go to this thing.

"I wore it to one. Figured I'd get one more use out of it."

"Oh yeah, the actress."

"One of my many mistakes. That whole life was." He gave a shake of his head, sending the golden locks over his left eye. "I'm hoping tonight isn't one of them. I don't know these people. We were never friends."

"It'll be fine. It's a reunion. People drink too much and reminisce about the dumb things they did in high school. You make new memories. New friends, maybe. Ten years changes things."

"People also gossip nonstop for days afterward." He reached into the coat pocket and passed her a small black velvet box. "On that note, will you do me the honor of wearing this?"

Zoe swore her fingers shook as she took the box from his hand. She opened it and gasped. Inside was the most beautiful ring she'd ever seen. Set into a 14-karat white gold setting, the ring had a brilliant-cut white diamond that was colorless. Set on each side of the center stone was a smaller, pear-shaped diamond. On each side of those were six tiny pavé set diamonds that twinkled in the thin band. Damn it. Why couldn't this be for real? Why did this fake act have her feeling as if she wanted forever with him? "Nick."

He took the box from her trembling fingers. "The diamonds are all recycled and handpicked. Each ring is handmade by artisans in Brooklyn."

The diamond caught the light and sparkled as he took it from the box. "Nick, it's gorgeous but I can't accept this. It's too much."

Wordlessly, he slid the band onto her finger, then lifted her hand to his. He placed a kiss directly above her knuckles that sent a tremor through her. "Humor me. Please. We can't go in there without a ring. What will they think of me? Of you? And I'm glad it fits. Megan showed me one of yours."

"Was that what the two of you were doing the other night after dinner when I heard her giggling?" She'd been ready to go find out what the two of them had been talking about, but then Megan had come barreling into the kitchen, wanting a cookie. Since they hadn't had any dessert following dinner, Zoe had allowed her daughter to have one.

"She helped me pick it out."

"Nick." Zoe tried not to nibble her lower lip. Megan was clearly getting attached to Nick.

He gently moved his hands to her shoulders. "Zoe,

it's fine. I just showed her some rings on a website and she picked one she thought you'd like. Don't make it a big deal. If we don't leave now, we will be late."

"Okay," Zoe caved, especially as her stomach grumbled, either from sudden nerves or hunger. Eating the pony shoe sandwich had occurred hours ago. She could argue with him over the ring when they returned. Already the band circling her finger felt as if it belonged, and she worried she wouldn't want to take it off. Despite great sex, none of this was real for long, and it would be best if she remembered that.

She put on her coat and the small cross body she'd transferred some essentials into, like her phone and lipstick. She locked the door behind her, and when she turned around, she paused at the top of the steps to her front porch and stared at the street.

Instead of Nick's rented Audi, a uniformed driver stood outside a waiting limousine. "I figured we'd go in style." Nick held out his hand. "Plus, I didn't want to fight for Ubers. I don't drive if I drink, and I'm sure I'll need a cocktail tonight. Hence, our ride. Besides, you deserve the red carpet treatment."

This had to be some dream she'd gotten herself into, and one that would end logically once he left. Perhaps she could convince him to stay...

She couldn't think about that now and risk ruining the evening. "I feel a bit like Cinderella," she told him as the limo pulled away from the curb and headed toward Winery Road and Jamestown Vineyards. "No worries. I won't turn into a pumpkin. Or a scullery maid. You must be used to riding in limos."

"Doesn't mean my nerves aren't fried." Nick poured her a glass of champagne. "This is like a return to high school. I didn't do the prom thing. Did you have a limo then?"

"Yes, but not to ourselves. We shared with other people." Zoe sipped the bubbly.

Nick took her glass from her fingers and leaned over to kiss her neck. "So you couldn't do this?"

"Uh, no," Zoe murmured as her body heated. His fingers slid along the ruffled *V* of her dress. Her head fell back against the seat as her body began to quiver. "Nick."

"The privacy glass is up."

"You'll ruin my makeup." It was the only excuse she could think of not to do this, making sure he knew she didn't mean it when she set aside her champagne glass.

"Trust me, I won't." Confidently he found the hollow at her throat with his tongue. His fingers drifted lower, under the ruffled hem at her knees. Zoe had debated wearing shapewear, but as Nick's fingers slid her panties down, she thanked herself for her foresight. The magic movement of Nick's fingers vanquished thoughts and doubts.

Before the limo began to ascend the hill to Jamestown's tasting room, Nick brought her to heaven. When done, he gave her a quick kiss and helped her become presentable.

"I don't even want to know if you and that ex of yours did this," Zoe said as the limo pulled up at the portico. She took another sip of champagne.

"We didn't, which is a reason I wanted to."

That fact eased Zoe's mind. She slid her arm through Nick's as they went through the double doors. They stepped into the Great Room, which also doubled as Jamestown's dining room and tasting room. Her dad had

modeled the space on the lobby of the Tenyana Hotel at
Yosemite. Zoe had always loved how the Great Room
was a huge, open expanse with two-story-high ceilings,
dark wooden trusses and rustic chandeliers. While he'd
rebranded many of the other wineries, Jack, Sierra's
husband, had kept everything the same at Jamestown.

They paused at a table to retrieve their nametags.
Because Zoe was a guest, her nametag didn't have her
high school picture. Nick had a square box placeholder
where his was supposed to be. Two women worked reg-
istration, and the one Zoe didn't know held Nick's tag
outstretched but pulled it back. She stared at his name,
then Nick, then the pictureless nametag again. "Nick.
I remember you. You've certainly changed since our
American history class."

Zoe recognized the other woman, Ann Alfred Cole.
She managed a high-end department store in Frontenac.
Ann peered at Nick's outfit. "Is that Armani?"

Nick didn't confirm or deny as he clipped on the
nametag. As they walked away, Ann held out the phone
to her table partner as if showing her something. "That's
this season's couture."

"Armani?" Zoe asked Nick as they walked away.
"Really, who are you?"

"Nick Reilly, Beaumont class of 2013" He guided her
into the tasting room. Unlike the smaller tasting rooms
of the other wineries purchased by Clayton Holdings,
Jamestown's tasting room was designed by her father
so that the length of the gigantic main room was double the width. A wall full of two-story-high windows
stood opposite the front doors. During the day, the windows provided a sweeping view of rolling hills. Tonight,

guests could see the glowing firepits that waited on the expansive deck in case anyone wanted to go outside.

She and Nick stopped at the long bar running along the entire left side. Behind her, on the opposite wall, an eight-foot-wide floor-to-ceiling stone fireplace held a roaring, wood-burning fire.

"What would you like?" Nick asked her.

"A glass of Norton is fine."

As Nick went to order, people Zoe knew came to greet her. When Nick rejoined her, she had just finished chatting with some of the other girls on the dance team. "I'd forgotten you were a Beaumont Belle."

"National champions my senior year." Zoe took the glass he held out. "But in reality, it was long ago and lives on as just another glory day memory. Another lifetime, really. And if you think I could do any of those hip hop routines now?" Zoe gave a small shake of her head and laughed. "I'd probably throw a hip out."

"Never. Not with the moves I know you can still make." Grinning, Nick placed his hand on the small of her back and guided her deeper into the room. In the center, the venue's kitchen had set up a huge dinner buffet. "Shall we eat first?"

She considered his suggestion. If she was going to drink, it'd be smart to get some food in her stomach. Already she had butterflies taking flight. Nick's touch created tingles. Her face heated as she remembered what his firm fingers had done to her in the limo. "That might be a good idea."

The buffet was served on round tables rather than rectangular, and Zoe grabbed a dinner plate and began to choose some of this and some of that. She added nuts and cheeses, baked lasagna, and salad. Nick added sliced roasted beef, salad, a slew of appetizers like can-noli bites and bacon-wrapped dates, and some pasta salad. When they turned to figure out where to sit, Zoe saw Ashley standing and waving at them. "Nick, Zoe. Over here."

Resigned, Nick nodded. "We can sit with them."

Zoe threaded her way through the crowd to the table.

"Take a seat," Dan invited. "Ashley's been saving them in hopes you'd show."

"You talked me into it," Nick told the group. Zoe noted he'd adopted a friendly, yet distant air, almost as if he was playing a part in a play. She frowned, but when Ashley patted the chair to her right, Zoe sat, with Nick seated to Zoe's right.

"I love your dress." Ashley leaned closer, into a con-spiratorial distance. "Thank you for dragging him. He cleans up well, doesn't he? Who would have thought Nick would wear designer duds."

"Did he not before?" Zoe asked, genuinely curious.

"Zoe, you're such a joker."

Zoe frowned. She hadn't meant the question as a joke, but rather for needed clarification. A memory danced at the periphery, out of reach, of this one kid at Beaumont…had his name been Nick? Before she could seek additional information, Ashley stood and began waving.

"There's Claire and her husband."

"Claire! Here!"

Zoe pushed aside the immediate disappointment. She and Nick sat at a table for eight, and soon the table held four couples. Most of them were interested in knowing what had happened to Nick once he'd left Beaumont High mid-year, so Zoe listened intently.

"Stanford," Nick told them. "Then I stayed in California and worked for a tech firm."

As the night went on, Zoe realized how little she knew about Nick. Or how his classmates, who might have known what he was like in high school, had either forgotten or been too tactful to bring up the past.

From the conversation, Zoe gathered he'd lived in that now-demolished trailer park at the edge of the historic part of town, just south of Main Street. Not everyone in Beaumont had been rich, so she didn't understand why he had never brought it up with her. As for other clues, the night kept them secret. Whenever anyone got too close, Nick deflected with some story about life in L.A. and people he'd known in Hollywood. "The tech company I worked for created green screen software," he revealed. "Some of our programs helped studios create higher-end special effects."

That had started a new tangent, delving into everyone's favorite movies, both then and now. Nick revealed some Hollywood insider scoops, with all hanging on his every word. Why wouldn't they? He'd charmed her just as easily. He'd been correct about the ring, with Ashley and Claire having to hold Zoe's fingers when they'd been in the bathroom together so they could study the gems. "He's got such good taste," Ashley said. "But then you know that if you're wearing this ring. You remember what he was like in high school. He hardly spoke to anyone. Aren't you so proud of him for rising above?"

She assumed Ashley meant poverty. Was that why his taste bordered on designer and such? Or why he'd hired a limo? Or why he needed to exorcise demons? But why hadn't he told her? Had she made him feel less than? Or embarrassed?

A sense of unease settled in Zoe's stomach. Or maybe it was the five toasted ravioli she'd eaten—she usually avoided fried food; it never truly agreed with her. But the ravioli—she sighed. The St. Louis tradition was delicious and worth every bite, even if it gave her a sour stomach.

The reunion committee had hired a DJ, and after a while he began playing the hits from the previous decade. At an upbeat number, Ashley stood and grabbed Zoe's hand. "This is my favorite song. Come on!"

Zoe allowed herself to be dragged onto the dimly lit dance floor, moving to the beat of the pop hit with Ashley and Claire. The partiers sang at the top of their lungs, and everyone threw their arms in the air as they grooved to the beat. Zoe couldn't help but laugh, go wild and have fun. Two glasses of wine plus the earlier champagne had loosened her inhibitions, and Ashley and Claire seemed genuinely kind and welcoming. A roving photographer took their photograph for the archive, and Ashley also proved to be queen of the selfie. "I'll give you my Insta," she shouted at Zoe as the music segued into another song. "And my TikTok."

When the DJ finally began to slow things down, Nick was there as if she'd conjured him. Zoe wrapped her arms around his neck and placed her head on his chest. His arms wrapped around her waist. "Enjoying yourself?" he asked.

Zoe could hear the thump of his heartbeat. "I am. I haven't danced like that in forever. Well, maybe a few songs at Sierra's wedding, but I had Megan with me and we left early. I forgot how much I loved to dance. Before Megan, I'd go out to the club on North Main and dance until my feet hurt." Sure, Ted had been there, but he'd sat at the bar and drank with his guy friends instead of joining her.

"I loved watching you dance. You have this verve and energy. You can see the fun written all over your face."

She wiped her forehead. "Are you sure that's not sweat?"

He leaned back so he could see her eyes. "No. It's gumption. Guts. It's one reason I'm so attracted to you."

"I'm attracted to you too," Zoe admitted. Heck, if she dug deeply, she might have to admit to herself that she was falling in love with him. Which was stupid. He was leaving. "But I don't know a lot about you. I've learned more about who you are from sitting at the table tonight than in the week we've been engaged. Air quotes around that last word." She'd make the motion with her fingers, but that would involve lifting her hands from around his neck, and she couldn't find the drive to do that. She liked touching him too much. "There's nothing to be ashamed of if you didn't have money growing up. Or having it now. It's clear your tech job paid well."

He tilted his head. "I wanted you to know the real me. I wanted time to know the real you, and not the girl I've had in my head all these years, the one I had the biggest crush on. Why do you think I came in all the time for cookies?"

"I wish I could remember that. It's on the edges. Maybe if I saw a picture of you back then." She moved her hand and pressed a finger to the square. "But you don't do pictures."

"Not if I can avoid it. It's easier to forget the past that way, especially when only parts of it are worth remembering."

As if fate mocked his words, the roving photographer

took a shot of the crowd and Nick quickly turned his head. But later Zoe had to give him credit for playing along when Ashley approached when the song ended and demanded a photo of the four of them. Nick slid his arms around Zoe as Claire took the shot with Ashley's phone. "Airdrop that to me, will you?" Nick asked, and Ashley obliged. "I'll give it to you later," Nick promised Zoe.

"Along with the rest of the story," Zoe pressed. "You owe me that."

A fast number started, and Ashley demanded everyone dance, saving Nick from having to reply. Zoe was delighted to discover that Nick was an excellent dancer. He had all the right moves, and Zoe couldn't wait until later tonight. She'd been home with Megan since Wednesday night, or the equivalent of three nights without being able to creep across the hallway into Nick's room at the inn. She'd missed loving him and holding him.

The hours flew by, and as the reunion came to an end, despite the invitations, Zoe and Nick begged out of the after-party.

"Did you give us your contact information?" Ashley demanded of Nick.

Nick gave her a hug and a wave. "Zoe knows how to find me."

"I do?" Zoe asked as he slid inside and closed the door. The driver put the car in gear and began to head down the hill toward Winery Road and the twenty-minute drive into historic Beaumont. "I mean, I have your phone number."

"Which means you'll always know how to find me. I won't ever leave without saying goodbye or letting you know how to contact me. I promise never to block you. Now, Ashley and them, don't let them know where I'm at until another ten years go by. Please. This was enough for a decade."

She didn't believe him. "You can admit you had fun and that you liked hanging out with them."

"I did, but only because you were with me."

Zoe sighed. Not exactly the answer she'd hoped for. Maybe if he had more friends he'd come back and visit more often. "Did the demons get exorcised?"

Nick uncapped a bottle of water and handed it to Zoe before opening one for himself. "Maybe a little. It was good being seen as the guy who I am now and not the one I was."

Zoe took a long sip of water. She hadn't realized how parched she was from dancing. "Who exactly was he? Besides from the trailer park. I noticed you deflecting. At times, you seemed to be acting instead of showing the real you."

"Isn't that what reunions are? But I'm not that way with you," Nick assured. He took another swallow and capped the bottle. "Ever."

Maybe the glasses of Norton had loosened her tongue. "Nick, our whole relationship is us acting the part of an engaged couple. I'm not sure what's real and what's not. Like the sex, I know that's real, at least it is for me. It's never been so good. But maybe you're just an excellent lover. You dated actresses. I'm a cookie store owner in Beaumont."

"You are more beautiful than they are."

Zoe couldn't help but scoff at his declaration. "I know what my reflection looks like. I also know a deflection when I see it."

He held her hand. "It's not. You don't have short-comings where I'm concerned. You, Zoe, are gorgeous and perfect."

"That's so unrealistic," Zoe protested. "We each have baggage. You have a past you won't share with me. I don't even know what you do, minus something in tech, but you can afford a plane and a ring like this and a limo, and…why won't you tell me the truth? Are you married or something? Or a felon? Or on the run from the law?"

"God no." Nick appeared genuinely shocked. "None of the above. I simply hate my past. It's not who I am. It's a nightmare I want to forget. Forget the past, Zoe. Why are you so hung up on it? The more you stay in it, the more it drags you down. Manifest what you want for your future and make it happen. That's what I do."

"It's not that simple. I wish it was." She thumped against the leather seat, frustrated. Logically, every-thing he said made sense. Nothing good ever came out of dredging up the past, but yet the rumbling in her head wouldn't relent. Didn't lovers share everything? How could they move forward if he kept secrets? Did she even want to move forward? Like Pandora being tempted to open the proverbial box, the voices Zoe heard demanded her to pry, urged her to make him tell her so she could judge him worthy of her love. So that she didn't have to fear losing him as she had Ted and Jared. Somehow that also seemed so wrong.

She heaved a great sigh and pushed back against the clamor. "Look, I don't want to fight about this. We had too much of a great night."

He appeared incredulous, as if she'd shocked him. "Zoe, this isn't a fight. It's a discussion. It's not even heated. We may not agree on things. We may not see eye to eye. But it's not a fight. I'm certainly not trying to take away any of your agency. Your opinions and concerns are valid. Perhaps we should table this discussion until we're both a little more sober. I want to take you home and make love to you until neither of us can walk. I hated not being able to hold you and kiss you last night."

"That does sound nice," she admitted. "I've missed you too. Terribly, if you must know. I like being in your arms."

He obliged her and drew her close. "You drove me crazy out there on the dance floor. I can't believe we stayed until the end."

"Me either, especially for someone who didn't want to go in the first place."

He stroked her hair. "It makes me happy to see you happy. You had a great time and I was glad of it."

"I needed to let loose and have a good time. I loved it. No one was judging me. Everyone's goal was simply to reconnect and have fun." She snuggled close. "You sure you have to go? You don't want to stay in Beaumont forever?"

"I'm not really sure of anything anymore except that we've reached your house and if we don't get inside soon this limo is going to be sitting at your curb for a long time."

Zoe laughed, her mood lightening. "Then we better get inside, shouldn't we?"

An hour later, Nick held Zoe while she slept. He planted a kiss and she shifted, the smile on her face never leaving. He wished he could sleep. Instead, his brain raced, the computer chip working overtime. She'd thought they'd been fighting.

Fighting was the story of his childhood. Of his mother's rages that would send plates flying for whatever reason—she seemed to like to break things. Never him, though. She'd never laid one finger on her son. When he'd gotten older and successful, it was a silent pact that they'd never talk about her life or her own childhood.

Nick, however, thought she'd been abused, and that it had continued when she dated men who also abused her. Once, he'd used his fists on one of her so-called boyfriends after the man had slapped her around.

Had there been others who'd done the same? He didn't know but assumed so. Her lifestyle had been volatile and erratic and he'd tried to stay as far away from home as he could. Even as young as first grade, he'd found ways, usually hanging out at the local library, the librarian taking pity on him and often sharing her dinner. When he'd gotten older, he'd remained at school doing whatever homework he had, or working in the computer lab until the building closed and the custodians shooed him away. Until he'd gotten the job washing dishes, Nick had been the local charity case. Once a church had dropped off a turkey dinner at Thanksgiving and ham at Christmas, along with a present from the local toy drive.

He'd hated it. Being poor had made him the weird kid. The one in the hand-me-downs. Thankfully, if his classmates had thought that about him tonight, none of them had had the guts to say it. Perhaps ten years was a great equalizer, especially as he'd told better stories than those at the table with him. He normally didn't trot those out, but he'd wanted to prove that he'd made something of himself. He thought he'd succeeded in keeping the demons of his past at bay, not that he felt super great about the evening. He'd felt exposed. Maybe somewhat fake.

Perhaps he'd simply exchanged a set of demons for another. None of the other women he'd dated or slept with had cared about who he'd been. Rather, all they wanted was what he could give them or how handsome he appeared on their arm. Those relationships had existed on a surface level, one that wouldn't lead to heartbreak or deep disappointment. In the limo it was clear that Zoe was the type of woman who wanted to know everything: past, present, and future. Hell, those three words had been the reason he'd bought the ring he'd given her. The center stone represented the future and the teardrops on either side the past and present. The creator's description said so, and the words had solidified the decision for Nick that this was the ring he wanted to buy. It was as beautiful on Zoe's finger, and part of him wished she'd leave it on forever, and that he'd share her bed and....

And there was danger in doing that. Therein lay the conundrum. She scared him. She was different from the others. She wanted to probe the layers. She wanted things Nick didn't even understand, for he'd never had that type of relationship. He didn't have a mother who was overbearing and showed up the next morning. Zoe might claim to want her independence from her family's interference, but she'd hate the alternative he'd had—a mother never there. Zoe rested secure in the love of her family. Even from the simple drop-off of Megan at her cousins' house, Nick could read the room. Family photos had lined the mantel. Hung on the wall. Jayne lived with her son so she could be near her husband, so she could visit him daily, even if his Alzheimer's meant he didn't know her anymore. That's what love was. That lifelong commitment. Once Nick had set his mom up financially and passed off the managing of her money to his broker, he and his mom hardly spoke, unless she needed something. It was rare she needed him as long as the broker gave her what she wanted, and Nick had given the man pretty much carte blanche to do that as long as she didn't break the bank he'd set for her. He'd made it clear no more would be coming.

Nick smoothed the hair on Zoe's forehead. She'd kill him if she knew he'd paid her HVAC invoice. But he couldn't let her deal with that bill, not when he could so easily take care of paying it. He wanted to take care of Zoe. She'd taken care of him, been a beacon of hope and light when he'd been in a dark place. Taking care of her seemed fitting, right.

Had he always loved Zoe? If he hadn't, he was over his head, in too deep now. He loved her, or at least he thought these feelings were love. Not having married role models, except for one of his college professors and his former business partner, Nick wasn't sure what real love would actually look like when it was his turn. He wanted that forever love desperately, though, and knew it was the one thing all his billions couldn't buy. The weight of the world settled on his shoulders. He was in bed with Zoe, snuggling her and listening to her breathe. He could stay here forever, but did she even want that? She didn't want people's help, and that was pretty much Nick's entire existence. From tutoring in math, to charitable donations, to paying for his mom, Nick lived to help others.

Kevin called him the fixer. Speaking of, Nick leaned over and grabbed his phone. Kevin had sent him a text urging Nick to check his email. Nick loaded the message and began to read. Kevin had another issue, this one with some new software. Nick frowned. If he couldn't solve the problem remotely, he'd have to fly back to California and be on-site to interface directly with the servers. He sent Kevin a reply that said he'd call him Sunday night. By then he'd be back at the inn.

Beside him, Zoe stirred. "What are you doing awake?" she asked, her voice husky and her eyes slumberous. She was so beautiful and precious. He didn't deserve her and owed her the truth.

"I'm too wound up to sleep. Sometimes my computer brain doesn't shut off. There's a lot on my mind." Like the fact he was deeply in love with her and didn't know how to tell her. He had no idea how to handle things. Or how to love her without revealing all the secrets he'd buried deep. She wanted all of him, something Nick had never given anyone. He'd never let anyone see the ugliness, the parts of him that didn't deserve the light of day. But Zoe made him want to throw caution to the wind, to embrace everything they might be able to be and create together. Like the fact he'd started exploring the idea of buying the candy store and expanding Zoe's empire. The future could be limitless, if he wasn't so afraid of exposure. Money couldn't buy respect or happiness. It certainly couldn't buy love. All millions could buy was stuff.

Zoe shifted, the sheet slipping to reveal her lovely breasts. As if sensing something had changed, instead of asking him questions, she reached out. "Come here and let's see if we can tire you out."

Shoving aside the new demons wanting to taunt him, Nick willingly went into her arms.

Chapter Eight

The romantic idyll lasted until Sunday morning, when Nick kissed Zoe goodbye. He returned to the inn. Zoe went to Auntie Jayne's. With Sarah recovered from her illness, Zoe didn't need Nick's help, which worked out perfectly as he'd told her he had a contracted project requiring his attention. "Some computer stuff."

She'd loved every minute she'd spent with him. Something had shifted between them since attending the reunion. They'd been closer, yet something invisible hovered between them, like a veil. Something unspoken and silent—like a cliché elephant in the room. She wished he'd share the demons that chased him, but instead she let things go and lived in the moment for once. She could do that, at least for a short time. She'd never dated a man like Nick. No, it was better to say they were having an affair. That word indicated something serious, yet casual, as their relationship had morphed from make believe into real, satisfying love-making that shook her core. She'd thought Jared a great lover. Nick, sweet Nick, set new standards. Would she ever find someone like him again? After all, they had no real commitment.

As she worked, various flavors of cookie dough thumped round and round in stainless steels bowls. Beaters spun and ovens beeped. Cookie sheets went in and out, flooding the kitchen with warmth and delicious aromas. Zoe functioned on autopilot; her employees had the sales floor covered.

After a busy Sunday with fantastic receipts, Zoe faced the wind that had started blowing overnight after a cold front came through. She drove the highway that took her into Kirkwood and her brother's.

"Zoe!" her mom said, craning her head to peer around her daughter and out the door. "Where's Nick?"

"He had some work stuff." Zoe unwrapped her scarf as Megan came tearing down the stairs, her cousins following on her heels. Zoe gathered her daughter into her arms for a huge hug before Megan raced off after them. "We'll be leaving soon," Zoe called after Megan's back.

Twenty minutes later, her family relocated to the memory unit. After buzzing in the locked door, they went to the dining area, where their dad waited. He rose to greet them. "Jayne! Zoe!" Emotions flooded Zoe at the recognition. He knew everyone: her brother and his wife. Her sister, Sierra. He didn't know Sierra was married, but he remembered that her husband, Jack, had "that really nice Mercedes" that he'd ridden in one night.

Grateful they had something to be thankful for,

the family fell into an easy rhythm as Jayne set out a Thanksgiving dinner, complete with roast turkey, mashed and sweet potatoes, stuffing, green beans, cranberry sauce, and both pumpkin and apple pie. Life was short, Zoe realized. Too short to not appreciate the blessings of family. She wished Nick had come, but she'd gathered his family wasn't close, like hers. He rarely spoke of his mother, and had told her he didn't know his father. Perhaps coming tonight would have made him uncomfortable. She also worried if he was pulling away, getting ready to end their arrangement. Knowing he was always going to be leaving, she'd held herself back. Tried and failed not to fall for him.

Part of her wasn't ready for him to go. She admittedly liked being part of a couple. Was it fair for her to ask him to stay because she didn't want to be alone again? To return to the boring, work-focused single mom who thought rom-coms legitimate weekend plans?

She slept fitfully on the lumpy Murphy bed in her brother's office. Her sister-in-law made a delicious pancake breakfast, and then Zoe and Megan drove home.

But even though they returned to Beaumont in plenty of time, Nick gave his excuses for not seeing them Monday night. He called her, sure, and as much as she'd loved hearing his voice, she missed seeing him more. But when she invited him for dinner, he begged off, saying, "You need to have a mother-daughter night with Megan. You won't see her again until Sunday."

With his words like a reality check ringing in her ear, Zoe avoided the brewing disquiet and made Megan's favorite food, spaghetti and meatballs. Earlier that afternoon, she'd taught Megan how to make pumpkin bread, and for their after-dinner dessert, they topped slices of bread with fresh whipped cream sprinkled with cinnamon.

Afterward, they worked on their puzzle, ate kettle corn and snuggled while watching a classic Pixar movie about lovable monsters. She told Megan goodnight and pulled her pink-and-white floral comforter to her chin. Ted would arrive around noon, so she and Megan would pack her suitcase in the morning.

"I love you." Megan kissed and hugged Zoe, and Zoe held on tight as she added "I love you too." Standing, Zoe smoothed Megan's hair as her daughter curled around her bunny. A soft nightlight glowed once Zoe flipped the switch to the overhead light.

Zoe went into the kitchen and cleaned. Aimless, she grabbed her cellphone, hating the weakness. "Megan's asleep," she texted Nick. "You were right. We had an epic girls' night."

"I'm glad."

"I'm looking forward to seeing you tomorrow."

"Me too."

She reacted to his message, sending a little heart. Too much? Probably. Zoe winced as she second-guessed herself. She wasn't good with texting. She wanted him to know she missed him, but maybe a "like" would have been better. Tomorrow she'd get Nick to herself. As much as she didn't want to be without Megan for both holidays, the prospect of spending the time with Nick excited and thrilled her, and not just because they'd make love. He'd mentioned flying somewhere, if Zoe could get away. She'd make it a priority if he mentioned taking a trip again.

She wandered around, checking the front door was locked, setting the alarm, and marveling over the new

"Okay." Megan skipped down the walkway, her winter coat unzipped. From the passenger seat, Marilyn waved at Megan. Megan returned her stepmother's wave and climbed into the back where her half-brother sat in his car seat. Her daughter was so friendly, personable, and kind.

"Who's Nick?" Ted's nasty tone easily conveyed his objections to his daughter's announcement.

Zoe sharpened her tone and held her ground. "None of your business."

Ted refused to concede. "It is when he's hanging out with my daughter. I'm not having her being around strange men."

Zoe snorted. "Good grief. Will you listen to yourself? As if I'm hanging out with strange men? Seriously, Ted, you have no right. We are divorced. My life is none of your concern."

"I have every right if it might hurt her. You're a loose cannon, Zoe. Are you going to put her through another relationship? You keep getting attached to people you can't keep in your life and you're hurting my daughter when you do it. It's vile."

"She's our daughter, and she's fine." Zoe bit back the curse words she wanted to hurl at him. Ted's verbal attack was a low blow, the kind Ted was best at. "You have no right to question my relationships or my parenting style. We are divorced."

"Yeah, because you wouldn't move to Seattle. You're the one who tore our family apart."

"I did not force you to move or to marry someone else. No one held a gun to your head." Tired of retreading the same ground every time Ted came into town, Zoe shoved her left hand forward, the ring glittering as she pointed a finger at him. "You're the one who left. You're the one who wanted a new life. You're the one who doesn't fly in and use his custody, days that you fought me for so you didn't have to pay as much support. You knew my dreams when you married me. Then you knew about my dad's illness and how I couldn't leave my mom. You knew I couldn't live far from them like Sierra. Stop trying to guilt me or tell me I'm the one who was wrong. Because I'm not. You are, Ted. You always were."

"Is there a problem here?"

Nick's voice cut through air and Zoe's emotions went from strung out to relieved to worried. Ted had been late, and Nick was on time. Nick's shrug accompanied an apologetic smile. "Sorry. I didn't know you'd still be busy."

"Who the hell are you?" Ted demanded, puffing like a peacock. Nick, to his credit, didn't appear as if he planned to enter a misguided turf war. And why should he? Nick's looks and integrity had Ted beat. Ignoring Ted's deliberate antagonism, Nick stuck out his hand. "Hello, Ted. I'm Nick Reilly."

Ted refused to shake hands. Instead, his face morphed into an incredulous expression and he faced Zoe. Derision dripped from his lips. "You're dating Nick? Nick! Of all people. Nick?"

Zoe didn't recognize Nick from the past, but Ted clearly had, or at least he'd known the name, and as Ted's animosity simmered, Nick wasn't having any of it. His blond eyebrows knit together and his mouth scowled. As thunderclouds brewed, Zoe couldn't help but feel she was missing something. Whatever it was, Ted's disgusting insult as to her love life could not be allowed to stand. She folded her arms, her defensive posture daring him to argue. "Is there something wrong with that?" she challenged. "We're divorced, Ted. Who I see is none of your business."

As Ted opened his mouth, Megan had hopped out of the car and came racing up the sidewalk. "Nick!" She threw herself into his arms and he bear-hugged her back. "You didn't come over last night."

"Had to work. You know how that goes."

She frowned first. "I finished all my homework. You should be done." Then she laughed. "I'm off for the week. Dad said we're going to have an adventure at Grandma and Grandpa's. But I missed you."

Nick returned Megan's smile. "I heard you had a girls' night with your mom and watched a movie. Girls' nights mean no boys allowed."

Megan considered. "True."

Before Megan began describing the movie she'd watched, Zoe put her hands on her daughter's shoulders. "How about you go back to the car so you and your dad can get going? I'm sure your grandmother is wondering where you are since she wants to see you so much." Zoe gave Megan another hug before staring hard at her ex. "Right, Ted? Don't you need to get going? Since you're already late?"

"We do. Go on, Megan."

The trio watched Megan skip back to the car and climb inside. Ted stared his displeasure at Zoe. "You and I are going to talk about this." Determined to get the final word, Ted spun around and walked away before Zoe could reply.

Despite the chill that had moved in overnight, Zoe remained on the porch until Ted's car pulled away from the curb. Then she wordlessly entered her house, waiting until Nick stood in the foyer before she shut the door with a tad more force than necessary. "The nerve of the man. To think there are times I actually feel guilty, that it's my fault for breaking up our family."

Nick drew her into his arms. "Come here. I didn't help by arriving right on time. Sorry about that. I didn't want things to be awkward."

"Ted was late. He thinks that I'm supposed to be on his timetable. And the way he acted around you." Zoe checked her growing fury. "You shouldn't have been subjected to his rudeness. Why didn't I see how he was in high school?"

"Because it was high school and all of us are myopic idiots." Nick's hand stroked her hair and Zoe felt some of the stress leave. She tipped her face and Nick dropped a kiss on her lips until she sighed.

"Why didn't I see you? I heard you, you know, that first night at the inn. Gosh, that seems long ago. You said you weren't worth seeing. Right before you shut the door, that's what you said to me. I heard you."

"I didn't mean anything by it."

Nick returned his lips to hers, but when the kiss broke, Zoe couldn't quite let it go. "You're worth seeing, Nick."

"Look, you're making me sound pathetic. Don't look back. It never leads anywhere good."

"Nick, I want to know. I need to know."

She felt him cave.

"Fine. Later. I'll tell you all the high school drama later, especially since Ted seems like he plans on dragging it up. But right now, I can't wait to hold you again." He shifted his hands, pressing her closer to him. Heat

shot through her body. "The future is much more pleasurable and I can think of so many better things to do
with my time. I've missed you."

"I've missed you, too." Promising herself they'd
come back to this thread, Zoe let Nick lead her into
the bedroom.

Nick's phone began buzzing a little after seven.
When he saw the caller ID glowing in the darkened
room, he remembered it was only five p.m. out west.
Beside him, Zoe didn't stir from the sleep she'd fallen
into following multiple long bouts of lovemaking. He
grabbed his phone, slid out of bed, threw on his jeans,
and made his way into the kitchen. He returned the
video call. "Hey."

Kevin's voice and face came through crystal clear.
Nick could tell he was still in his office. "We're stuck.
I need you on-site."

Nick groaned. "This is not the week for that."

Kevin's face scrunched sheepishly. "I know it's the
week before Thanksgiving. If you leave tonight I promise to have you back by Thursday. I'll charter something
so you don't have to refuel and…"

Nick cut him off. He would not leave Zoe, who'd
come into the kitchen wearing a loose pink t-shirt and
drawstring shorts. His pulse quickened. "I can't leave
tonight. That's final."

Zoe frowned, but Nick realized her expression wasn't
directed at him but at the phone in her hand. "Hold on,"
he told Kevin. Nick pressed the mute key and paused
the video. "What is it?"

Zoe set her phone on the counter. "Ted says Megan
forgot her stuffed animal and she refuses to sleep with-

out it. He's on his way. I've tried to talk him out of it, but he insists. I'm going to put a robe on, grab the bunny and meet him in the living room."

Nick gave her a quick kiss. "I'll be here finishing my call. It's work related. Yell, if you need me." He unmuted and resumed the video. "Let me see if I can walk you through it."

Kevin still hadn't fixed the problem by the time Zoe returned. Nick's forehead creased and his eyebrows knit together as he read the shocked expression in her wide eyes, and saw the overwrought, tight lines of her lips. Nick told Kevin the issue would have to wait until morning. Clearly, Ted had put Zoe through the ringer, same as he'd been doing when Nick arrived earlier. The guy was a complete jerk.

Nick shoved the phone in his back pocket. "Hey, what's wrong? What did he say to you?"

Her lower lip quivered. "He was…he was horrible. Why didn't you tell me who you were? Why did I have to hear about it from Ted, of all people? Do you think I cared? Did you think I'd judge you?"

Nick spread his fingers, trying to release the tension. "Zoe, I didn't tell you I was a tech billionaire because I didn't want you to see me differently. I wanted you to know the real me and not see me with dollar signs attached like so many women do."

"What?" Her eyes turned into dinner saucers. As she screeched the word at him, Nick knew he'd made a major misstep. "There's more you haven't told me?"

He winced and returned her question with one of his own. "What was it Ted said?"

"That you're Nutty Nick."

Disgust made Nick's stomach roll. He hated that

nickname. How many times had he heard the elite of Beaumont High call out, "There goes Nutty Nick?" Or yell at him, "Hey, Nick the Prick, you going to the library again?" Or worse, "Hold your nose, there Nick goes," before dissolving into peals of laughter. Nick especially hated the last one. He'd bathed, damn it. He simply hadn't owned good clothes.

Zoe shook her head and planted her hand on her hips. "You should have told me who you were. While my memories were hazy, I…" she broke off.

"I wasn't a charity case," Nick shot back. "Everyone thought I was. Except you. Or at least I didn't think you gave me free cookies because you felt sorry for me."

"No, I never felt sorry for you. I treated you like any other customer who came in. I don't know why you kept this from me as if it was such a state secret."

"Then you don't understand childhood trauma," Nick blinked as all the bullying of high school rushed back. This is what he'd been afraid of—always being known as that guy who'd been Nutty Nick. "Did you even know your boyfriend called me names?"

Zoe gave a shrug. "He called everyone names. He thought he was the big man on campus. Hell, he called me names. But no, that's no excuse for how he treated you. Why didn't you trust me enough to tell me who you were?"

"I didn't tell you so you wouldn't be staring at me, like you are now, with complete disgust."

"I'm not disgusted. I'm angry because you kept things from me!" Zoe's chest heaved as she fought for breath. "There's little difference between holding things back and lying outright. It's splitting hairs. How do you think I feel? First, guilty for not realizing he was a jerk to you. Then terrible for not stopping it back then. Add to it that I'm frustrated that you couldn't trust me enough to tell me now because you thought I'd judge you. Instead, my ex-husband lorded it over me. He yielded it as a weapon. Your omission left me defenseless."

"And that's what really matters. That you lost ground with Ted."

"You'd understand if you were divorced with a kid. It always matters." Nick watched as Zoe went to the cabinet, grabbed a glass, and pressed it against the dispenser on the refrigerator. "He made me feel small. Like I've been sleeping with a total stranger. Sharing my secrets. My life. My bed." She took a long drink, coiled tension evident. "I've tried to get you to tell me, as recently as earlier today. Yet, you clammed up every time. Why? Why didn't you trust me?"

His therapist had once told Nick he had trust issues. But patterns were hard to break. The closer she got, the more she pressed, the more he retreated. "You've been living a lie as well, Zoe. You tell yourself you hate being alone but you're never truly alone because you have your daughter and a family. You've always had people there, unlike me. But rather than stand up for yourself, you told them we're engaged so that it would be easier."

She gestured upwards. "Which you made me ask you for real. Who does that?"

"That way it wasn't a lie. And because..." he yanked a hand through his hair. "Maybe I wanted to believe that you wanted and needed me. What I feel for you... Never mind. We don't make sense. None of this does."

Except that he knew one thing: while this wasn't like

any fight he'd been in or seen his mother in, he knew this was an argument, which meant someone would lose.

As Zoe set her glass down and tugged on her finger, Nick knew it would be him. She took the ring off and handed it to him. Nick refused to take it. His voice hollow, he gestured and waved the offering away. "Keep it."

"I'm not a charity case." She shoved her knuckles into her mouth. "I'm sorry. I shouldn't throw your words at you. I didn't mean…"

He folded his arms across his chest. "You're right. You're not a charity case. But I was, and it's always going to be a part of who I am, and it's how you'll remember me, Zoe. It's always going to be an issue with people who knew me when. Ted won't be the only one. It'll taint what we have until it's poisoned, like what's happening now. It's probably wise if we both end this before we say things we might regret. Our relationship has probably run its course anyway."

For even though he loved her wholly and completely, because of his past, he couldn't stay in her life. He couldn't open past wounds and let the blood run again. He'd been battered enough years ago by living in this town, and he refused to have Zoe tarred with that brush. Once Ted spread his secrets, everyone would see him differently and, in turn, her. They already thought her a loser for letting go of Ted and then Jared. He couldn't make things worse for her.

Besides, Kevin needed him in California, where people only cared about his money and his computer skills. His time in Beaumont had been an interesting and heartbreaking walk down memory lane, but to Ted and his ilk, Nick would never be good enough. No matter how many billions he had.

Zoe's jaw locked in the way he'd seen on the morning she'd told Larry and Hal she wouldn't be using the town's heritage fund. She was stubborn, his Zoe. No, not his. Not any longer. Her lips quivered but she didn't cry. Not that he wanted her tears. He felt terrible enough. "You might be right. You were always going to leave, and well, I'm not. I'm staying here to run the store."

"Exactly. You belong here." Nick had known that indisputable fact the first moment he'd seen her behind the counter in Auntie Jayne's. "I don't. I'm going to get my things and leave. Work needs me."

He strode past her into the bedroom. He dressed quickly and found Zoe standing in the living room. He didn't approach her. She'd made her decision. He'd made his.

"You paid for my HVAC, didn't you? And for my room at the inn." She leveled the flat-toned accusation from where she stood near the couch.

He put his hand on the doorknob, the metal cold to the touch. "Yes. You deserve to have it all, Zoe. You deserve to be happy and I want that for you. I wish I might have made you happy, but... I'm sorry. Tell them the breakup is all my fault. Put the blame on me."

Without waiting for her reply, Nick closed the door behind him. He jogged his way to the inn, not caring his shoes weren't the best for running. When he reached the porch, he called Kevin. "Get me on a plane and I'll be there tonight."

He found Mrs. Bien in the dining room, preparing for the next day's breakfast. "No need to fix anything for me. I'm checking out immediately. I've got a work emergency and I have to fly to California tonight. Don't worry about any refund. Keep it as a bonus for a great stay."

Her face appeared distressed. "Oh Nick. I hope everything's okay. Will you be back soon?"

Nick shook his head, grateful his floppy hair provided some protection so Mrs. Bien couldn't see the hurt reflected in his eyes. "I don't know when I'll be back, if ever. But you've been fantastic. This inn is top notch. I'll be certain to recommend. Thanks for everything."

"I'm so sorry. If there's anything I can ever do?" Her face radiated concern—for him and not her online rating. She was everything he wished his own mother could have been. But what was that saying? No use crying over spilled milk. "You will let me know," Mrs. Bien insisted.

He sent her the best smile he could manage. "If there ever is, I promise I will tell you."

"Let me at least pack you some pumpkin muffins for the flight."

"That would be lovely."

Twenty minutes later, Nick left his car at Beaumont's airport, and flew his Cessna to Chesterfield, where a Gulfstream waited, with a pilot and crew ready for takeoff the moment he boarded. "Would you like anything to eat, Mr. Reilly?" the male flight attendant asked. Nick shook his head and handed him the box of muffins. "Share these with everyone. Best you'll ever have, hands down."

Nick poured himself two fingers of twenty-year-old Macallan and leaned back against the soft leather. He let the heady fire of alcohol burn down his throat as the plane engines roared to life. Took another sip as the jet launched into the air and left Beaumont behind for good.

* * *

He'd gone. Zoe sat at her dining room table staring at the puzzle she and Megan had been completing. In her palm rested the same piece she'd been holding for the last twenty minutes. In the living room, the television blared, tuned to a late night talk show. A guest promoted her new movie, which sounded like something Zoe might want to stream, if she remembered the title. She couldn't muster the energy to write it down.

How had a night that had started so right with such sweet lovemaking turn out so terribly wrong? She'd known things with Nick had to end at some point, but not like this. Not with him thinking she believed the worst about him. That she'd been disgusted by the person he'd been in high school.

Just as she didn't want anyone's pity now, Nick didn't want anyone's pity for what he'd lived through. Once Ted had eviscerated her and made it click, Zoe remembered all the rumors and gossip—mostly spread from Ted and his ilk. They'd had to have someone to pick on to feel superior, and Nick's social class and home life had made him an easy target. But Zoe had been raised differently. And Ashley hadn't seemed to view Nick as a pariah, and she'd cared enough to wonder what happened to him. At the reunion, she'd seemed genuinely happy he'd turned up doing so well. And Nick hadn't even told them how much money he had and they'd still liked him.

Zoe realized no one at Beaumont High had given Nick enough credit, and he'd risen to the top despite every obstacle in his path. Most of Zoe's peers had judged him on appearances. On his home life. On his poverty. He'd outdone all of them. To be able to buy a plane, or drop fifteen thousand on an HVAC system or nine thousand on a ring without even breaking the bank? Zoe had no idea what having that much money would be like. Would it be freeing? Or its own kind of trap, like Nick indicated?

As for her role, she was guilty as charged. While she hadn't necessarily treated Nick like he was dog poop on her shoe during high school, she hadn't defended him from the bullying either. Frankly, she'd done exactly what he'd said—she hadn't seen him. He'd been another faceless entity on a lower rung of the social tier, far beneath her own world.

Her past made her ashamed. Had he been right? That when he'd come into the shop, she'd handed him extra cookies because she felt superior and charitable, as if she were benevolent and kind, doing something nice for someone less fortunate? She hoped not.

But she had been a passive bystander, caught up in all that high school drama that really was a useless time suck and irrelevant years later. She set the puzzle piece down, not liking the person she'd been. No wonder why he didn't want her to remember him from back then. He'd been a nobody who'd had a crush on her anyway. That hurt even more.

Especially as Zoe, in the blindness created by her own popularity and perfect high school life, hadn't ever tried to see the real him. Like most did with the homeless who lined certain St. Louis city streets, Zoe had moved on by without a glance, her world superior and out of reach. She'd been untouchable. She should be rightfully ashamed.

Zoe muted the TV as guilt consumed her. No wonder he'd lied. All his life he'd been judged by his past, not by his present, and he'd wanted a chance to get to know her. Nick hadn't wanted her to make comparisons between then and now. Ted had been proof positive of Nick's worry.

Zoe wished her ex had never come back for the stuffed rabbit. He'd been angry about having to make the trip, especially blasting Zoe that it was her fault that Megan kept crying after she'd discovered she'd forgotten "Bunny." Ted might have had more tolerance had the rabbit been a gift from Zoe, or Zoe's mother, or even Zoe's sister, but Nick? Ted had been livid. He'd stormed into the living room and let Zoe have it with both barrels, sneering at her. He'd enjoyed telling her she was dating trailer park trash.

"I can't believe you're seeing Nasty Nick. You've really lowered your standards, Zoe. You'll be the laughingstock with our classmates when they find out. You know I'm going to enjoy telling them."

Of course Ted would. He'd convinced most of the town to take his side in the divorce. Her ex lived for adulation, and he reveled in the sympathy her subsequent failures provided. She'd given him so much mileage over the years.

Add tonight to her failures. Tonight, caught in old patterns as Ted had shot forth a multitude of insults, she'd stood there, incapable of firing anything back. She'd been in shock. Why hadn't Nick told her the truth? She understood his embarrassment, or his worry that people like Ted would throw things in her face. That they wouldn't accept him. But she didn't care about that. What hurt was that his deliberate omissions had left her unprepared to mount a defense, much less an offense. Ted had left with a smug sneer on his face, his sense of superiority firmly in place. She felt so small and blind-sided—by both men. Nick, she might be able to forgive. With Ted she'd lost ground in their perpetual "war."

Zoe's stomach churned. She couldn't remember what she'd eaten, so she rose and stretched out stiff legs. She cut another slice of pumpkin bread and took a bite. The delicious pastry sandpapered her tongue and Zoe rinsed the morsel with some water and put the rest aside. She'd lost her appetite. She'd googled Nick once he'd left, and using his name, the word computers and the name Kevin, she'd managed to find an article on the sale of his company. He wasn't lying when he said he was a billionaire or a tech genius. With her, he'd been Nick.

A regular guy.

A man who took her to heights unimagined in bed.

A guy who'd only wanted to help her out of a jam.

The facts gave her conflicting feelings, with none of them making sense. He'd lied to her—by omission if not in fact. She should be angry and furious. But as the residual shock wore off, she simply hurt and she wanted to crawl in bed and sleep for the next twenty years.

Adding insult to injury, her phone pinged and a text came in from Ashley: I forgot to send the pictures. Here they are! Hope to see you again soon! Don't be strangers.

The image was of Ashley and Dan and Nick and Zoe. She enlarged the shot, hovering over Nick's face. He was so beautiful. And he'd loved her so well. But in the end, he had to go home, and she already was home and would never leave. The fact gave her little solace. In fact, it felt like a cement block tied to her feet. Zoe James Smith, the woman who couldn't leave Beaumont.

With nothing to do and no one to confide in who

wasn't already asleep, Zoe headed into her bedroom, stripped the sheets and put on new ones. She located the ring and then stored it in a safe place. Tomorrow might be a new day, but for Zoe, it was time to face the music. She wouldn't put it off any longer. She'd tell everyone the truth. Zoe James, sadly, was single again.

She told her mother the next day, when she came out to help bake for the Black Friday rush. "I need to tell you something."

"That sounds ominous," her mom said. Jayne stopped the mixer and wiped her hands on her apron, giving Zoe her full attention.

Zoe took a deep breath and plunged in. "Well…"

When she was finished, both she and her mom were crying. "I never meant to be domineering," her mom said, wiping her tears with her apron. She drew Zoe in for a hug. "Never. I'm sorry you felt inadequate. That was never my intention. You're strong, Zoe. Strong."

Nick had said much of the same thing but hearing it from her mom was balm for Zoe's battered soul.

"I never meant to lie. I was overwhelmed and the debts were mounting and I didn't want you to worry. I wanted to prove to you I could do this. And then Nick swooped in and he seemed like an easy escape."

"Until you fell for him. Oh, honey."

"I think my heart's broken," Zoe said, tears still streaming down her face. "Look at me. I never cry. Ever. I didn't think I was capable of it."

"Maybe what you feel for Nick was real. Do you love him?"

"It started wrong. It was a mistake from the moment it started." Zoe reached for a paper towel and wiped her face. She and her mom had moved away from the counters where cookies in various stages waited for their return. "How can he love me when I hurt him so badly? While I know I'm not fully at fault, I played my role in this. I don't get off freely. I deserve some blame, especially after how things ended. I'm an adult. It's time that I acted like one."

"Perhaps the real question is, what does Zoe want?"

Nick. His name popped into her head, but Zoe shook it, her hair not budging because of how she'd pinned it so she could bake and not worry about it escaping. "People keep asking me that but it doesn't matter what I want. I have a store and a child to consider. My life is not my own."

"That's where you're wrong. That's the mistake you're making. Maybe what's best for the store and for Megan is for you to be happy. You need to figure out what would make you happy."

Nick. Again, his name danced on the tip of her tongue. In college, she'd taken a psychology class and learned about Carl Jung's word association test. The researcher says a word and the respondent said the first thing that came to mind. Zoe's subconscious kept coming back to Nick.

What would make her happy? Being with Nick. He'd completed her in a way she didn't deserve but had loved. He let her be fierce and independent. Could she be mad at him for wanting to help? Her mom wanted to help because she loved Zoe, not because she believed Zoe couldn't handle it.

Could Nick love her? This farce on its surface had been nothing more than a show. But the moments they'd spent together had been real. Her feelings had not been faked. The lovemaking had been glorious and transcendent.

What would make Zoe happy? When Ted had left, it had been the store and Beaumont. When Jared had left, it had been the store and familiarity. This was her home.

And with Nick, home had been more than a place to live. Home had been in his arms, secure in feelings that played deep in the subconscious, bouncing around trying to break free so they could knock some sense in her.

Fresh tears started. "I love him."

"Of course you do," her mom said, handing her another paper towel. "He's a good man. Even as a boy coming in here, I could tell he was different."

Another sob wracked Zoe's frame. "I didn't see him."

"Because he wasn't yet yours to see. But he saw you. And no, it's not creepy he's held some crush all these years. He's not a stupid man. He came into the store with blinders off, but then you blinded him all over again. I could tell, you know, that morning."

Zoe blew her nose again, the paper towel rough on her nose. "You knew I was lying?"

"I knew something was going on. But I let it play out because of how he looked at you."

"And what way is that?"

"The way your father looked at me when we dated. The way he still does now, even if he doesn't always remember my name. Deep in his heart, he knows we're soulmates. That's enough for me."

"But I blew it."

"Nothing is ever truly lost. You're strong, Zoe. You may not know this, but I had to remind your sister of the same when she was starting to see Jack. I raised brave, strong women. You're a fighter, too, Zoe. If you want him, you'll figure out what to do."

"Zoe?" Sarah came into the kitchen and stopped short. "I'm sorry."

"It's fine," Jayne told Sarah. "Grab the batch that's on that prep tray and carry it out. We'll get back to work in a minute."

Sarah did as told, eager to escape the private moment she'd walked in on.

"We need to get baking." Zoe tossed the paper towel in the trash and went to wash her hands. Tomorrow was Thanksgiving and the store would be closed. She'd spend the night at her brother's house. Her whole family—minus Megan and her dad—would be in attendance, including her brother Vance who was driving in from Chicago with his husband. It would be weird without her dad there, but they'd visit him earlier around lunchtime. She'd had a video chat with Megan yesterday and Ted's mom was spoiling her rotten.

What did Zoe want? Family. Friends. Home. Nick. And not necessarily in that order.

Oh, and a win in the cookie competition in three days. "You're smiling a little more," her mom noted.

"I think I have a plan. But I can't implement it until after this weekend." She nibbled her bottom lip. "Do you think he misses me?"

"I'm sure of it." Her mom swapped out her apron for a new one. "I think he misses you a great deal."

"I miss him too. It's going to take a grand gesture for me to prove he can trust me again. I hurt him pretty badly. But I have to try." Because she loved him. Nick. Past, present, and future.

Her mom set the mixers to whirring. "What do you have in mind?"

Zoe put cookie trays into the oven. Thanksgiving occurred late this year, meaning this upcoming Sunday would mark the first of December. Strong women had to be strategic. "I have a few moving pieces to put in place. As soon as I lock them down, you'll be the second person to know."

Chapter Nine

In the past, Beaumont's cookie competition hadn't been anything super formal. However, since the opening of the Main Street Makerspace, the event had morphed into something larger and grander. The first floor flex room had been divided into two general areas. In one space, long tables covered with white linens showcased display trays of Christmas cookies. With over twenty entries, Zoe wasn't certain she'd win, but her Madeleines certainly garnered attention. The judges were sampling the wares and making notations on clipboards. For luck, Zoe crossed her fingers as she moved to the area of the floor hosting the gingerbread contest.

This space also contained six-foot-long tables, but instead of linens, these were covered with white paper and divided by a straight line drawn down the middle.

Zoe had the right side of the table—spot number four. She'd partnered with her sister.

"You'll have an hour," Makerspace owner Luke Thornburg announced to the contestants. "Then the judges will make their rounds."

"Do me proud," Zoe and Sierra's mom called.

"We're fortunate we did one of these each year for our family holiday," Zoe said as she began piping icing on the sides.

"I'm glad you're the one decorating. I was never good squeezing icing," Sierra said.

"It's the fine motor stuff." As Zoe finished decorating each gingerbread flat, her sister began the assembly. They'd chosen to create the cookie store, right down to using coconut for a snow-covered lawn, blue icing for the door, and red candies to form the brick sidewalk.

As the time counted down the minutes they had left, the gingerbread store took shape, including the sloped roof with gumdrop Christmas lights. Around them, couples laughed. One or two groaned as their structure collapsed, but Sierra, with her master's degree in engineering, had created the right amount of tension so their creation held together.

"Time!" Luke called. "Hands up!"

Zoe and Sierra complied, and then scooted back from the table. One final task was moving the gingerbread store to the display table. The walls wobbled but held and soon it rested fourth from the left. Zoe took a picture with her phone. Then her mom took a picture of both Zoe and Sierra standing behind their creation. Jessica and Sarah manned the store in the absence of the James women, helped by some of their college friends hired as temps for the holiday rush.

Mirabelle walked by with her house and set it in spot six. Traditional in shape and design, it leaned somewhat to one side. She saw Zoe's. "Your store. That's cute."

Zoe smiled. "Thanks."

It would probably be the closest thing to a compliment Mirabelle ever gave her. "Shame Nick couldn't be here."

Ah, there was the Mirabelle she knew well. Zoe's smile never faltered. "It is, but my sister and I wanted to do it together."

"Sierra Clayton." Sierra stuck her hand out and gave Mirabelle's limp fingers a firm handshake. Mirabelle said nothing but Zoe watched as she shook her hand before she walked off. Sierra's wicked grin bloomed. "Sorry, couldn't resist. There are times when I really do like my new last name. Speaking of, there's my man now with my in-laws. They flew in for this event especially. I know people had their doubts, including me at first, but they really do want what's best for the area. Do you still need to talk to Jack for Operation Nick?"

"I do."

"I'll make sure you get the time. Let me do some wrangling." Sierra greeted her husband with a kiss and a "Zoe needs to talk to you."

A cough sounded through the speakers, and Luke began tapping on the microphone. "Attention. Our judges have the cookie contest results."

Adrenaline pulsed through Zoe. This was it. Luke held a folded piece of paper in hand. "The third place Christmas cookie goes to Mrs. Kim Coil for her sugar cookie Santa Clauses."

Zoe clapped. Mrs. Coil owned the jewelry store. "In second place, Zoe Smith with her Madeleines."

Disappointment surged, but Zoe smiled and took it in stride as she accepted her ribbon. Then Luke announced the winner: "First place goes to Mrs. Laura Bien for her Christmas shortbread."

But of course. Zoe turned to her mom and laughed. "Has Mrs. Bien ever lost a baking contest?"

"Not that I can remember. The fact that you're second is a high honor." Zoe's mom went to congratulate her friend. "That's the best I've ever done."

Then it was time for the gingerbread competition, and Zoe held her breath as the first two spots went by. She'd either placed first, or she'd not placed at all. But then Luke was calling "Zoe James Smith and Sierra Clayton," and happiness permeated Zoe as she and Sierra went to get their ribbon. "It was your decorating," Sierra said.

"It was your engineering." They smiled for a photo for the local paper, standing alongside the other winners. Then, as it was nearing four, people began leaving the Makerspace to head back to their businesses as they'd close in an hour.

With Sierra speaking with his parents, Jack approached Zoe. "What's up?"

"I need your help." Saying those words, words she wouldn't have said even a few weeks ago, felt powerful. Asking for help was what strong people did. And having a brother-in-law like Jack Clayton put her in a good position to get what she wanted.

"What can I do for you?" Jack asked.

Zoe took a deep breath. She'd mulled this question over the entire week since she and her mom had talked: what would make Zoe happy?

Zoe had come to a conclusion, and her decision had

been empowering and freeing. She gestured, and Jack followed her to a corner of the Makerspace. "I want to sell the store."

Nick's fingers flew over the keyboard. He glanced at the time in the upper right corner. He'd been coding for hours. He'd lost himself in the problem Kevin had given him to solve. He didn't mind. This was his world and he was good at it. Combining zeroes and ones didn't lead to heartbreak. Music blared through his earbuds as he worked, reprogramming the servers. He'd been working on them since he arrived, which kept him from thinking about Zoe.

Okay, so he was thinking of her now. Same as he did whenever his mind wandered. He'd been here two weeks—or was it three now?—immersing himself in the job that needed to be done. Sometimes he spent the night in the breakroom, catching sleep here and there on the lumpy couch that had seen better days and smelled like old shoes. But time was money, and every moment he hadn't solved the problem cost the company thousands. Nick and coffee had become best friends.

Besides Kevin dragging Nick to his house for Thanksgiving dinner, Nick's entire world otherwise had become the servers or the hotel suite he visited whenever he needed to shower. Which hadn't been often. He had eight hundred square feet of five-star accommodations he didn't use. Frankly, even though it was tastefully decorated, it didn't contain the warmth and personality of the inn. And then thinking of the inn brought him back to Zoe and...

"You look like hell." Startled, Nick removed an ear-bud and accepted the bottle of water Kevin handed him. "Have you even eaten dinner yet?"

"I had a handful of cashews earlier. If I keep at this, I'll be done tonight. I had a breakthrough."

"And then what?"

Nick blinked. He worked in a low light environment, his focus on the screen in front of him. As Nick tilted his head from side to side to work out the kinks in his neck, Kevin came into focus. "Then I'm done."

"Are you leaving again? Where will you go? What are your plans?"

"Aren't you the nosy one. I honestly don't know. I had my plane flown back here. Don't really feel like flying anywhere now. Probably will hang around here for a while."

"And do what, mope? Damn, Nick. You either gotta get over her or you have to go win her back. Because while you're great at fixing this," Kevin gestured to the servers, "you need to fix your life."

"Not all of us get happy marriages like you," Nick shot back. "My mother didn't even have a husband. I'm not from good lineage here."

"That's bull. You're smarter than half the guys I know."

"I'm not getting into a nature versus nurture debate."

Kevin planted his hands on his hips. "Stop deflecting. Don't get irritated at me for speaking the truth. Your mom wasn't necessarily a good mom. That doesn't mean you have to follow her example. You do get to have it all, Nick. You do deserve it."

"Money can't buy love, Kevin. Even you have to admit that." Nick figured that zinger might get his friend off his back. He'd been far too overly concerned lately. Nick felt fine. He was doing okay. He'd get over Zoe. He'd gotten over—what was her name? The actress. The woman before Zoe. See? He couldn't even remember her or her gold-digging ways.

Eventually he'd forget Zoe too. And how he felt about her. He could be cold and analytical. Like a computer. His brain was one. Why not his heart? Logic said that way he wouldn't hurt anymore.

His phone chimed, and Nick glanced at the number. He didn't recognize it. He kept his phone by him at all times, not that Zoe had reached out. But he'd wanted not to be away from the device in case she did. He'd promised not to block her and he hadn't. She simply hadn't contacted him. But maybe she might. Someday.

"Nick." Kevin's tone held infinite patience. "You're following the Beaumont social media feeds. Admit to yourself that you're not over her."

"Simply keeping current with the news." So what if he'd set a search engine alert for her name? How else would he have known she'd won the gingerbread contest? Or that her Madeleines had taken second to Mrs. Bien's shortbread? Nick had sampled both. The judges had chosen wrong.

He raked his hand through his hair, making it stand straight. He should go to the hotel and take a much-needed long shower to wash away the grunge he'd acquired. "I've turned into a mess, haven't I? A cliché? I'm a real loser."

"Never. But you walked away from something wonderful. Maybe you should go back and try to make things work."

Nick tilted his head, still trying to remove the stiffness. "Not an option." He waved Kevin off before his former partner got in a word edgewise. "You need to leave me alone. Besides, if you don't go, I won't finish this project. This has been a mess."

"I'll check on you soon." Kevin turned heel and walked away.

Nick returned to coding. He'd tried to describe what he did in lay terms once—the idea of peeling back various layers to get to where he wanted to go so he could fix what was broken. When he got there, keystrokes corrected the problem. Then he leaned back, watching as the program began to execute and restore itself. Nick smiled. Problem solved and better than ever.

The same couldn't be said for him. But before his brain began processing the problem of how to figure out what to do next, Nick decided to check his voice-mail. The earlier caller had had a Missouri area code. He pressed play.

"Hi, Nick, this is Florence from GLF Realty. At one point you'd inquired about the candy store. While that's been purchased, I've got a line on another Main Street business coming onto the market, Auntie Jayne's Cookies. Zoe Smith will be listing it with…" She named the agency. "It's a fantastic opportunity. You'll want to move fast. The building alone is in a prime location and…"

Nick didn't listen to more. Zoe was selling? Where was she going? What had happened? This was the store's busy season. Her receipts from sales should get her through to spring, when the Clayton Holdings contract started. She was giving up? Quitting her dream?

Her actions didn't make sense. Had he caused this shift? He couldn't live with himself if he had. Guilt plagued him and Nick ambled to his feet. His body ached from sitting for so long, but blood began to flow as he stretched out his legs. He found Kevin. "It's finished."

Kevin peered at him through his tortoise shell frames. "And? Are you going to finally do something smart with your life for a change? Maybe go back and win over the girl?"

Nick sighed. "I'm not sure that's possible. While you're good with what I just fixed, I found another vulnerability that can be exploited. I've still got work to do until you're all clear."

Kevin shook his head. "Nick, go back to Beaumont."

"And risk you getting raked over the coals for what I discovered? You don't own this company anymore. You actually have a boss. He's not going to like it if I leave this and you get hacked."

Kevin conceded with a wistful smile. "True. Do you miss it sometimes? Owning something?"

Nick shook his head. "Nah. I miss the thrill of solving problems. I don't miss all the subjectiveness and dealing with investors and all that. Computer problems I can handle."

At least the computer ones he could. His life—that was hopeless. Now a computer—that was his element. Where he was competent and respected. "You need me so I'll stick around and help out for a while. At least through the holidays."

"Of course. We'd hire you full time if you would agree but that's not what you want long term," Kevin said. "But you know my wife will insist you come to our place for Christmas and happy wife equals happy life and all that crap, so you're coming. No argument."

Nick shrugged. "Got nowhere else to be."

"You know I'm going to keep working on you to fix yourself."

Nick hastened to the door. "No time. If you'll excuse me, I've got a vulnerability to fix."

Zoe had a buyer for her store. Several days after listing the place and two weeks before Christmas, her sister-in-law called with the exciting news. "The contract is all cash plus ten percent over asking. The buyer isn't requiring any inspections of the building, but insists on retaining control over the Auntie Jayne's name and the proprietary recipes. Jack's attorney reviewed it and that's standard.

"Are they crazy?" Zoe asked.

"To ask for your recipes? That's standard."

"I meant to buy something with no inspections. This building is ancient. If it's anything like my house, it might not even be up to code. I expected to make some concessions. Do we even know who the buyer is?"

"It's some trustee for a blind trust. They want all rights. You can bake, but not compete with Auntie Jayne's. Maybe they want to franchise. Anyway, with nothing standing in the way, the title company can get the paperwork done by Friday, ensure the cash is there, etc. Whoever they are, they forked over fifty thousand dollars in earnest money for the building. To retain the rights to Auntie Jayne's, they provided a transfer of one hundred thousand dollars as proof of their good faith. Zoe, I don't think you'll get another offer this good."

The numbers were astronomical. When Zoe had first thought about selling the store, she hadn't realized that meant more than the building. But her brother-in-law Jack had been an invaluable resource. He'd purchased tons of wineries in the area, and he'd had his lawyer walk Zoe through everything, such as did she want to keep the rights to the recipes and the name? Did she want to sell only the building? What did she want?

Zoe wanted to be free, which meant selling everything and walking away. She wasn't certain what she'd do next, career-wise, but the decision she'd made to sell felt right. She no longer wanted to run Auntie Jayne's. For too long she'd let the store define her life. Trying to force success in what she thought was her dream had blinded her to the fact that she wasn't happy. The store wasn't her destiny. Jared and Ted—they'd been stepping stones on her journey. Good relationships, perhaps, for a time, but not enough to be forever love. But they had taught her things. Ted, that people change and that it's okay not to change with them. Jared, that sometimes love wasn't enough to go the distance.

And Nick, sweet Nick. He'd taught her that she needed to love herself first and break free from the chains binding her. Like that airline safety demonstration—she was no good to others unless she put on her oxygen mask first. To be a good mom, friend, sister, daughter, partner, etc., Zoe had to take care of herself and for once, put her happiness first. By doing so, she'd make those around her happy as well, which is what she wanted. A feeling of calm and serenity soothed Zoe's soul. This was the right choice. Financially, she'd be set.

Her sister-in-law broke the silence. "Zoe, are you there? Are we accepting their offer?"

Zoe clutched the phone. What was that old saying? Leap and the net will appear? She said one last prayer that adage was true and that she wasn't throwing herself off into a deep chasm and making yet another mistake. She didn't think so and her strong tone conveyed her conviction.

"Yes. Yes we are."

Two days before Christmas, Zoe wrote her signature one final time on the seemingly endless stacks of legal documents she'd had to sign. Before she'd even set the pen down, the title agent swooped in and bundled everything for notarizing and photocopying. Zoe remained in the small conference room and sent a message to her mother. "It's done."

Her mom sent back an encouraging "I'm proud of you, Zoe."

Zoe lifted the coffee cup and sipped the now-cool hazelnut blend. Her hand trembled slightly. As soon as the account funded, she'd hand over the keys. As the title agent had patiently explained, "It's not like in the movies. It doesn't transfer instantly."

Having sold one house and bought another, Zoe knew that. But the amount from the sale of her and Ted's house was nothing like what she received today. Even after settling what she owed to her parents—the title company would pay that lien using the proceeds— Zoe had enough to pay off her mortgage several times over. And then some.

She'd decided to put off making any other major decisions until after the holiday. She was the last holdout in Beaumont for the James family, and for the first time ever, Zoe itched to leave. The title company representative returned with Zoe's papers, all secure in an elongated plastic portfolio with the title company's name embossed in gold. If Zoe's nephew hadn't been sick, her sister-in-law would have been here. Instead, Zoe had been alone.

It seemed rather fitting, she decided. She carried the papers back to Auntie Jayne's. She'd leave the keys with Sarah and Jessica. Both had agreed to stay on to train the new manager and baker. They'd be paid at three times their regular salary for one week, and then after the New Year adjust to a more realistic, yet still increased hourly rate.

As Zoe entered the shop from the kitchen, Sarah lifted her gaze from arranging cookies on the sales floor. Jessica worked the point-of-sale device, getting it ready for the busy day ahead. Zoe's title company appointment had been at nine-thirty, so the store didn't have much time before it opened. "Is it done?" Sarah asked.

"It is."

"Seems sad." This came from Jessica.

"It is, but I'm ready for a change." Zoe held up the gift bags she'd retrieved on her walk back from the title company. She passed a bag over to Sarah, who squealed when she opened the necklace and earring set Zoe had gotten her.

Jessica held out her necklace. "This is so perfect. Thank you." Jessica gave Zoe a hug. Echoing Jessica's thanks, Sarah hugged Zoe as well.

The moment was bittersweet. "I wanted to say thank you for being great workers. I'm leaving the store in good hands. Now, if you'll excuse me, I've got to go. Especially because I'm about to cry and I never cry."

Zoe scurried back into the kitchen. Over the weekend, along with her family's assistance, she'd cleaned out all the family's personal items. They were safe in the basement of her brother's house. Zoe set her keys on the counter and gave one last look around. Then she picked up her papers and refused to look back as she walked to her house.

She set the papers inside and glanced around. She'd already packed. Her first stop—flying Megan to Seattle to drop her off for Christmas with Ted. It remained his holiday, and Zoe would miss her daughter terribly. However, she and Nick had unfinished business and the break would give her time to take care of things. There were things she had to say.

She'd also put Ted firmly in his place. Thanks to the sale, she had more money than he did. A "don't make me take you back to court" had called his bluff about the lawyer and put her back in the driver's seat.

As for travel arrangements, since Jack and Sierra planned to travel to the West Coast for the holiday, they'd arranged for Zoe and Megan to join them on the Clayton Holdings' corporate jet. It would stop in Seattle first to drop off some employees who lived in Washington State, as well as to drop Megan with Ted. Then Jack and Sierra would continue on to Portland, leaving Zoe to make the final leg to California by herself. Zoe was glad she and Megan wouldn't be flying by themselves with total strangers.

Megan had spent the night with Zoe's mom, meaning Zoe would meet her daughter at the plane as Sierra would pick her up since she was closer. Zoe climbed into her car and drove into Chesterfield. While Clayton Holdings had a runway in Beaumont that Nick used, until the larger hangar facilities were finished, the company flew out of Spirit of St. Louis airport. Her car would be safe in the gated lot until she got back.

The December day was sunny and the wind calm, the complete opposite of the tumult Zoe felt. The last time she'd been in this terminal, she and Nick were heading to Springfield on their date. Weeks had passed since then, but if anything, the sense of loss had intensified. Her nerves clamored. She was going to do this. She'd confront Nick and set things straight.

She walked inside, and Megan raced over to hug her. "Sierra says we're going to fly."

"We are." Zoe knew how much progress her sister had made on managing her PTSD, enough to handle the four-plus-hour flight to the West Coast. After the crash by her student during flight instruction, Sierra hadn't been able to even go near an airport, much less sit in a plane. Yet, here she was. Nervous, but ready.

"Great, now that we're all here, let's get going." Jack took charge, ushering them out the door to the tarmac.

Zoe and Megan comprised the rear, with Megan insisting on rolling her "big girl" carry-on suitcase she'd gotten as an early Christmas present. Parked across the way from the Clayton Holdings' Gulfstream was another Gulfstream, this one as sleek but slightly smaller. The door opened, and as if pulled by an invisible string, Zoe stopped to watch the passenger debark. She knew the set of those shoulders, that blondish hair that appeared as if a sunset had streaked through it. Long strands feathered over a perfect forehead whose tiny lines Zoe had traced with her finger. Her heart raced and her breath drew short. Surely she'd conjured him and this was an illusion. "Nick?"

It wasn't a mirage. As if he'd heard a voice calling his name, he stopped short. His glance found her like a heat-seeking missile finding its target. "Zoe?"

She walked toward him, meeting him in the middle. "What are you doing here?"

"Why did you sell the store?"

"Because I…"

"Zoe!" From a short distance away, Sierra glared at Nick. "We need to take off and you could be in the way of aircraft trying to park."

"Where are you going?" Nick asked.

Everyone except for Sierra and Jack had boarded. Megan waved at them, but Sierra had forbidden her niece to run over to greet Nick. This was an active aircraft zone, after all.

"I'm dropping Megan off in Seattle and then I was coming to find you. She's going to visit her dad for the holiday. Sierra and Jack were going to bring her back right after New Year's."

"I want to talk with you too. It can wait until you get back."

He began to turn and Zoe put her hand on his arm. "It can't. Come with me. Megan will be devastated if you don't say hello."

Nick followed Zoe over to where Sierra, Jack, and Megan stood. "Hey, Megan," he said.

Megan frowned for a moment, as if about to give him a piece of her mind, but then she threw her arms around Nick and gave him a hug. "I missed you."

"I missed you too."

"Did you miss my mom?"

Nick glanced at Zoe. "Very, very much."

"We need to get going." This time the reminder came from Sierra. Zoe pulled her aside while Nick talked to Megan. "I need a favor."

"Let me guess, you want me to take Megan and you stay here."

"I need to talk him. I can fly, but then I need to come right back here. It can't wait. Not this time."

Sierra nodded. "We were going to pick her up, so as long as you fill Ted in on the change of plans, that we're dropping her off. It'll give me some quality time with my niece, and I need the practice anyway for when I have my own child."

"Don't let her scare you out of having one," Zoe teased.

"Oh, too late." Sierra's hands went protectively to her stomach.

Zoe's excitement bubbled and she threw her arms around her sister. "You didn't say anything."

"We were waiting until after the holidays. We just found out."

Happy tears moistened both Sierra's and Zoe's eyes. Jack approached with a grin and an "Ah, I see the secret's out."

"She's my sister," Sierra defended as he drew her into his arms.

"Megan?" Zoe called. Megan walked over, followed by Nick. "Megan, I need to talk to Nick. Are you good with flying with Aunt Sierra and Uncle Jack both ways to see your dad?"

Megan nodded. "There's games and movies on the plane, right?"

"There is," Sierra confirmed. "Do you think I wouldn't know how to have fun?"

"Okay," Megan said. She hugged and kissed her mom, and climbed aboard. Jack followed and returned with Zoe's suitcase. Then he went back up the stairs. Sierra boarded last.

"You let me know what happens," Sierra said from inside the door. She pointed two fingers at her eyes and then at Nick. "I'm watching you. Don't you dare hurt her again."

"I'm not planning on it," Nick said.

Sierra nodded. "Good." With that, she disappeared and the door rose.

Nick and Zoe went over to his plane, where he'd left his bag. They rolled their luggage into the building and then outside into the parking lot "How about I follow you back to your house?" Nick suggested.

"How about we go to neutral ground. Say, the inn?"

"That's where I'm staying."

"Then the parlor at the inn it is."

Zoe's drive back from Chesterfield took forever, as if time had slowed to a crawl, similar to the traffic that for some reason snarled once she crossed the Missouri River, as if everyone was on the two-lane road to Beaumont. Zoe parked in the lot behind the inn, with Nick's rental SUV arriving within seconds to take the spot beside her. Mrs. Bien greeted Nick warmly and relieved him of his wheeled suitcase. As if sensing the two needed privacy, she shut the wooden sliding doors to the parlor, enclosing them in the Victorian-decorated space.

Zoe drank Nick in. He appeared slightly worn and haggard, as if the last few weeks had tired him out. He wore a flannel shirt over a white tee, and a pair of jeans with ragged cuffs, the strings hanging loose over brown boat shoes. "How did your project go?"

"Fixed one thing and found another. Then realized I had to fix the one thing that was most important."

"What's that?"

Nick shuffled from side to side. "Me."

Confusion knit her brows together. "You're not broken."

"Maybe not exactly, but my coding's certainly off if I walked away from you. I let my past come in between us. I judged you based on my own bias. We entered this relationship as a fluke. I wanted to be your knight in shining armor and ride to your rescue. Be a protector. But you didn't need me to be any of those things. You needed me to listen and support you in what you wanted. You didn't need me to save you. You could always save yourself."

"I didn't defend you. Even though I was blindsided by who you were, that's no excuse. I could have done better. I reacted badly because my history with Ted colored my actions. I'm also guilty of letting my past come between us. While the past will always be the past, I want a future with you, Nick. You. Not anyone else." She drew a breath. "I sold the store. I don't know what I'll do next, but I was coming after you to figure it out. I've never done that for anyone else—go after them. I cried after you left. I've never done that either. I'm stoic. Emotionless. Ted told me I'm cold and heartless."

"He'll always be an ass in my book. Those two descriptors are the last things you are. You're laughter and warmth. Rainbows and sunshine. I had such a crush on you in high school. I worried that accounted for my behavior. But after being without you, I realized I was wrong. This is no misguided crush or lust. When you ran into me at the airport, I was coming back to make things right because I love you. You, Zoe. I love you."

His words curated an emotional tidal wave that overflowed her heart and warmed her soul and her heart overflowed. "Well, I was on my way to California because I love you, Nick. You and only you. You are my future. My forever." Her purse was on the side table and she reached into it and withdrew a small black velvet box. She opened it and the ring flashed. She dropped to one knee and raised it up. "I'm doing this correctly this time. Nick Reilly, will you marry me and put this back on my finger?"

Nick hauled her into his arms and crushed her against his chest. His mouth covered hers and he kissed her in that star-seeing, mind-blowing way that sent quivers everywhere. "I assume that's a yes?" Zoe asked when they surfaced for air.

"That's a hell yes. I'm going to make you happy, Zoe."

He slid the ring on her finger and tears of happiness began to wet the corners of her eyes. "My mom asked me what would make me happy. The first thing I thought of was you. You already make me so happy, Nick. I don't know what the future holds, or what job I'll do or what happens next, like if you want us to live in California or whatever, but I'm willing to do it. I'm ready to leave Beaumont if it means having you in my life." She slid her hand to his cheek, the stubble prickly. The diamond caught the light as she pressed the little dip in his chin. "I've missed you so much."

"Same. I thought I could lose myself in computer programming, but I never stopped thinking about you. We'll make it work because I love you and want to be holding your hand when we're old and gray and playing with our grandchildren and traveling the world, whatever we want."

"I'll have time. I'm not as rich as you are, but I certainly don't need to work. Eventually I'll want to do something, but there's no hurry. I sold the store. It's someone else's problem. I have time to figure things out."

"About that," Nick said. He grinned sheepishly. "Don't hate me."

"Hate you? Why would I hate you when I love you?"

It dawned on her what he was about to say at the same time Nick said, "I bought the store."

"You're my buyer?"

"I didn't want you to regret selling it. It's ours to do what we want with it. You can work full time, part-time, or not at all and train people to run it for you." He held her hand in his and brought it to his lips. "Forgive me, but I couldn't see it in the hands of anyone but family, and I've never owned anything in Beaumont. It seemed a good time to put down roots. Not that we can't live anywhere in the world."

Zoe brought her mouth to his, kissing him between each word. "You. Wonderful. Man." He captured her mouth fully as she tried to say "I love you." She kissed him back, marveling at how each time they kissed their bond grew, as if it were something tangible she could actually feel beyond the desire powering through her.

His hand slid around her waist, drawing her to him. "We probably need to take this somewhere more private," Zoe whispered as she nipped his earlobe.

"I have a room upstairs."

They pushed open the parlor doors, finding no one in the main foyer. Nick's room key sat on the table in the center of the room, and he snagged it. Mrs. Bien had put him in the suite, his luggage already delivered.

She could get hers from the car later. Zoe grabbed his hand, and together they raced up the wide, front stairs to the second floor, where Nick took her to paradise and beyond.

"You know everyone will think us crazy," Zoe said as she lay in his arms following a frantic bout of love-making, her head on his chest.

"Exactly. Crazy in love."

Zoe shifted. His fingers were already moving. Before he made her moan, she managed to tease him. "You know, we could work on revising some of those nick-names. Make them fitting."

"How so?"

She shifted so she gazed down at him. Her hand reached lower and she leaned to whisper in his ear. "Instead of sweet nothings, I'm going to make them nasty. What do you think? Can we be nasty? Want to be nasty, Nick?"

"I think you're incredibly wicked and I'll let you do whatever you want. I love you," Nick said.

"And I love you too."

After Zoe took them to heaven and Nick returned the favor, they held each other tight and the old inn, which had seen many a reconciliation, honeymoon, and an-niversary, seemed to give a great sigh when it settled down for the night. Far below, the Woman in White glided by and Nick and Zoe, gazing out the window, swore she glanced at them and smiled.

Epilogue

Three years later

Nick and Zoe stayed in Beaumont. For the first several months they lived in Zoe's small house, until Nick insisted they had to buy something else. Instead of purchasing, though, at the insistence of Sierra and Jack, Nick and Zoe had moved into Zoe's childhood home, which had been sitting there empty since the James family sold their winery and land to Clayton Holdings.

Zoe was the third generation to move in, and she couldn't have been happier with the way things turned out. After their time at the inn over that magical Christmas, she and Nick had made a quick pit stop in Vegas to get married. Then both she and Nick had picked up Megan from her dad's. Zoe missed her daughter and hadn't wanted to wait for Sierra and Jack to bring her back to Beaumont. Besides, Zoe loved flying with Nick and even years later, they'd take trips as often as they could. Sometimes Megan tagged along. Sometimes they left her with her grandparents or at Anna's house.

Zoe wasn't sure what Nick had said to Ted when he'd pulled her ex aside that first time they'd gone to get Megan, but Ted had never said another word about Nick's past. From that moment on, co-parenting with Ted became far easier. Which was good, as now Zoe had a pair of identical twin boys to deal with, who at almost eighteen months, were into anything and everything. Nick was a great father, and Zoe couldn't have asked for a better partner. When they threw parties for family and friends—and they'd become close to Ashley and Dan—Nick was the best host and organizer. No one ever had a bad time.

Nick had even found his business soulmate in his brother-in-law, and he and Jack had quietly started buying even more businesses and properties around the area. They did so in order to stabilize the businesses and keep the community strong. They didn't target the owners, but rather bought whenever the owner was ready. When Mirabelle Adams's husband had received a job transfer, Nick and Jack had jumped on the opportunity to purchase another building on Main Street.

With the twins taking most of her time and energy, someone else ran the cookie store. Zoe instead worked from home—well, from the state-of-the-art commercial kitchen Nick had built in a cute little outbuilding on their acreage. Cookies by Zoe were custom made and exclusive to the Clayton Hotel chain. At some point, Zoe knew that she'd need to expand.

But not yet. She pressed her hand to her stomach as

she finished packaging an order of Madeleines. *Had she?* Yes, she had. She smiled, feeling the first sensations of movement. They were expecting a girl. She and Nick were over the moon. Megan was ready to have a younger sister so the boys didn't outnumber the girls.

As if sensing her thinking of him, Nick entered the kitchen. He kissed her as strongly and deeply as he had the day they'd had their second wedding, this ceremony for family and friends. Zoe had always wished to be happy, and to use the silly cliché, her cup ran over. "You about done for the day?" he asked. "Because I finished my project and need some adult time with my wife."

Megan was at school and the twins were with her mother, who'd insisted that after raising four kids herself, she could take her grandchildren to the St. Louis Zoo by herself.

"You need adult time, huh?" Zoe shot him a wicked grin as she put the package on the shelf in a small vestibule, where the delivery man would retrieve it in a few hours. "You want us to take off the entire afternoon?"

Nick's arms were already around her. "That's an unequivocal yes."

Zoe took his hands and moved them to her stomach. There the sensation was. "I felt it!" Nick was as incredulous as he'd been with the twins. He kissed Zoe's lips. "She must know her mom needs some adult time."

She kissed his neck. "I'm always ready for some adulting."

The spring day was glorious, with new growth on the trees and the flowers budding. Hand in hand, they raced to the main house, onto the porch and into their bedroom. Afterward, Zoe rose and went to the window. She loved the view of the land sprawling before her, especially in the afternoon sun. Nick came and wrapped his arms around her. "It's a great view."

She lifted her lips and returned his kiss. She'd finally found what she'd been looking for. A soulmate. Love. Home. All because of Nick. She held his gaze as she drew him closer. "This view's better."

* * * * *

Chapter One

Layla pushed the swinging door that led to La Cabane de La Mer's kitchen and stepped inside. The sounds of simmering pots and sizzling grills filled the air. She smiled and sucked in a deep satisfying breath.

She moved to the first prep station. A petite young blonde with a pixie haircut stood bent over the metal counter chopping potatoes. "Hi, Lucie." Her *chef de partie* was the only kitchen staff who had agreed to stay on when Layla had purchased her grandfather's restaurant nine months ago, after he and Nonny retired to Florida. She'd needed to hire three line cooks to replace those on her grandfather's staff who'd thought her crazy when she'd announced she'd turn his place into an upscale French bistro. So what if New Suffolk wasn't Paris? She'd make it work.

Antoine's smug image floated into her brain. *Lying, cheating bastard.* He thought she couldn't make it without him? *Hah!* She might not have her three Michelin stars yet, but she would. She'd turned his restaurant into one of the top places in Paris. She'd do the same here.

"Would you like to taste the lyonnaise potatoes?"

She gave herself a mental shake and concentrated on the task at hand. "Yes, please." Layla scooped up a thin slice covered with caramelized onion with her disposable tasting fork. She inserted it into her mouth. The potatoes were cooked to the correct consistency. Not too soft, not too crunchy. "Perfect."

Pitching the fork in the trash as she passed by, she wandered to the next prep table. "Hi, Luis."

Her *poissonnier* mumbled something she couldn't make out as he presented tonight's special.

Layla swallowed to clear her dry throat. Had she made the wrong decision in hiring Luis? She would have preferred to hire another female prep cook to replace Gabrielle when she'd moved away last month, but with his impeccable references, Luis had been the most qualified candidate who'd applied for the position.

Yes, he could be gruff at times, and a bit temperamental. Still, it wasn't like he wouldn't take direction from her.

Not like Pierre.

Her blood boiled every time she thought about how her ex, Antoine, had insisted she hire the arrogant souschef, and refused to allow her to fire his condescending ass when he kept going over her head every time he disagreed with her.

Stop it. Not all male cooks had a problem working for a woman. After all, Luis couldn't be a better fish cook. He really got her menu, and everyone on the team liked him. She shouldn't look for trouble where none existed.

Grabbing another disposable fork from her pocket, she scooped up a bite. "The sole meunière is delicious."

She gave a satisfied nod and turned her attention to her sous-chef. "You're in charge of the kitchen, Olivia. I'll be in my office if anyone needs me." She needed to meet with Zara to review the restaurant finances. Her sister had insisted they discuss some supplier invoice matters now that couldn't wait until their scheduled meeting in three days.

Layla exited the kitchen and strode down the hall to her office. She opened her laptop and logged into the reoccurring Zoom meeting. Her sister's face appeared on screen. "Hey, Zara. How are things in Manhattan?"

Thank goodness Zara had agreed to stay on as well after she'd purchased the restaurant. With five years' experience managing Gramps's place, her knowledge was invaluable.

"How are you feeling?" They'd skipped last week's review because Zara had come down with a stomach bug. This was the second time in as many months Zara had caught a nasty virus that had left her bedridden.

Layla scrutinized her sister's image. Truth be told, she didn't appear one hundred percent recovered. Not if her washed-out pallor was anything to go by.

"Let's get started." Zara's weary expression tore at Layla's heart.

"You know, we can reschedule if you're still not well."

Zara didn't respond. Instead she shared her screen

and pulled up a QuickBooks entry. "Here's the information from last week."

Layla scanned the invoices sitting on her desk and compared them to the entries in Zara's file. "I don't see the butcher payment. Can you go to the next page, please? Maybe it's just in the wrong place."

The color drained from Zara's face. She looked as if she might get sick.

Layla sucked in a quick breath, concern overtaking her irritation—after all, she'd stepped away from dinner service for this meeting! But her sister's well-being had to come first. "Okay. Enough is enough. You need to go back to bed and get over whatever bug you've got. We'll finish this when you're feeling better."

Zara dragged a hand through her long brown hair. "Layla, I—"

"Don't argue, Zara. Just get some rest and feel better soon." Layla waved and ended the call.

She sighed and added the two remaining invoices to the pile in the corner of her desk along with a sticky note reminding her to confirm the payments when she and Zara met next.

Damn. Zara had never voiced her concerns. She couldn't imagine what Zara might want to discuss when the invoices appeared to be in order. Hopefully, she'd be feeling better soon and they could talk about whatever was on her mind.

Shrugging, Layla rose from her chair and exited her office, walking the opposite way down the long hall. She stepped into the conservatory of the colonial mansion, now a spacious dining room, with to-die-for views of the Atlantic Ocean.

Three couples sat at intimate tables for two. She

glanced at her watch. Seven at night. She would have expected more people on a Friday evening. No matter. Layla straightened her whites and readjusted the toque atop her head. Smiling, she approached the first table. It was time to meet and greet.

"Frank, Kim. It's so nice to see you." She wouldn't have expected the Bay Beach Club members—New Suffolk's version of a country club that catered to the affluent visitors who summered in the little beach town—to be in town at this time of year.

"Layla." Kim smiled. "We just had to stop in while we're in town for a little getaway from the city. We so enjoyed coming here last season."

"Yes," Frank agreed. "My coq au vin was delicious." He pointed to his empty plate.

"And you have one of Frank's favorite wines." Kim pointed to the almost empty bottle of Louis Jadot Echezeaux Grand Cru.

"You're on par with some of the finest bistros in Paris," Frank added.

A rush of pride flooded her chest. "Thank you. I'm glad you enjoyed your meals. Enjoy the rest of your weekend."

"We will. We'll be back again before we head back to the city," Kim said.

Layla wanted to pump her fists in the air and do her happy dance. She wouldn't, of course. Instead, she pinned a polite smile in place and gave a nod of her head. "I look forward to seeing you."

Layla moved to a couple seated by the window. "Good evening. I'm the executive chef, Layla Williams. Thank you for dining with us tonight."

"Hello. I'm Winnie and this is my husband, Tom."

"Is this your first visit to La Cabane de La Mer?" She didn't recognize the fiftysomething-year-old couple.

"Yes," Tom said.

"My clients at the Mermaid talked about this place all last summer, so we thought we'd try out your place," Winnie added.

The spa at the beach club. "A fellow New Suffolk business owner. I'm glad you came for dinner tonight." Layla made a mental note to return the favor once the club opened for the season. "How were your meals?"

Tom opened his mouth to speak, but his wife cut him off.

"Excellent, but a bit pricey for beef stew if you ask me. The diner down the street serves a similar dish for a lot less."

Layla shuddered, but her smile never faltered. Of course her elegant boeuf bourguignon was more expensive. Her dish couldn't compare to something served in the local greasy spoon. And probably labeled "pot roast" to boot, she thought.

"Now, darling." The man reached across the table and patted his wife's hand. "It's our anniversary. This is a special occasion. You don't need to worry about the cost tonight."

"Happy anniversary." She gave a discreet wave and motioned for the server to come to the table. "Please enjoy dessert and a glass of champagne, on the house." She always treated customers when they came in for special occasions. It was just good business.

"Thank you." Winnie's eyes lit up with excitement.

"You're welcome. Enjoy the rest of your evening." Layla moved on to the next table, but she couldn't banish Winnie's remarks from her mind.

After speaking with the last couple, she returned to the kitchen, nodded to the line cooks and walked into the back room to take inventory for the next day's menu. She scrubbed her hands over her face. What was wrong with her tonight?

There's nothing wrong. She gave herself a mental shake and yanked open the cooler with more force than she'd planned. The door ricocheted off the outside wall and came flying toward her. She jumped out of the way to avoid being hit.

Layla stepped inside the cooler. She'd already cured the duck legs for the cassoulet. At least no one would compare that traditional dish to anything made in the local diner.

Stop it. The diners tonight had liked her food. No, they'd *loved* her dishes. So, why complain about the cost? This town needed an upscale restaurant. Right?

They could patronize Gino's. It might not be in New Suffolk, but it was only five miles from here. Her shoulders sagged. The Italian food was superb and the prices... *Even better. Enough.* She needed to stop this madness. People liked La Cabane de La Mer. She was proud of what she'd built over the last nine months. With a little more time her place would be even more successful.

Layla double-checked the rest of the ingredients she'd need and exited the cooler.

Emily walked in as Layla returned to the kitchen. She grabbed a salad from the cooler.

"How's it going out there?" Layla asked. "Any more customers come in in the last hour?"

Emily nodded. "Table three would like to speak with you." She let out a little chuckle.

Layla arched a brow. "What's so funny?"

"It's Mrs. Clement."

Oh, Lord. The elderly woman who always tried to fix her up with her nephew every time she came in. "No problem. I'll go and speak with her now." She'd politely decline to meet Mr. Wonderful—this according to his besotted aunt—just like she'd done all the times before. She wasn't interested in a relationship. Not with Mrs. Clement's nephew. Not with any man.

Her hands clenched into tight fists. She wouldn't allow any man to make a fool of her ever again.

Layla would focus her energy on what mattered most—her restaurant.

She straightened her shoulders. Holding her head high, she marched back into the dining room.

"Hey, Wall Street. That was pretty good work you did tonight—for a newbie."

"Hah, hah, Cruz." Shane Kavanaugh snorted as the ambulance rolled to a stop in the New Suffolk regional community medical building. "I left New York six months ago. I'm an EMT." Step one of his life plan—complete. Step two... He couldn't wait to start paramedic classes in the fall.

Duncan Cruz rested his hands on the steering wheel and faced Shane. "Gotta say, it's a heck of a career change."

Shane viewed the switch as refocusing on his original goal—a career in the medical field—something he'd wanted to do from the time he was six years old and his father, Victor, first got sick. Dad would have preferred he join Turner Kavanaugh Construction, the company his father had started with his best friend more than thirty years ago—but Shane was sure Dad would be proud of him for being true to himself—even if he hadn't lived long enough to see the man he'd become. Above all else, Victor had wanted his kids to be happy.

New York had never made him happy. He'd tried like hell for a long time to believe it would, but he couldn't fool himself any longer.

The money was great. He couldn't deny that. He'd been like a kid in a candy store buying every treat he could find in the beginning. Having cash to spare had been a powerful draw for a guy who... Well, while he couldn't classify his family as poor—not by any stretch of the imagination—but growing up, there definitely hadn't been money in the Kavanaugh home for frivolous things.

What was the old saying? *Money can't buy you happiness.* Yes, that was it. Whoever came up with that saying was spot-on.

"Let's just say the city life's not for me." He missed walking down Main Street and greeting his fellow neighbors by name. Missed the sense of community that came with small-town living.

"You're a small-town boy through and through, huh?" Cruz let out a roar of laughter.

Absolutely. "Hey. I like it here in New Suffolk."

Life in Massachusetts suited Shane just fine. Always had. He never needed to pretend to be something— someone—he wasn't. He was good enough—as is. He'd finally realized that.

Duncan pulled the keys from the ignition. "Hey, wanna go down to Donahue's and shoot some pool after we restock the ambulance?"

He nodded. "Yeah, sure. Sounds good. Loser buys the first round."

Duncan grinned. "I guess you'll be buying then."

Shane shot him a disparaging glance. "We'll see about that." He jumped out of the ambulance and strode to the stockroom.

Thirty minutes later Shane drove his F-150 up to Donahue's Irish Pub. As always, the place was rocking on a Saturday night. He hoped they wouldn't have to wait too long for a pool table. He pulled into a spot in the back of the lot and hopped out of the truck.

Snow fluttered from the clear night sky as he exited the driver's seat. The first day of spring might officially arrive in twenty days, but it felt as if the warmer weather would never get here. Shane zipped his bomber jacket, shoved his hands in his coat pockets and picked up his pace as he strode toward the entrance.

Loud music accosted him as he stepped inside. A group of local musicians rocked out on the stage in the back of the room. The song ended and the singer announced the band would take a thirty-minute break. Shane strode down the short narrow hall that led to the bar area.

He scanned the room. A woman standing near the front entrance caught his attention. Shane studied her as she moved in his direction.

Tall and thin with long dark curly hair, her hips swayed ever so slightly as she moved through the throng of people. She wasn't Hollywood gorgeous, but he found her quiet beauty attractive nonetheless. Who was she?

She disappeared from his view.

Shane searched the crowd for a few minutes but couldn't find her anywhere.

"Excuse me," a female said.

He jerked his attention toward the voice. His mystery woman stood in front of him. Tonight was his lucky night.

"Could you please move?" The woman offered a winsome smile. "I need to leave." She pointed to the door behind him. "I can't get by."

"Oh, I'm sorry." He grinned and stepped aside.

"Thank you." Her gaze connected with his and she stiffened. "Shane."

How did she know his name? He scrutinized her face, then recognition slowly hit him.

Holy hell.

"Layla?" *No way.* The Layla Williams he remembered had shoulder-length light brown hair. Not long, dark, silky curls and certainly not the sexy curves this woman sported.

"Yes. It's me." Her gaze darted around the space.

"It's been a while." At least a few years.

"Yes," she agreed.

Why wouldn't she look at him? "How are you doing?" he asked.

"Fine. Um... You?" came her clipped reply.

Nothing had changed over the years. The rich Manhattan socialite still wanted nothing to do with a townie. Would she be as standoffish if she viewed his bank statement? Most women found him—his portfolio, he mentally corrected—quite attractive.

His wealth may have secured admittance into New York's upper echelon, Melinda *had* married him, after all, but admittance and acceptance were two different animals. He'd learned that the hard way.

"I'm surprised to see you." He couldn't hide the disdain in his voice.

"I'm...hanging out with some friends."

Here? Shane's jaw almost hit the ground. Donahue's wasn't a dive, but... He'd never have guessed a Williams would enter such an establishment. They'd frequented the Bay Beach Club during those years they'd summered here. He ought to know. He'd waited on her and her family often enough over the years.

"At least I was. I'm heading over to my restaurant now."

He'd heard she'd purchased her grandfather's place when he retired.

"I opened La Cabane de La Mer last summer." A look of pride flashed across her expression.

She'd have been better off sticking with a name for her restaurant that sounded less uptight, pretentious. Something with wider appeal, in his opinion. "How is your restaurant doing?" He'd noticed fewer cars in the parking lot when he passed by on the way home each day. Then again, many of the businesses in town suffered from a turndown in commerce during the winter months, when tourism tended to slow in the coastal towns.

Layla flashed a wide smile that stole the breath from him. The way it lit up the room, and transformed her face from...well, she'd always been beautiful, but the warmth and joy radiating from her now jolted through him like a bolt of lightning.

"It's great." She glanced at her watch. "But I have to go."

Same old Layla. A bitter smile crossed his face. "Of course." He gestured for her to pass by.

As she walked by him, murmuring a distracted "Bye," and disappeared outside, it was as though he'd imagined the transformation of a few moments ago. An odd feeling of disappointment shot through him before he shrugged it off and continued down the hall.

Shane walked into the bar and peered around. Several patrons sat in the high-back chairs along the length of the long glossy wood bar to his right. He spotted Levi Turner at the far end. Walking over, he clapped his friend on the shoulder. "Hey, man. What's up? How did you get out of the house tonight? I thought you have Noah on Saturday nights."

Levi turned sideways in the chair and faced him. "I usually do, but he's with his mother tonight. I'm supposed to meet Cooper here for a beer, but he's late."

"How is your little brother?" Shane waved at the bartender and he came toward him.

"I'm fine." Cooper Turner walked over and grabbed the seat next to Levi. "Sorry I'm late."

"No problem." Levi slid a pint toward his brother. "It might be a little warm now."

Cooper snorted.

"What can I get you, Shane?" the bartender asked.

"I'll take the New Suffolk IPA, Ben."

"Me, too," Cooper added and shoved the warm glass of beer aside.

Ben nodded, grabbed a couple of frosted glasses and headed to the tap a few feet away.

Shane scanned the room but couldn't find Duncan anywhere. They'd left the EMS building at the same time. He must have stopped somewhere along the way.

He directed his attention to Levi and Cooper. "So—"

Someone slammed into him from behind. Shane

whirled around and caught an older man before he landed on the ground.

"Sorry 'bout that," the man grumbled.

Shane stared into the man's vacant gaze. Something about his weathered features seemed familiar.

"Another bourbon, Ben," the man called.

"Not a chance. You've had enough, Gary. You're shut off."

"Gary Rawlins?" Shane's gaze widened.

Gary jerked his blurry gaze to him, and snarled, "Yeah. What of it?"

No wonder the man had looked familiar. This was his best friend's father. He held out his hand. "Shane Kavanaugh."

Gary did a double take and a small smile crossed his once handsome face. "Well, I'll be damned." He pumped Shane's hand. "Haven't seen you in years." He wobbled, but straightened himself before he fell. Clapping Shane on the shoulder, he said, "Mind ordering me a bourbon?"

Shane's mouth fell open. "How about I call you a cab instead?"

Ben returned, and set full mugs down in front of him and Cooper. "Already done. The cab will be here any minute."

"I'm not ready to go home," Gary objected.

"Okay, but you know the rules." Ben pointed to the door. "You're banned from this place if you don't leave when I tell you."

Gary groused some more as he made his way to the exit.

"Sorry about that," Ben gestured to Gary's retreating form.

"No problem." Shane waved off Ben's concern. "Does this happen often?" Jax's father tended to indulge on certain occasions, but he'd never seem him this bad before.

"Often enough." Levi snorted.

Ben shook his head. "We've had an arrangement with the cab company for years."

"Ever since Jax left town," Cooper added. "You ever see him when you lived in Manhattan?"

"Sometimes." Shane nodded. "When he was around, which wasn't much."

"Who would have thought one of New Suffolk's own would make it big?" Levi said.

"Rachel and I went to one of his shows last year, when his photos were featured at a gallery in Boston," Cooper added.

"Hey, look who just walked in." Cooper pointed to three women who stood by the front entrance.

"Who are they?" Shane asked.

"The middle one with the blond hair is big brother's fiancée," Levi scoffed.

Cooper elbowed Levi in the side. "Would you just stop already?" To Shane he said, "Her name is Isabelle."

Shane's eyes widened. "Nick is engaged? When did this happen?"

"Yesterday." Levi snorted and shook his head. "Worse—"

Cooper cut in before Levi could continue. "Not all marriages end up in the toilet. You just need to meet the right person." He jerked his head to Shane, a back-me-up-here expression on his face.

"Don't look at me for confirmation." He wouldn't be

making his way down the aisle again. Not in this lifetime. *That's for sure.*

"Oh, come on." Cooper rolled his eyes skyward. "Don't tell me you're a card-carrying member of the He Man Woman Haters club, like my brother here." Cooper gestured to Levi.

Levi snorted. "I'd say the answer to that is no, given he was checking out a hot little number not more than five minutes ago."

"What are you talking about?" he asked.

Levi leaned back in his chair and shot a challenging glance in his direction. "You're going to deny you were checking out Layla Williams?"

Shane opened his mouth but Levi jumped in before he could say anything.

"I saw you when you came in. I waved, but you obviously didn't see me." Levi arched a brow and flashed a smug smile. "You were otherwise engaged."

"Didn't you used to have a wicked crush on her when we were kids?" Cooper asked.

Levi smirked. "Oh yeah. I forgot about that. You had it bad for her."

"I don't know what you're talking about." *Lie much?* Because yeah, he'd just told a whopper. Yes, he'd fallen hook, line and sinker for Layla all those years ago. That fourteen-year-old boy had been naive enough to believe their backgrounds wouldn't matter. *Yeah, right.* Lifting his mug to his mouth, he swallowed a gulp of his beer.

"Not much has changed, has it?" Levi nudged him in the ribs. "She wouldn't give you the time of day back then and it looked like tonight was no different."

"Whatever." He gave a dismissive gesture. Shane could care less. He might find Layla attractive, but he sure as hell wasn't interested in pursuing her. He'd had his fill of Manhattan socialites, enough to last the rest of this lifetime and into the next. "I'm focused on my career right now. I'm not looking for a relationship."

"Amen to that." Levi lifted his mug and clinked it with his.

"Oh, come on," Cooper insisted.

He shook his head. Love wouldn't last. It never did. He ought to know.

When it ended… His gut twisted. *Never again.*

The reward wasn't worth any amount of risk.

Chapter Two

Layla woke on Sunday morning to the bright light blazing into her bedroom. She jumped out of bed and walked to the window. Sunshine glowed in a cloudless blue sky. A few people meandered along Main Street, even at this early hour.

Although she enjoyed this view of the town green from her place above the Coffee Palace, she missed the serenity of waking to the sounds of surf crashing on shore and the waves rolling in from the sea. Layla wished she could have continued to live in the second-story apartment above La Cabane de La Mer. Lord knew the space would have been more than enough for her, and she could have saved the monthly rent she paid to live here, but the private lender she'd used to secure the loan required to finance the restaurant renovations wouldn't allow it.

She glanced around the room. For now, the gray Ikea modular couch and black lacquer rectangle table would suit her fine. Not to mention the perks of living above a fabulous coffee shop and the friendship she'd found with Elle, the woman who lived across the hall, and Abby, the coffee shop owner.

Layla turned from her view and headed down the short hall to the bathroom. After a quick shower and dressing in warm clothes, she descended the exterior back staircase and walked around to the front of the building once she reached the parking lot. She walked inside and stepped up to the counter.

"Good morning, Layla. Oh, my. Do I have something to tell you. Things got quite interesting after you left Donahue's last night." Abby tucked a lock of titian hair behind her ear. She shuffled to the display case containing a selection of confections.

How lucky was she to have been inducted into the sisterhood? For the first time in her life, she had steadfast female friends she could rely on. Although truth be told, she was still getting used to the gal pal thing. Her sister was the outgoing one of the two of them. Zara loved to party and be surrounded by swarms of people, while she'd always preferred to be with Gramps in his kitchen.

Gramps never thought she was weird because she'd rather cook than go hang out at the mall or get her nails done. He never shoved her in front of a boy she'd crushed on and laughed when she'd almost lost her lunch trying to talk to him.

While she might have outgrown the nausea, her cautious, wary side still made frequent appearances—but she was working on that thanks to these wonderful, supportive, funny, loving women.

Layla grinned. "Do tell."

"You know who," Abby pointed to the back room, "finally plucked up the courage to ask that cute guy she'd been drooling over, for the last few weeks, to dance."

"By you know who, she means me." Elle sashayed in from the kitchen. Her long blond hair was piled on the top of her head in a haphazard bun. The hairstyle added a good four inches to Elle's petite stature.

"So..." Layla grinned, enjoying the comradery. "What happened after you danced?"

Abby let out a low whistle. "Just the dancing was pretty hot. The two of them were stuck together like Velcro. And that kiss..." She fanned herself.

"Get your mind out of the gutter." Elle's cheeks flamed.

"Someone had a good night. That's all I'm sayin'," Abby retorted. "Anything to eat today?" she asked Layla.

Layla studied the trays of sweets. "I can't decide which one I want. Surprise me."

Wax paper in hand, Abby reached inside the display case and plucked a figure-eight Danish from one of the trays on the top shelf. "Cherries and cheese okay?"

She nodded. "Sounds yummy."

"Excuse me." A short woman with a chin-length brown bob appeared.

Elle glanced over her shoulder. "Oh, hey. This is Mia. She just started here today."

Something about the woman seemed vaguely familiar, but Layla couldn't place a finger on what. "Hi, Mia."

Layla extended her hand over the counter. "Have we met before?"

Mia cocked her head to the side and scrutinized Layla's face. "I was just wondering the same thing."

"Maybe you two have bumped into each other here." Abby moved to the coffeepot and filled a large to-go cup. She added cream and sugar and handed it to Layla. "She and her three girls come in on the weekends along with Mia's mom, Jane Kavanaugh."

Shane. She remembered their brief exchange at Donahue's the other night. Yep. She couldn't have made a bigger fool of herself if she'd tried. The minute she'd recognized him... Can you say shy fourteen-year-old with a schoolgirl crush complete with sweaty palms and a topsy-turvy stomach? At least she hadn't lost her lunch. *Thank You, God, for small mercies.*

She'd annoyed him, for sure. *No news there.* He'd always found her irritating. *Poor little rich girl.* Oh, he'd never called her that to her face, but she knew damn well he believed it, according to some of the other locals who'd worked at the Bay Beach Club those years her family summered in New Suffolk.

"Layla?" Elle's voice cut into her thoughts.

"Sorry. I remember now," she said to Mia. "Your mom introduced us here at the Coffee Palace a few months ago—right before Christmas. The five of you had stopped in for a treat after taking your daughters to see Santa at the community center. It's nice to see you again."

Recognition dawned in Mia's gaze. "Right. It's nice to see you, too."

The bell above the door chimed. A tall man entered the shop.

"Shane." Mia's eyes widened. "What are you doing here?"

Layla whirled around. Lord, it was as if her thoughts had conjured him.

Shane swaggered over to where they stood. His big grin sent a tingle down her spine and made her insides go soft and mushy.

What was wrong with her this morning? So what if Shane had a great smile? He meant nothing to her.

"Ladies." He gave a brief nod of his head. "I'm here to support my big sister."

"By all means." Abby stepped aside and motioned for Mia to replace her at the counter.

"Hi, Shane." Layla's words came out in a rush.

He jerked his attention to her. "Layla. Hello." He gave her a polite smile.

A smile was good. So much better than the frown he always wore around her all those summers ago. "It's nice to see you again." Layla sucked in a deep breath. She wouldn't freeze up again. "I mean I haven't seen you in years and now it's been twice in two days." She gave a nervous laugh.

"Right." He eyed her as if she were delusional.

First, she couldn't string two words together, and now she couldn't stop talking. *Bumbling fool.*

Shane turned his attention to his sister. "I'll take a large black coffee, one of those giant cookies with M&M's and an apple fritter."

"Hungry much?" Mia aimed a smirk at her brother.

"Ha, ha. The second pastry is for Mom. She's outside." He jerked his head toward the entrance. "I ran into her in the parking lot, but she got a call. I said I'd order for her."

The chime sounded again and Jane Kavanaugh stepped in. "Good morning, everyone."

"Hi, Jane," Abby and Elle said at the same time.

"Hello." Layla smiled. Would Shane's mother remember her?

"Layla." Jane gave her a hug. "It's so nice to see you again."

Shane frowned. "You two know each other?"

"Of course we do. I've known Layla for years. I used to see her all the time when she visited her grandparents."

Layla prayed Jane had never suspected the truth about those occasions—that she'd arranged to run into Jane on purpose—so she could find out how Shane was doing and what he was up to.

Yes, she'd crushed on Shane something fierce in those days. Heat crept up her neck and Layla suspected her cheeks had turned red.

That was a long time ago.

"Do you want something to drink, Mom?" Mia asked. "Shane only ordered one coffee."

"No. I've got a mug in my car." Abby rang up the order while Mia filled a cup and placed each sweet in a paper bag.

Jane picked up her order. "I'm off to run a few errands."

"Bye," Layla called.

"Me, too." Shane grabbed his bag and cup and turned to the door.

"Have a great day." Layla winced when he just stared at her. She breathed a sigh of relief when he exited the shop. "I've got to get going, too. Take care." Coffee and Danish in hand, Layla headed toward the exit.

"Wait a minute," Elle called. "I almost forgot. Are you in for tonight?"

Layla turned to face the women. Their weekly Sunday night poker game. Those cutthroat women took the game seriously. Layla couldn't blame them. Not with such high stakes at risk. Reese's Peanut Butter Cups Miniatures, Hershey's Nuggets, and the occasional fun-size Hershey Bars thrown in for good measure. "Heck, yeah. I can't wait."

"How about you?" Elle turned her attention to Abby.

"Absolutely. And cousin or not, you get none of my winnings," Abby replied to Elle.

Layla cocked her head and jutted her chin. "You think you're going to win, do you? We'll see about that."

Abby crooked a smug smile. "Yes, we will."

"What about you, Mia? Care to join us for a little fun?" Elle asked.

"Are you sure? I wouldn't want to intrude."

"Positive," Abby responded. "The more the merrier."

"I agree," Layla added.

Mia smiled. "I'd love to. Let me see if I can get my mother to watch the girls for me. I'll give her a call during my break and let you know."

"Great." Elle gave a little wave and strode to the back room. Mia followed.

"See you later," Layla called over her shoulder as she walked to the exit.

Layla stepped outside. The blazing sun glinted off the white snow covering the town green. She sipped her coffee, passing the new boutique that had opened right after Thanksgiving, the local courthouse and the police station as she made her way through town.

She turned right when she reached the public beach

access. The peaceful tranquility of the waves crashing on shore calmed her mind and body. Who cared if most of the sand was covered with a foot of snow? Not her. She proceeded down the boardwalk and trudged through the gleaming white snow toward the ocean. High tide had washed away some of Mother Nature's white blanket, leaving a strip of sand visible about two feet from the water's edge.

Sipping her coffee, she meandered along the narrow path taking care to avoid the water to her right and the snow to her left.

The pavilion came into view. A lone man stood inside; his elbows propped up on the railing. He stared out at the waves crashing on shore.

Shane. Layla recognized him as she approached. She studied him from this vantage point. Dressed in jeans and a hooded sweatshirt, he cut an imposing figure.

High cheekbones, a rugged square cut jaw. He'd always been handsome, although her fourteen-year-old self wouldn't have used that term to describe his tall, lanky frame, his wavy brown hair that was just a little too shaggy to be considered clean-cut, and those mesmerizing sapphire-blue eyes. *Don't forget his smile.* It had made her innocent heart slam in her chest. If she were honest, it still did.

Shane spotted her. His piercing gaze bore down on her, scrutinizing, assessing.

Something flashed between them. Intense, fiery, it threatened to consume her.

She blinked. Shane was gone when her eyes fluttered open.

Her mind whirled, a chaotic swirl of emotion.

What had just happened between them?

* * *

Shane glanced at his watch. Ten more minutes and he'd need to leave for work. He munched the last of his cookie as he stared out at the sea and breathed in the crisp clean air.

A man raced along the beach chasing after two young children who laughed and played in the snow. It reminded him of the walks he used to take with his dad when he was a kid. They'd stop at the Coffee Palace, where Dad would get a coffee and he'd get a cookie. They'd walk along the beach and end up here, at one of the tables in the pavilion. Shane would tell him about his week at school and Dad would tell him about whose house they were renovating or building and how much he looked forward to Shane joining the family business one day.

Shane smiled into the wind. Despite what he'd told his father about wanting to work in the hospital so he could make people better, like the people who'd made Dad better—at least they had in the beginning—he'd taught him how to wield a hammer and by the time Shane reached his early teens, he'd accompany his father on small jobs.

He caught sight of someone else approaching in his peripheral vision. Layla. Shane shook his head. Leave it to her to come along and disrupt his thoughts.

Shane blew out a breath as she continued walking. He studied her face now that she was closer. How could he have forgotten who she was? She still looked like the girl he'd met in her grandfather's kitchen all those years ago.

His mind drifted back to that day.

"Boys, would you like some lemonade?" Mrs. Wil-

liams stepped over the short stack of two-by-four planks on the floor as she entered the bedroom in the upstairs apartment above the restaurant.

Shane glanced over at her as he held a piece of Sheetrock in place while his father tacked the gypsum board to the new frame they'd just made.

"I've got fresh-baked cookies, too," Mrs. Williams added. "They're right out of the oven."

"You guys go ahead," Dad said to him and Levi. "Take a break. Just be back in fifteen minutes."

"Follow me," Mrs. Williams said.

They walked into the living room. Shane marveled at the paintings that hung in gold frames on the walls and the decorative...what had his father called the large vases that sat atop the glossy wood tables? Urns. Yeah, that's what they were. He'd never seen anything so fancy in his life.

"It's this way, boys." Mrs. Williams walked into the kitchen.

Shane's mouth fell open when he spotted the young girl about his age standing with a tray of chocolate-chip cookies in her hand. Her hair was tied back in a ponytail and freckles dotted her nose. His stomach flip-flopped all over the place. She had to be the prettiest girl he'd ever seen.

"Boys, this is my granddaughter. Layla, this is Mr. Turner's son Levi." She pointed to her right. "And Mr. Kavanaugh's son Shane." She gestured left to him. "They're helping with the renovations to the bedroom we're redoing for you and your sister to stay in when you come here for visits."

"Hey." Levi grabbed two cookies from the plate on the counter and a glass of lemonade.

"Hi." Shane smiled. He couldn't take his gaze off her.

"These are really good," Levi mumbled.

"See, I told you, Layla," Mrs. Williams said.

"You made the cookies?" he asked.

Layla nodded.

Shane reached for one and bit into the gooey treat. "They're awesome."

Layla's cheeks turned bright red, but she smiled at him.

A rush of warmth flooded through him. His pulse went through the roof.

He smiled back.

Shane blinked. Why was he wasting time on memories that didn't matter anymore? He returned his focus to the surf.

Layla's gaze connected with his.

Something zipped between them, powerful and strong; his heart pounded even faster for a moment.

Shane inhaled a lungful of air and blew it out slowly as he tried to steady his erratic breathing. Why was he allowing her to affect him this way? Like Levi had said yesterday, she hadn't given him the time of day back then and nothing had changed as far as he could see.

It's nice to see you again. Her words flashed into his mind and the genuine smile on her face…

There went his traitorous heart again.

Shane banished the *what-ifs* banging around in his head. He'd already learned the hard way; girls like her brought nothing but heartache.

Shane strode into the empty locker room at the regional medical building and Duncan followed.

"I can't wait to get home and put up my feet for a

couple of hours. It's been a long day." Duncan grabbed his jacket from his locker and shrugged it on.

Shane nodded. "You got that right." Three trips to the hospital over the last eight hours had kept them busy.

"See you later." Duncan exited the locker room.

Shane finished changing into his street clothes. After packing his uniform into his duffel bag, he slung the strap over his shoulder and headed toward the exit to the parking lot.

He spotted a light on in Mark Burke's office as he made his way down the dimly lit hall. What was the EMS director doing here on a Sunday evening? Shane started to knock but held back when he heard voices.

"I'm well aware of the limited town budget," Mark said.

"You keep saying that," someone else responded.

Shane stopped and listened. The voice sounded familiar, but he couldn't connect the voice with a face.

"We can't afford to lose anyone, Lionel."

Was that Mayor White? Had to be. There wasn't another Lionel in New Suffolk as far as he knew.

"We're already operating the EMS at minimum staffing levels. If we lose even one person, we can't properly serve the community," Mark added.

"We may not have a choice. You know the EMS budget relies heavily on donations and other revenues generated," the mayor said.

"We've got the gala fundraiser coming up in roughly six weeks," Mark responded. "I'm sure we'll be able to raise the funds we need."

"You'd better hope so," Lionel said.

Shane sucked in a breath. Would Mark really have to cut personnel if the upcoming gala couldn't generate enough money? Damn. He could be one of those people. *Last in, first out.* That's the way it usually worked— in the business world. How many times had he seen it happen to his friends on Wall Street? Enough to know what happened when times got tough.

"Duncan and the rest of the volunteer committee for the gala are meeting tonight at seven here in the medical building. You're more than welcome to attend and see for yourself how the planning is going," Mark offered. "Better yet, you can offer your services. The committee can always use extra people."

If Duncan needed help, Shane was about to volunteer.

The community college Shane wanted to attend next semester required six months of EMT on-the-job experience as a prerequisite for acceptance into their paramedic program. Sure, there were other programs in the state that didn't make such requirements, but they were already full for the fall.

If he lost this job now...

No. He'd worked hard to get this far and he wasn't about to let his dream slip away now.

Shane would do what needed to be done to ensure he kept this position. No matter what.

Have a last-minute committee meeting for the gala this evening. Can't make our weekly game after all. Layla sent the text to Elle. Grabbing her purse, she slid from the car. A gust of wind blew and she shivered. Zipping her jacket, Layla quickened her pace as she strode toward the entrance of the EMS building.

Stepping into the empty main hall, she stopped in front of the wall containing the years-of-service plaques. She still got a kick out of seeing her grandfather's plaque on the top row with the five other founding members.

"I remember working with Joe when I first started here. Your grandfather was a great paramedic."

She jumped and whirled around to face the newcomer. "Oh. Hi, Mark."

"Sorry. I didn't mean to startle you," the EMS director said.

"No. That's okay." She gestured to the wall behind her. "I like seeing his picture up there." She was proud of his contributions to the community. Even after he'd retired from the EMS department, he'd continued his support.

"I see you're following in his footsteps."

Brows furrowed; she cocked her head to the side. "What are you talking about?"

"Allowing us to use your restaurant for the fundraiser. Joe hosted at least one EMS event a year when he owned the place. I can't wait to see what you've done now that you've taken over."

She beamed a warm smile at him. "Don't wait until the ball. Come by anytime. Tell your friends, too."

"Will do."

"We should get going." She gestured down the hall to where the community rooms were located. "The fundraiser meeting will start soon."

"I can't make it tonight. I have a family commitment. It was nice seeing you, Layla. Thanks again for helping with this event. It's people like you and the rest of the committee that make it possible for us to raise the money we need to better service the district."

"You're welcome. I'm glad to help." Giving was important. A responsibility as far as her parents and grand-parents were concerned, for everyone. If you can't give financially, find another way, Gramps would say.

How could she have lost track of those values over the last few years? Antoine's image appeared in her head. The fact that he didn't share her beliefs should have been a red flag. Yet she'd dismissed the facts, choosing to see what she wanted. *Foolish, all right.* Layla wouldn't make that mistake again.

She continued down the hall and stopped at an open door on the right. The fundraiser team sat inside on ei-ther side of two long banquet tables which stood side by side. She grabbed the last open chair.

Her eyes widened when she caught a glimpse of the man to her right. What was Shane Kavanaugh doing here? He seemed as surprised to see her as she him.

Duncan Cruz rose and called the meeting to order. "Thanks for coming, everyone. We're a little less than a month and a half from our event. I have something I need to share with you, but first, I want to introduce a new committee member." Duncan gestured to Shane. "For those of you who don't already know him, this is Shane Kavanaugh. He joined the department about a month ago."

Mr. New York Stock Exchange was an emergency medical technician? *Like Gramps?* No. That couldn't be right. He wasn't anything like her beloved grandfather.

He was a Wall Street Wolf. Wasn't he?

Shane cringed when Layla walked into the room. Wasn't it just his luck she'd be involved with the ben-efit? He couldn't catch a break.

He straightened and gave a little wave to acknowledge Duncan's introduction.

"Let's get started." Duncan explained the situation with the town budget and how they needed to generate as much revenue from this event as possible. "I'm looking for ideas we can easily implement since we don't have much planning time left."

Hal Smith raised his hand. "What if we changed the seating to family style instead of individual tables?"

Shane nodded. "Great idea. We can seat more people that way, which means we can sell more tickets."

"Can we do that, Layla?" Duncan asked.

"Sure. I don't have long tables, but we can string several of the small ones together and create the same effect."

Duncan grinned. "I like it. What else?"

"What if we do a themed event?" Layla said.

Duncan pursed his lips as if considering. "What did you have in mind?"

"We'll go upscale. Black tie for the men, fancy dresses for the women."

Faith nudged her husband. "Looks like I'm going shopping."

The group chuckled.

Layla grinned. "We'll have fairy lights, gold candelabras on the tables. Lots of glitz and glamour."

"We decorated the fire trucks with white lights for the parade last Christmas," Quinn Cain said. "I'm sure the chief will allow us to use them."

"Sophisticated Blooms can donate flower arrangements," Sophie Bloom added.

A round of *yeses* and *sounds goods* ensued.

Layla's eyes lit with excitement. "We can even do an ice sculpture in the main entry."

An ice sculpture? Seriously? Talk about over-the-top.

The rest of the group agreed with him if their silences were anything to go by.

"You don't have to answer now." Layla laced her fingers together and rested her hands on the table. "Just think about it."

He rolled his eyes skyward. Man, she was just too much.

"While I love your enthusiasm," Duncan started, "and I'm not saying we shouldn't go ahead and snazz things up a bit—because I think we should—our ultimate goal is to generate as much cash as we can. I'm not sure a themed event would bring in the extra money we need."

"Not to mention we'd exceed our budget to pull it off." Faith sighed. "I'm still shopping for a fancy dress." She winked at Layla.

"Me, too." Sophie smiled. "And I'm still willing to donate the flower arrangements."

"I'll string the lights," Quinn added.

"Great." Duncan nodded. "What else can we do?"

"What about a silent auction?" Hal suggested.

"That's always a good moneymaker," Shane agreed.

"We can get donations from local businesses," Sue added.

"I can make that work," Layla confirmed. "We have plenty of space."

"Now you're talking." Duncan gave two thumbs up.

"Sue and I will work together." Hal pointed to his wife sitting next to him. "But we'll need other volunteers to help."

Shane raised his hand along with several other members of the group.

"Tina and Yvonne." Duncan pointed to the two women who sat closest to him. "Sally and Tom." He indicated two others who'd raised their hands. He scanned the group. He pointed to him. "Shane. You team up with Layla."

Work with Layla? For crying out loud. Can't catch a break, indeed. He slanted his gaze in her direction. She seemed less than thrilled with their pairing. Shane straightened his shoulders and held his head high. Well, that was too damned bad. He was as good a partner to work with as any of the others in the room.

Deal with it. He would.

So, they'd spend a few hours together collecting donations. No big deal. The fundraiser would generate the extra revenue they needed. He'd keep his job.

What could go wrong?

Chapter Three

Layla glanced at her watch. They closed at nine on Friday evenings in the winter—no use staying open when the whole town shut down early—but she'd leave the front entrance open so Zara could get in.

Something was up with her sister and Layla was worried.

Zara's call last night had set her on edge when she'd told her she was on her way to New Suffolk. This week should have been a Zoom call according to their schedule of weekly remote meetings and one face to face a month, but she'd insisted on meeting in person.

Even more bizarre, she'd pressed Layla to meet today. They always held their in-person meetings on Saturdays. That way Zara wouldn't miss a day of work.

And the thing with her showing up here late this afternoon and insisting they perform the review immediately was *really weird*. She'd seemed...almost panicky when Layla couldn't drop what she was doing and accommodate the request.

"Layla," her sous-chef called.

"Coming." She hoisted the case of Château Lafite Rothschild Pauillac into her arms and strode toward the bar. Lifting the four remaining bottles from the cardboard box, she set each one atop the glossy wood surface.

"Oh, here you are." Olivia approached. "The kitchen's all set. I'm heading out now."

"Okay, thanks. See you tomorrow." Layla brushed a stray lock of curly hair from her sweaty face.

"Oh, the mailman delivered a certified letter earlier. Couldn't find you so I signed for it and left it on the chair in your office."

That was weird. Who would send her a certified letter? "Okay, thanks for letting me know." Layla headed down the back hall toward her office. She flicked on the light. Sure enough, a large manila envelope sat propped against the back of her brown leather swivel desk chair.

Her brows furrowed as she read the letterhead in the upper left corner. It was from the private lender who'd issued the loan she'd taken out to finance opening the restaurant, using the mansion as collateral. Grabbing the envelope, she tore it open and dropped into the cool seat.

Layla removed the letter and scanned the first page. Her eyes bugged out. "What the hell?"

"Hey, Layla. Where are you?" her sister called.

She rushed out of her office, through the empty restaurant to the front entrance to meet her. "What is this?" Layla clenched the document in her hand.

"What is what?" Zara asked.

Layla thrust the document at Zara. "Notice of Default." She shook her head. "I don't understand. They're going to force me to sell the mansion to pay off the loan in full if I can't make the loan current by the end of the first week of April." She lifted her gaze to Zara's. "Why would they believe the loan isn't current?" Her finances might be a little tight, but she hadn't missed a payment.

Zara wouldn't answer. She just stood there with a deer-in-the-headlights expression on her face.

Layla sucked in a lungful of air and tried to relax. Yelling at her sister wasn't going to straighten out this mistake. Zara was obviously as surprised by this as Layla. They'd figure it out together.

She walked into the bar. Setting the document aside, she pulled two wineglasses from the rack and set them atop the glossy bar top. "Red or white," she asked when Zara sat in a chair on the opposite side of her.

"Doesn't matter," Zara grunted.

Layla opened a bottle of her favorite Bordeaux and poured two glasses.

"I'm sorry—" She and Zara spoke at the same time.

Layla heaved out a sigh. "Let me go first. I shouldn't have yelled at you. I'm just…in shock, I guess." She drew in a deep breath and let it out slowly. "Do you have any idea what's going on? How could the lender make such a mistake?"

"It's not a mistake." Zara's voice held a note of panic.

Layla stiffened. Her eyes went wide. "Excuse me? What do you mean? There must be some kind of processing error." If there wasn't… Nausea churned in her stomach and burned a path up her throat.

Zara scrubbed her hands over her face. "I couldn't cover the loan amount due in January or February."

The shaking started in her hands and spread like wildfire throughout her body until she shook from head to toes. But she tried to keep calm. "Why would you miss two payments?" How could that happen? She would have noticed the discrepancies during their weekly finance reviews except... An image of her sister's washed-out face formed in her head. "Oh, my God. You've been hiding this from me. Were you even sick, or was it all a sham so you could keep the truth from me?"

Tears formed in Zara's eyes.

Layla rubbed at her temples and started to pace back and forth behind the bar. "Why would you do such a thing?"

Zara's head lowered and her voice shook when she spoke. "I wasn't... I didn't think..."

She marched over to where Zara sat. Her hands clenched into tight fists. "Why couldn't you make the payments?"

"You're not making enough money."

"Are you kidding me?" Okay, yes. The tourists who'd filled her dining room to capacity every night last summer had departed at the end of the season, but still...

"These days, you barely make enough to cover day-to-day operating expenses." Zara sounded as if she were dealing with a stubborn child who refused to listen.

The image of a nearly empty dining room popped into her head. Her shoulders slumped. "Why didn't you tell me when we missed the first payment?"

"You didn't seem worried when things slowed down after the holidays and I figured we'd make up the missed payment in February."

"But we didn't, and still you said nothing. And how the hell would I make it up in the off-season, of all times?" A heavy weight settled in her chest making it hard to breathe. "For God's sake. You agreed to manage the finances, Zara. I *trusted* you."

The color drained from Zara's face. "I know. I'm trying, but managing *your* restaurant isn't anything like what I did for Gramps, or what I do for the nonprofit. You have so many more moving parts to juggle, new suppliers every week. Just when I believe I'm caught up, you surprise me with another invoice to pay. That coupled with the fact that I hadn't anticipated the steep decline in business in January and February meant I wound up short when the loan payments were due.

"I'm sorry. I really am." Zara's crushed spirit tore at her insides. "I spoke to the lender yesterday. They told me about the letter. I wanted to tell you myself this afternoon. It's why I came up."

Layla scrubbed her hands over her face. She didn't know what to say.

"Please don't hate me," Zara pleaded.

Her heart squeezed. This was her sister—her best friend through thick and thin—not archenemy number one. She wouldn't have made it through those initial days after her split from Antoine without Zara's love and support.

Lord, what a mess they'd made of this.

Zara wiped tears from her eyes. "I never thought it would come to this."

"But it has." Her breaths came in short, sharp gasps. Everything she'd worked for. All her dreams. Gone.

Done. At last. Shane yawned. He couldn't wait to hit the hay. He pushed the door open and exited the EMS building. Stars twinkled in the dark sky and the full moon negated the need for lights as he strode through the parking lot to his truck.

Once there, he tossed his duffel bag on the passenger seat and hopped inside. Shane pulled out of the parking lot and headed east. He drove through the now silent town and turned left at the light and headed toward home.

The bright lights shining at La Cabane de La Mer surprised him. He wouldn't have guessed the restaurant would be open at this hour. Of all the people on the gala committee, wasn't it just his luck he'd end up paired with Layla? Shane blew out a harsh breath. Now that his work schedule was set for the next two weeks, he needed to speak with her and set up a time they could collect the rest of the silent auction donations. Now was as good a time as any. He made a U-turn and headed back.

The parking lot was empty when he pulled in. Maybe he'd been wrong, and the restaurant was closed? He was here, so he may as well check. Shane hopped out of his truck and walked toward the entrance.

Silence greeted him when he stepped inside. "Hello? Is anyone here?" A loud crash came from the room to his left. "Who's there?"

"We're closed," a female voice yelled.

He moved toward the sound but couldn't find anyone. "Hello," he called again.

"I said we're closed." The sound came from behind the bar.

"Layla?" Shane walked over and peered over the marble countertop. She sat in a heap on the floor with three broken wine bottles beside her and spilled red wine on the floor. He rushed to her side. "Oh, no. What happened?"

She shot an accusing glare at him. "It scared the heck out of me when I heard your voice and I knocked over the bottles that were sitting on the bar top. How did you get in?"

"The front entrance was open. Here, let me help you." Shane extended his hand and pulled her to her feet. "Are you okay?" He scanned the length of her to make sure she didn't have any visible cuts.

"What are you doing here?" Oh, yes. She was mad at him all right.

"I saw the lights were still on, and I wanted to talk to you about the silent auction donations we're supposed to—"

The look on her face had him stopping midsentence.

"What's wrong?" Maybe she'd been injured after all? "Are you sure you're not hurt?"

"Not hurt." She shook her head and looked away. "Letter..."

Shane couldn't understand. "What are you talking about?"

She turned to face him. Her distraught expression stole the breath from him. "Close down... Lose everything."

She wasn't making any sense. Maybe he should leave and come back another time.

A single tear fell from the corner of her eye. "What am I going to do?"

Her vulnerability tugged at his heart. "Come on. Let's go sit down, and you can tell me what's going on."

He walked to the closest table and Layla sat.

"Would you like a glass of water?" he asked.

She scrubbed her hands over her face. "Y-yes, please."

"Okay. I'll be right back." He stepped behind the bar.

Shane picked up one of the broken bottles. He let out a low whistle when he read the label. *Château Lafite Rothschild Pauillac.* A bottle went for six hundred dollars, maybe more. He couldn't imagine anyone in New Suffolk spending that kind of money on a bottle of wine with dinner. The wealthy tourists who summered in their quaint little beach town, maybe, but the locals who catered to those vacationers… Most couldn't afford such luxuries, especially during the slow season.

Shane tossed the bottles in the trash. He'd help her clean up the rest of the mess later. It was the least he could do, considering he'd been somewhat responsible for creating it. *First things first.* Grabbing a glass from the shelf, he filled it with water and returned to the table. "Here you go."

"Thanks." Her large watery eyes gazed at him. Layla sipped from the glass and set it back down on the table.

"Now tell me what's got you so upset." Shane sat in the seat across from her.

She blew out a breath and recounted the story.

Shane stared at her wide-eyed. "Most banks give you more than thirty days before they make you liquidate your collateral."

Layla nodded. "I used a private lender my sister, Zara, was acquainted with."

Sounded more like a loan shark to him. *Wait.* Thirty days would put them at the end of the first week of April. "What about the gala?"

"We'll have to cancel." Tears welled in her eyes again.

"No way." The EMS department was counting on the funds this event would raise. He was counting on the money to ensure he'd keep his job. "We've sold almost all the tickets, and it's too late to find another comparable venue."

"What do you want me to do?" Layla jumped down from the chair and started pacing back and forth across the room. "We don't have the money needed to make the loan current."

"I can help you." The words erupted from him before his brain could engage.

"How?" She stopped walking midstride and turned to face him.

Shane expelled a resigned sigh. It was either help her or risk getting cut from the EMS team. "Former business investment consultant here. I can review your finances and make some recommendations on how you can make more money." Eliminating the purchase of six-hundred-dollar bottles of wine came to mind for starters.

She studied him, a hopeful glint in her gaze. "You would do that for me?"

"Yes. You have enough for the March payment, right?"

"I'll make sure of it." A tentative smile formed on her face.

"Great. We'll find a way to keep your restaurant open." At least he'd try to make that happen.

Layla walked back to the table and sat in the seat she'd vacated moments ago. "Why would you want to do this? What's in it for you?"

He wouldn't pull any punches with her. "We both know the EMS department needs the money the gala will generate. I want to make sure it happens. It's a win-win for both of us. So, what do you say?"

"Okay." Layla extended her hand to him and he shook it. Sparks of electricity sizzled through him the moment his palm touched hers.

He jerked his hand away and shoved it in his jeans pocket. What had he gotten himself into?

Layla pulled her car into the driveway of the 1930s Cape-Cod-style home on Monday evening and peered around. Strategically placed spotlights brightened the sweeping snow-blanketed front lawn. She imagined what it would look like in spring, the beds of bright fragrant blooms in a multitude of species with green Hosta and tall beach grass intermixed.

The calming ebb and flow of the ocean waves crashing on shore filled her Mini Cooper, even with the windows closed. She took several deep breaths, willing herself to stay calm.

Layla grabbed her purse and the thermal take-out bags from the passenger seat and exited the car. She walked up the blue stone walkway and rang the doorbell.

Minutes passed and no one answered the door. Had Shane forgotten he'd told her to stop by tonight? They hadn't spoken over the weekend. She should have texted him this afternoon and confirmed. She turned and started back down the walkway to her car. The snick of the lock had her stopping. She whirled around.

The door opened.

Shane appeared wearing a pair of black sweatpants slung low on his hips and… Oh, dear Lord, nothing else. No socks, no shoes. No shirt. Holy moly. She swallowed. *Perfection personified.*

"What are you doing here?" he asked.

Yes. He'd forgotten, all right. Layla cleared her throat. "You asked me to stop by tonight and bring the restaurant financial information with me. Remember?"

"Right." He nodded. "Come on in." Shane stepped

aside and gestured for her to enter. "Sorry, I just got off shift and was in the shower." He shrugged into the sweatshirt she hadn't noticed in his hand.

Layla stepped inside. "Oh, my gosh. This is an amazing home." She could see through to the opposite side of the house where floor-to-ceiling windows and sliding glass doors lined the outside wall.

His gaze narrowed and every bone in his body stiffened. "It might not be much now, but wait until the renovations I have planned are complete."

"No, no." Layla shook her head. "I wasn't being sarcastic. This place is gorgeous. You must have an amazing view of the ocean from every room in the house."

He stared at her, a curious expression on his face. "Sorry. I guess I'm a little sensitive when it comes to this place. Like I said, it needs work. And yes, the views are stunning. They're what sold me on the place. The rest I can fix."

"You're doing the work yourself?" At his puzzled expression she added, "Right. Of course you are." How could she have forgotten? TK Construction had renovated her grandparents' apartment. It was where she'd met him all those years ago. Where she'd experienced her first real crush. Oh, who was she kidding? She'd fallen head over heels for him, but how could she compete with all of those Bay Beach Club teenage beauties who flirted relentlessly with him when she couldn't master the art of speech in his presence?

At least she'd finally conquered that particular phobia—funny how the threat of losing everything that mattered to you gave you something else to focus on. She had bigger problems to worry about than making a fool of herself in front of him.

That's what she'd always been afraid of, but it didn't matter anymore.

"Want a quick tour before we get started?" he asked.

Her eyes widened. She wouldn't have expected him to offer such a thing, to be so…friendly. He'd made it clear from the start he was only helping her because it benefited the EMS department. "A win-win," he'd said. That was fine with her. She expected nothing more. Still, her curiosity got the better of her. She couldn't resist now that he'd offered. "Yes. I'd love to hear what you have planned for each room."

"Follow me." Shane walked past the staircase on the right and moved into the interior.

Layla stood in the center of the home and peered around. A large kitchen sat on the right in front of the staircase and a gigantic living room with a wide fire-place on the left. "Oh, wow. I love how all the spaces are open to each other and the view you have…spectacular."

"It wasn't that way when I bought the place. Each room was separate."

"You've done an amazing job making it so open." She wondered why he'd decided to pursue careers in finance and medicine when he obviously possessed the skill and talent to excel at the kind of work his family had been doing for years.

"I'm going to add an island in the kitchen."

"I can picture it there. In front of the dining table." She pointed to the open floor space in front of where the wall of cabinets stood. "A long, wide one with lots of counter space." The perfect place for preparing a meal.

Shane smiled and nodded. "That's exactly what I'm thinking."

She turned toward the living room. "What will you do in here?"

"I'll rip out the nasty carpet. There's hardwood underneath that matches the rest of the flooring on this level."

"Sounds perfect. All you need is a comfy sectional in front of the fireplace and a huge TV over the mantel and you're all set."

"You're reading my mind." Shane stared at her, a stunned expression on his face. "There's not much else to see on this level. We'll work at the table." He turned toward the fridge.

"Wait, please." She placed a hand on his arm to stop him.

He faced her. "What is it?"

"I just wanted to thank you again for helping me. My restaurant is…" She hesitated. How could she explain what La Cabane de La Mer meant to her? "It's more than just a job. Cooking is a part of who I am. To be able to do that on my own terms… It's a dream come true."

He studied her for long intense moments before saying, "I'm glad to help. Go ahead and grab a seat." Shane pointed over his shoulder in the vicinity of the table. "Want something to drink?"

"Actually, I brought you dinner and a bottle of red wine. I figured it's the least I could do." Layla handed him one of the thermal takeout bags and pulled a wine bottle from her purse.

His mouth gaped. "You did?"

Layla beamed a tentative smile. "You mentioned you had to work until six. I figured you wouldn't have much time to eat before we got started, so I thought we could eat while we worked."

"Thanks." A puzzled expression crossed his face. "Where's your meal?"

"Right here." She held up a second bag.

"What'd you bring?" Shane jiggled the bag in his hand.

"Burgers. I hope you don't mind." She'd been in the mood for one. Sometimes you just got a craving for something greasy.

His eyes widened, and was that excitement in his astonished gaze? "Are you kidding? I love burgers."

Layla laughed. "Looks like we've got something in common because I love them, too."

"Thanks again for bringing this." Shane went straight for the table and sat. He unzipped the warming bag and slid the clear container from the bag. "It looks amazing."

"I stuffed the meat with Gaperon cheese and we had extra brioche rolls this evening."

"You made it?" Shane yanked the lid off one-handed. He stared at the burger as if he'd found the holy grail.

"Of course I did. Like I'd serve you fast food from—" She stopped midsentence when he grabbed the burger and took a bite.

"Oh my God." His eyes closed for a moment and a look of ecstasy crossed his handsome face. "It *is* delicious. You're an amazing cook."

A rush of warmth flooded through her. "Thanks."

"Is this on your menu? If not, you should add it." Shane bit into the burger again.

Was he kidding? Of course he was. She owned a gourmet French restaurant, for goodness' sake. "Right." Layla grinned.

"This is really fantastic."

Layla gawked as he consumed the rest of the burger in one bite.

"Sorry." His cheeks flamed bright red. "I, ah... missed lunch and dinner." He lifted a napkin from the holder perched in the center of the table and dragged it across his mouth.

"Why did you miss lunch and dinner?"

His blue eyes sparkled and...he looked like a kid at Christmas.

"I became a godfather today." A wide happy grin spread across his face.

"A godfather?" She frowned. "Did someone have a baby?"

"Yes." His smile grew brighter and his eyes... Holy cow. They danced with delight. "I delivered my first baby this evening," he added at her confused expression.

Work. Of course. "What happened?"

"Woman was alone at home and in labor. She couldn't reach her husband and called 9-1-1." Shane grabbed a fry from the container and munched. "She was one hundred percent dilated when we arrived. No time to get her to the hospital so we delivered the baby at her home. I'm happy to say mother and son are doing great."

He'd brought a new life into this world. Helped someone when they couldn't help themselves. "That's incredible." Now she understood why he'd chosen this profession. He loved his work.

"It really is." His look of wonder made her smile.

Amazing home renovator, successful Wall Street career, EMT extraordinaire, lover of burgers. Let's not forget those fabulous abs and biceps. So many layers to this complicated man. What else made him tick? Layla wanted to know.

"The parents made me an honorary godfather."

She grinned. "Congratulations."

"Thanks." Shane stood and walked to the fridge on the far side of the room. He returned a moment later carrying a bottle of ketchup.

"Oh, you don't need that. There's some in the bag."

He set the bottle on the table and lifted the small cup filled with the dipping sauce she'd included. "This doesn't look like ketchup." He tilted the plastic cup for her inspection.

"That's the honey mustard mayo. The curry ketchup is in the other container."

"Curry ketchup?" He shot her a dubious look.

"It's good. Trust me."

Shane dipped a fry and stuck it in his mouth. His eyes opened wide and a look of surprise crossed his face. "You're right. I thought it sounded a little weird to mix curry and ketchup, but this is great."

"I'm glad you like it." She grinned.

"Okay." He licked the salt from his fingers, grabbed his laptop from the counter and brought it back to the table. "It's time to get to work. Are you ready?"

Layla reached inside her purse, withdrew the Jump-drive containing the restaurant financial records and handed it to Shane. "Let's do this."

Don't miss
A Taste of Home *by Anna James,*
available now wherever
Harlequin Special Edition books and
ebooks are sold.
www.Harlequin.com

#2989 THE MAVERICK'S SURPRISE SON
Montana Mavericks: Lassoing Love • by Christine Rimmer

Volunteer firefighter Jace Abernathy vows to adopt the newborn he saved from a fire. Nurse Tamara Hanson doubts he's up to the task. She'll help the determined rancher prepare for his social service screening. But in the process, will these hometown heroes find love and family with each other?

#2990 SEVEN BIRTHDAY WISHES
Dawson Family Ranch • by Melissa Senate

Seven-year-old Cody Dawson dreams of meeting champion bull rider Logan Winston. Logan doesn't know his biggest fan is also his son. He'll fulfill seven of Cody's wishes—one for each birthday he missed. But falling in love again with Cody's mom, Annabel, may be his son's biggest wish yet!

#2991 HER NOT-SO-LITTLE SECRET
Match Made in Haven • by Brenda Harlen

Sierra Hart knows a bad boy when she sees one. And smooth-talking Deacon Parrish is a rogue of the first order! Their courtroom competition pales to their bedroom chemistry. But will these dueling attorneys trust each other enough to go from "I object" to "I do"?

#2992 HEIR IN A YEAR
by Elizabeth Bevarly

Bennett Hadden just inherited the Gilded Age mansion Summerlight. So did Haven Moreau—assuming the two archenemies can live there together for one year. Haven plans to restore the home *and* her broken relationship with Bennett. And she'll use every tool at her disposal to return both to their former glories!

#2993 THEIR SECRET TWINS
Shelter Valley Stories • by Tara Taylor Quinn

Jordon Lawrence and ex Mia Jones just got the embryo shock of their lives. Their efforts to help a childless couple years ago resulted in twin daughters they never knew existed. Now the orphaned girls need their biological parents, and Jordon and Mia will work double time to create the family their children deserve!

#2994 THE BUSINESS BETWEEN THEM
Once Upon a Wedding • by Mona Shroff

Businessman Akash Gupta just bought Reena Pandya's family hotel, ruining her plan to take it over. Now the determined workaholic will do anything to reclaim her birthright—even get closer to her sexy ex. But Akash has a plan, too—teaching one very headstrong woman to balance duty, family *and* love.

Get 4 FREE REWARDS!

We'll send you 2 FREE Books plus 2 FREE Mystery Gifts.

FREE
Value Over
$20

Both the **Harlequin® Special Edition** and **Harlequin Heartwarming™** series feature compelling novels filled with stories of love and strength where the bonds of friendship, family and community unite.

YES! Please send me 2 FREE novels from the Harlequin Special Edition or Harlequin Heartwarming series and my 2 FREE gifts (gifts are worth about $10 retail). After receiving them, if I don't wish to receive any more books, I can return the shipping statement marked "cancel." If I don't cancel, I will receive 6 brand-new Harlequin Special Edition books every month and be billed just $5.49 each in the U.S. or $6.24 each in Canada, a savings of at least 12% off the cover price, or 4 brand-new Harlequin Heartwarming Larger-Print books every month and be billed just $6.24 each in the U.S. or $6.74 each in Canada, a savings of at least 19% off the cover price. It's quite a bargain! Shipping and handling is just 50¢ per book in the U.S. and $1.25 per book in Canada.* I understand that accepting the 2 free books and gifts places me under no obligation to buy anything. I can always return a shipment and cancel at any time by calling the number below. The free books and gifts are mine to keep no matter what I decide.

Choose one: ☐ **Harlequin Special Edition**   ☐ **Harlequin Heartwarming**
(235/335 HDN GRJV)   **Larger-Print**
(161/361 HDN GRJV)

Name (please print)

Address   Apt. #

City   State/Province   Zip/Postal Code

Email: Please check this box ☐ if you would like to receive newsletters and promotional emails from Harlequin Enterprises ULC and its affiliates. You can unsubscribe anytime.

Mail to the Harlequin Reader Service:
IN U.S.A.: P.O. Box 1341, Buffalo, NY 14240-8531
IN CANADA: P.O. Box 603, Fort Erie, Ontario L2A 5X3

Want to try 2 free books from another series? Call 1-800-873-8635 or visit www.ReaderService.com.

HARLEQUIN
PLUS

Try the best multimedia
subscription service for romance
readers like you!

Read, Watch and Play.

Experience the easiest way to get
the romance content you crave.

Start your **FREE TRIAL** at
<u>www.harlequinplus.com/freetrial</u>.